FROZEN FIRE

Art of Murder Series
Book 4

PAM FOX

Bright Fox Books

Bright Fox Books
Copyright © 2019 by Pam Fox
ISBN-13: 978-1-7328799-3-5

This is a work of fiction. Names, characters, places and incidents are the products of the author's imagination or are used fictitiously. Any resemblance to actual events or persons, living or dead, is entirely coincidental.

ONE

At the top of the hill, Kate Corliss slid her left ski back and forth, then her right, partly to make sure the kick zones under her boots were free of clumped snow and partly from excited anticipation. Her cross-country skis had stayed in the closet the previous winter because she'd been depressed by the break-up of a long relationship just before Christmas. Now the white stuff piled up by a late November storm in western Massachusetts looked like it was made for her to play in, and her favorite way to do that was on skinny skis.

She'd only had to step out the door: this park, Topper Reserve, was right next to the house where she was staying.

Thin flakes were still falling from a bright but cloudy sky. It was unusually cold, in the mid-teens. Kate's eyes watered, and she pulled her balaclava higher on her face. The hill's blinding white was interrupted only by a tangle of bushes near the bottom, at the edge of woods to the right.

She pushed off with both poles. The snow was fresh and fluffy, so her skis sank until only the tips were visible, small triangles flinging crystal sprays to both sides. The new snow meant slow going until she made enough passes to compress it, each run making her tracks faster.

She curved left, then right, toward the bushes. Just as she shifted her weight to arc left again, she saw somebody's lost glove, pale blue, caught in low branches. She hated litter, intentional or not, and made a mental note to pick the glove up on the way back.

The exercise warmed her. She unzipped her purple anorak and the zip-neck top under it, then addressed the long shallow hill that rose above her. It wasn't steep enough that she needed to herringbone, was it? She'd try the faster method first, walking with steps forceful enough to give a good grip.

That meant pulling one ski up out of the snow and half-jumping forward onto it, then the other. Quickly. As each ski surfaced, snow slid off the purple and gray graphics of her boards and she could see individual flakes. Pretty.

No, she was slipping. She'd have to herringbone, skis pointing to ten and two o'clock, inside edges cutting into the snow. After a few such duck-footed steps she was flushed with heat and wished she'd taken off the balaclava.

Working on technique, she didn't notice the man in the red jacket until he was halfway down the hill.

Crouched for speed, heading right at her.

"Stop!" Too late, surely.

Seconds before they would have collided he flipped sideways into a hockey stop, spraying her with snow, then turned his skis downslope again and coasted gently against her. One of his skis slid between hers, and she found herself looking up into a pair of dark brown eyes.

He put his hands on her shoulders, his poles hanging by the wrist straps, and grinned at her through a generous black beard. Then doubt swept across his face. "Oh, no, you're not Cammie!"

Confusion is not good for coordination. And skis are not built to go backward, especially up a slope. The man slid back, tried to turn, slipped, waved his arms wildly, and went down. The ski between Kate's whacked her calf and she fell with him.

She felt as well as heard him laughing. It was a deep, resonant sound, and a few seconds of it was enough to make her laugh too.

Eventually he said, "Houston, we have a problem."

"I'd help you, but I can't move because you've got a leg across one of mine."

"I also am unable to move." He had an accent, although Kate wasn't sure what kind. "All of you is lying on top of all of me."

"This is like a party game," Kate said. "The kind I never played."

"The snow is a party. The best kind." A last rumble of laughter came more softly, like thunder from a storm that's moving away. "I apologize for my boorish behavior. My only excuse is that I thought you were my fiancée. She wears a similar coat."

"I wouldn't say boorish," Kate said. "Impetuous, maybe. But you did an amazing job of not running me over." Even though her right mitten had come off and her hand was cold, she fished through the snow under the man's leg for her left binding and pressed its release. The same on the right. She'd have to lift each boot with her hands to get the toe-bar to come out of the clip, and that wouldn't be easy with the buried foot.

He'd worked a hand free to put between his face and the snow, a napping position to keep his cheek from freezing—although the risk should be low with a beard as thick as his. "I'm Azul, by the way."

"Hello, Azul. I'm Kate." She sat up and pulled off her balaclava, then reached awkwardly toward her trapped foot. Cupped a hand under the boot. "I'm getting us out of this pickle. You may feel a little kick."

"You would kick a man when he's down?" English may not have been his first language, but he knew the idioms.

"As gently as possible." She pulled her boots out of the bindings and crawled away from the big man. A clump of snow slid into the opening at her neck and melted, sending tendrils of ice-water down her chest.

Her new acquaintance popped his boots free and sat up. Picked a tasseled red hat out of the snow and shook it, jammed it on his head and looked at her. "Are you at the college, Houston?"

"No. I'm a free-lance artist." Kate floundered a bit, getting her feet under her. "Since you're calling me Houston, are you admitting you're a space cadet?"

"Ah, you have found me out. But I'm glad you are not of the academic persuasion. My reputation among the faculty will not be sullied."

"I'm visiting my aunt and uncle. He's a professor. Does that count?" Apparently it did: Kate laughed as Azul's eyes widened. "He can spread all kinds of vicious gossip. I'll see to it."

"What department is your uncle in?"

"Is there a botany department? He's a botanist." She stood, up to her knees in snow, and breathed into her cold fist, looking around for the lost mitten.

"Plants get filed under Biology," Azul said, looking relieved. "My department. What is your illustrious uncle's name?"

"Peter Stewart."

"Ah, Pete. The royalty of root systems. His wife is a good friend of Camila, the light of my life." He was up, too, brushing off his jacket. "My fiancée. Who will defend me."

"Light of your life? That's a lovely phrase."

"Ah, if only it were mutual."

"I can't imagine you're anything but the light of her life." Five minutes wasn't much to judge by, but he seemed like a total charmer. "Women don't get engaged to men they don't love."

"Her life is lit by hundreds of adorable faces. With bright brown eyes and black whiskers. Like mine, only on a smaller scale. Her attraction to me, alas, may lie in the similarity."

"Students?" Otterlin College must have non-whiskered, women students. Kate was at a loss.

"Mice," Azul said.

The gloom on his face had to be a bit of play-acting. She laughed. "Mice? Seriously?"

"The black-footed field mouse. Most seriously."

"You hardly look like a mouse. Or act like one." Her skis were set at right angles to the slope and she stepped onto them, the click of the bindings loud in the white day.

"The black-footed field mouse is endangered. You may not think it important, but I assure you it is. Urgent, in fact." He was facing her, his skis also perpendicular to the grade. He held a pole below the handle and shook it at her for emphasis, the wrist loop flopping. "As the black-footed field mouse goes, so goes the planet."

"So let me get this straight. The woman you are going to marry, Cammie, is in love with hundreds of field mice, and they—she and the mice—are going to save mother-ship Earth?"

"You have perceived the situation correctly," Azul said, "except for one detail. Camila Chavez, Ph.D., a woman of fire and vision, a woman with the heart of a wolverine and the breath of a dragon, would scorch anyone who called her Cammie."

"Except you."

"Except me. And if you will excuse me, I will now go in search of my sweet she-dragon, who went out last night to gather data on her furry subjects and has not yet come to my house for the long and luxurious breakfast she promised to let me cook for her." He angled his skis down the slope and pushed off, the tassel on his hat swinging.

"Don't let the dragon burn the toast!" Kate called after him, and he waggled a pole over his head in acknowledgment.

Ah, the mitten, half-buried where she'd fallen. She used the basket at the end of her pole to pull it to her. Packed with snow, it didn't look the least bit warm, so she shook it empty and tucked it in a pocket. Wearing only one mitten was distracting, so she pocketed the second. After putting her balaclava back on, she considered the mayhem recorded in the snow.

Herringbone tracks going up, straight-line tracks coming down, a cavernous hole where the two lines met. The story was easy to read, and passing skiers would wonder if the injuries had been serious.

Or, depending on their temperament, they might have a good laugh.

She herringboned to the top of the rise and glanced at her watch. She didn't have a lot of time before she needed to make lunch for Aunt Sarah, who'd broken her arm earlier in the month when the outside staircase on the back of her house had collapsed under her. The accident was the reason Kate was in Massachusetts: with Uncle Pete teaching and working on his new book, it became clear Aunt Sarah needed help while she recovered, and Kate had agreed to be that help.

It meant interrupting the year-long trip in her truck camper across the continent, from Maine to Arizona, but Kate could easily change plans. She'd been laid off from her job as a newspaper reporter the previous spring, and it had been almost a year since her partner had asked her to move out of the house they'd shared. She was perhaps more free than she wished. This aunt had been a second mother during some crucial childhood years in Tucson, and Kate was happy to nurse Aunt Sarah back to the busy, independent life she'd built for herself.

Kate's slide-in truck camper was winterized—the tanks empty and anti-freeze in the water lines—and parked in Aunt Sarah's driveway. An extension cord ran from the house to power a coffeemaker and small heater so she could use the camper as a studio to do the artwork that had become her passion. She'd rediscovered it the previous summer at an artists' colony in Maine run by an old friend, and had even sold some work at a previous stop on her trip, in Pennsylvania. She could work here in western Massachusetts.

In her new nomadic life, she could work anywhere.

She turned the way she'd come and looked down the slope, choosing her course. Went down in Azul's tracks for a little speed and then cut left around the crater the two of them had made. The blue of the shadows in its center reminded her to look for the fallen glove she'd seen in the bushes.

Professor Dragon. She laughed as she thought of Azul's comic description of Dr. Camila Chavez. If she was in Uncle Pete's department, maybe Kate would meet her soon.

* * *

She paused in the dip between the two hills, near the scraggle of bushes and the cryptic messages their branches wrote on the snow's blank page. The sky had darkened and a gust of wind carried wet flakes. The storm wasn't over after all. Lunch sounded good, not just as a duty to Aunt

Sarah but as an answer to Kate's own growling stomach. She glanced up the rise to her aunt and uncle's house, its small back yard cluttered with the ruins of the fallen staircase. She'd be in the kitchen in minutes.

Ah, the pale blue glove, a lonely touch of color in a landscape otherwise as black and white as an Ansel Adams photo. Kate moved into the bushes, dead twigs breaking as she brushed past, her skis sinking. She stepped as if on snowshoes, lifting each ski out of the powder and setting it down so it wouldn't get snagged by a branch.

The glove was low, near an oak tree. The trunk had a well around it, the snow shallower because of the shelter the big tree provided. She planted her left pole for stability and reached with her bare right hand.

Recoiling, she almost lost her balance.

The glove wasn't empty. It was solid, with small wrinkles at each knuckle, and nails.

It wasn't a glove at all, but a hand.

A frozen hand.

Another gust of wind slipped under her collar. An eddy swirled the snow around the blue hand and exposed the sharp edge of a jacket cuff. Beyond, a long mound of snow spoiled the symmetry of the well around the oak tree.

Kate shivered and pulled out her cell phone. Instead of calling 911, she searched for the Hunterville Police non-emergency number.

An emergency had struck, but it was over.

* * *

Lunch was harried. Kate answered questions from a large, polite policeman while she made sandwiches and heated soup from a can. He took off a gray wool hat and mittens, and his stiff blue coat dripped onto the linoleum floor while he tapped notes into the tablet he'd propped on the kitchen island.

She offered him a cup of coffee, which he drank in short order. She couldn't tell him much, only what she'd found and that she'd seen one other person in the Reserve. The cop had left by the time she had a tray ready to take up to Aunt Sarah, who had been "condemned" to bed rest, as she phrased it. Her arm had broken in two places, requiring surgery. The "wretched" cast would be part of her life for six to eight weeks.

The poor woman was nearly frantic with curiosity, sitting up and craning her neck toward the two small windows. They faced the street, and she could see a couple of police cars parked out front. Kate's bedside efforts to focus attention on the barley soup and cheese sandwich were successful only after she promised to make a full report about what was happening behind the house.

"You've always been smart, dear," Aunt Sarah said. "Now you can provide intelligence." Kate rolled her eyes and stood.

Downstairs, from the bay window in the dining room, she had a clear view of the action in the Reserve: men in bulky jackets, on snowshoes, circling the area. At first they took photos, then they searched, slowly, heads down, seeming to cover mere inches at a time, some of them swinging metal detectors in front of them. They looked like sleep-walking golfers.

Eclipse, the resident black cat, curled up on the window seat and snored lightly. Human mishaps were not his concern.

Kate's temporary bedroom had a good view, too. Originally an attached garage, it had been converted to a double study, with a desk at each end separated by a sleep-sofa. When Aunt Sarah felt well enough to move back into the master bedroom, the small guest bedroom would go to Kate and then Uncle Pete could decamp from the living room, which he was using as an office. Papers were stacked so high on the glass coffee table that Kate wondered if it would snap. In ordinary times the couple adjourned to the former garage after dinner—Uncle Pete at one desk, grumbling at student papers, Aunt Sarah at the other, keeping up with friends online and browsing Audubon Society and Sierra Club news.

Domestic arrangements in the little bungalow were in disarray.

"It's ridiculous I can't sleep with Pete, but he's restless and he bumps my arm and it hurts and I don't get any sleep," Aunt Sarah had said when Kate arrived. "Who knew those back porch stairs were going to give way? They looked fine. I was taking birdseed out to fill the feeder and the next thing I knew I was ass over teakettle. Landed with my arm on the edge of the cement pad under the stairs, and then a piece of wood came down and gave me a second break. Now why did it have to be my right arm?"

"Those damn stairs have sabotaged my marriage," Uncle Pete had grumbled to Kate over the phone on her first day in Hunterville. Aunt Sarah had just finished saying he'd be stuck in Boston by the storm when he called to say exactly that. Kate was struck by the loneliness in his voice.

After lunch she cleaned up the kitchen and ran upstairs a couple of times to answer Aunt Sarah's questions. The house was old, the staircase steep, and Kate felt a pleasant ache in her thighs from skiing as she climbed it.

"You're not missing much," she reassured her patient. "Half a dozen guys wandering around in the snow, as slow as hunting herons. They look like old people. Exercise time in a geriatric ward."

"Watch it," Aunt Sarah said. "I'm an old person now. I don't know how it happened. I thought it would take longer, but here I am."

"You? Old? I don't think so," Kate laughed. She had to think a minute: her Ma was sixty-three, so that made Ma's only sister Sarah sixty-seven. Yikes. She was getting up there. Still, the sixties weren't considered old these days.

Later, most of the men walking around Topper Reserve had brooms. Brooms? Yes, it made sense to brush away an inch of snow at a time. The storm had lasted—was lasting—for more than two days, so to move downward through the accumulation was to time-travel. Like archeologists at a dig.

The back steps were off limits until the carpenter showed up, so she followed the path she'd shoveled from the front porch around the side of the house to the back yard. She unscrewed the lid on the five-gallon, raccoon-proof container, normally stored under the back stairs and now left beside their wreckage. Kate had extricated it when she'd first arrived, along with a stepladder and trash can. All three items, made of plastic and aluminum, had fared far better than Aunt Sarah, showing just some scratches and dents.

After filling the birdfeeder with three scoops, she carried the stepladder to the front of the house, opened it next to her truck camper and swept off the roof. Two inches of new snow since the last time she'd done it.

Chores finished, she swept off the camper's back step and climbed aboard. Sat at the dinette with her sketchbook.

Five minutes. Ten. The paper was still blank.

The problem was more than the distraction of the investigation going on behind the house, the occasional policeman walking past her window to or from the cruisers parked in the driveway and on the street. Kate had to admit she was rattled by the morning's discovery. Now that she wasn't talking to the polite cop or to Aunt Sarah, the terrible cold of the hand she'd touched came back to her.

Like shaking hands with death.

She closed her eyes. She'd so looked forward to spending time with her aunt, who'd not only nurtured her as a child but had also been a warm and wise counselor who'd kept her from dropping out of college. The upcoming Christmas with Aunt Sarah and Uncle Pete had promised to be a peaceful time, and mutually beneficial: helping her aunt, Kate would also be recovering from recent events at a campground in Pennsylvania. Two women had been murdered, and she'd had a close call herself.

When she'd seen the weather report she'd put in enough driving time to skitter into Hunterville just before the major Nor'easter. The city was New England picturesque, with old saltbox houses that had survived at the edges of the newer, commercial downtown. She'd had plenty of time to admire the city hall, a handsome brick building, since she'd had to stop in a line of cars held up by some kind of demonstration. People streamed from an overflow parking lot across the road to the gabled front doors, bundled in winter coats and waving signs that said JOBS FIRST. Kate fiddled with the truck's radio, trying out half a dozen stations while she waited until the traffic jam cleared.

She hadn't visited her aunt and uncle in two years, and was excited to arrive on their front porch as the first flakes trickled down. Aunt Sarah, it turned out, was alone. Her smiles and hugs were enthusiastic but awkward because of the big plaster cast and sling.

Kate opened her eyes and ran her hand over the blank page, feeling its texture. She wondered when Uncle Pete would make it home and hoped the meeting with his publisher had gone well. *Root and Leaf Systems Architecture: Adaptation Strategies* wasn't going to show up on the *New York Times* best-seller list, but it would make its author's life considerably easier: Uncle Pete had griped long and loud about patching course material together with photocopied pieces of other botanists' textbooks. "My book is organized in the most logical sequence, with just the right amount of explanation and lots of illustrations. I can't understand why somebody else didn't write it first," he'd told her on the phone.

"I hope it sells like ice cream in August."

"Thanks, Kate," he'd said. "Most of what it makes goes to the publisher, though. My royalties won't pay for the gas to get out here a couple of times a year."

She looked at the pencil in her hand and set it down. Too distracted to work. Restless, curious about the goings-on behind the house, she dropped out the door at the rear of her camper and had a look.

The police were being thorough, she had to give them that. Three of them inched around the snowscape, shuffling like penguins. Some unfortunate soul had fallen in the deep snow and died, probably of hypothermia, but any unattended death requires an investigation. Perhaps a homeless person. Perhaps they'd find evidence of alcohol, an empty flask or bottle.

Engine noise behind her. A snowmobile came down the driveway and passed her, the helmeted driver giving her a nod. Hitched behind him, a boxy trailer rode high on its skis, empty. Kate knew what it would carry on the return trip.

She'd seen enough. She climbed into her warm camper and stood at the dinette. The blank page looked up at her.

Oh, hell. She had to draw it, the thing that hung in her mind and wouldn't leave. The hand. The hand reaching up from the white underworld below the oak tree.

She picked up the pencil and willed herself back to the moment she'd touched the cold skin.

Twenty minutes later, she looked at her work.

An upturned palm cupped snow. The fingers curling over it were slender. Nails cut short, neat, clean. The edge of the cuff was crisp.

Not a homeless person, then.

A woman, most likely: the hand was the size of Kate's own.

TWO

Kate was shoveling off the front steps the next day when the sky-blue Volvo came down the driveway, lights on and classical music blaring. Good thing she'd gotten up early; she'd finished the driveway in the nick of time for Uncle Pete. The job hadn't been too bad, of course, since she'd cleared the driveway once to get her truck parked close to the house. She'd made extra space near the street, as Aunt Sarah had asked, to make room for visitors' cars.

She waited beside the Volvo. She'd forgotten how tall her uncle was: he seemed to get out in stages, like an extension ladder. At five feet eight she wasn't short, but when she hugged him it felt like she'd grabbed the bottom of a tree trunk.

"Katie, dear, thank you for coming. Thank you for all the shoveling you've done." Nobody called her Katie except her father and Uncle Pete, and she hadn't seen her father since he'd disappeared when she was eleven.

"It's a little narrower than I hoped—I ran out of places to put the snow. How was the drive?"

"Awful. Spin-outs all over the place. I probably should've waited. But good old Jenny got me through." He patted the roof of the car, then surprised Kate with a second hug that lifted her off her feet. He waltzed her a few steps and set her back down. Nothing low-keyed about her Uncle

Pete. He'd lost some hair and added a few pounds around his waist, but his energy and affection were unchanged. "It's just so great to see you."

"Likewise."

He took a small suitcase out of the back seat and handed it to Kate. "If you don't mind? You're getting a deal, mind you. It's light compared to this puppy." He pulled a cardboard box into his arms and bumped the door shut with his knee.

She started toward the house. "Copies of your botany book?"

"Yep. I wish the darn thing had been ready for me to use this semester like it was supposed to be. The publishing world isn't much better than academia for keeping to a schedule."

She held the front door open and followed him in, then ran into him when he stopped short in the middle of the dining room.

"What the heck, Katie? What happened out there?" He was staring out the big window. Yellow tape with POLICE LINE DO NOT CROSS on it in black was tied to trees and bushes in a wide circle around the place the body had been found. He rested the box on the back of a chair.

She came up beside him. "Somebody got hypothermia and died. Yesterday. I—I saw her hand—reaching out of the snow—"

He gave her a quick look and then her third hug of the morning, one-armed and awkward because of the box he was balancing. "Oh, how awful. I'm sorry."

Tears prickled. "Just a hand. It could have been worse."

"Yes." The snowy window reflected in his glasses like headlights. "Good Lord, that's a shame." He shook his head and let the box slide onto the table. "Can't have helped poor

Sarah's spirits any." He started toward the stairs and took them two at a time.

Kate hefted the box of books, carried it into the living room and set it on the floor. Then she stood in the dining room, absently stroking Eclipse, who was curled in his favorite place on the window seat. She gazed out at the Reserve. The wind was busy with its endless work. Let all low things be smooth and white, it said. Let memory be erased. It nibbled at the edges of footprints, blurred the tracks of the snowmobile and trailer that had carried the body away. It fluttered the edges of the plastic police tape, left it. Returned.

Uncle Pete came down the stairs. "She looks tired. I want her to get better faster." He hung up his coat and gestured out the window. "Who was it?"

"Don't know." Kate sat on the window seat, her back to the yellow tape the wind couldn't erase.

"It happened yesterday? The police might know by now. Probably make the front page of the local paper."

"It's in the kitchen," she said. "I found it on top of the snowbank the plow left."

"Yeah, the delivery guy just pitches it out the car window these days. Hardly slows down."

"It was in a plastic sleeve, so at least it didn't get wet."

"I delivered papers when I was a kid. Right to people's doors." He went to the kitchen and poured himself a cup of coffee, snagging the paper on the way to the dining room. "Join me, Katie?"

"Great." She got up and had just filled her cup when he shouted something, startling her. She dashed into the dining room, but he'd exploded up the stairs, the coffee in his cup still vibrating beside the open paper.

CONTROVERSIAL PROFESSOR FOUND DEAD, the headline read. Beneath it, in smaller type, ACCIDENT CLAIMS CAMILA CHAVEZ.

Camila Chavez—oh, no. That lovely man she'd met yesterday, Azul, had said Camila was his fiancée. The picture beside the story showed a fierce-looking woman holding a TREES = AIR FILTERS sign. Kate read the article, which sounded like an obituary after the first paragraph. Stanford, then M.I.T. for graduate work, a bunch of national awards—the woman had been brilliant.

The footsteps coming down the stairs were heavy. "We've lost Camila," Uncle Pete said, dropping into a chair.

"Was she a friend?"

"Friend? If an attack dog can be a friend. Her students called her the Dragon Lady. She did us a lot of good, though—she had more energy than the rest of the department put together." He threw his glasses on top of the newspaper, rubbed his hands over his face and looked out at the yellow tape. "Sad that she died a stone's throw from this house. So close to help." He looked up at Kate. "We didn't always see eye to eye, but she was a force of nature. Sarah was closer to her than I was."

Upstairs, Kate sat in the chair next to the bed and took her teary-eyed aunt's hand.

"Camila was a mover and shaker," Aunt Sarah said, her voice quavering. "She put this college on the map. Anybody who cared about the environment knew her name, and that meant they knew Otterlin's name. Oh, God." She got her voice under control. "She went after corporations and individuals, anyone she found polluting or weaseling their way around regulations. She was tough."

"She studied field mice?"

"More than studied them. She was their advocate, their champion, their den mother. Wrote her dissertation on them ten years ago and discovered their numbers had dropped drastically. Only a couple of places where the population was holding its own, and one of those was right in my back yard." She nodded in the direction of the snowy Reserve. "I used to see her out there all the time."

"I'm sorry. Uncle Pete said you were close."

"Yes. She chose her friends carefully, and I was honored to be among the few." She wiped her eyes with the hem of the bedsheet. "She didn't care much for Pete, though."

"That must have been awkward."

"No, Pete's good at ignoring what he doesn't like." She let her head fall back on the pillow. "Being her friend was work. She was high-energy, talked a blue streak. Completely dedicated to her work. She used to stop in here for tea sometimes, often very late, after she'd checked the cameras."

"Cameras? I didn't notice them when I was out there yesterday."

"You wouldn't. They're down low, hidden under bushes or near the stone wall. It's hard to find them even without a foot or two of snow," Aunt Sarah said. "They're digital, and remote controlled, so there's not much to do by way of maintenance. But sometimes a leaf or twig gets blown up against the lens. I used to help her when I could. Not since this, though." She raised her cast an inch.

"You'll be up and about again soon." She didn't tell Aunt Sarah that she looked weak and shaken. Having a friend freeze to death practically in her back yard had to be a shock, one Kate hoped wouldn't turn into a medical setback.

"Azul will be devastated. She was moving into his house, and they were making wedding plans." Aunt Sarah looked past Kate, out the window. "I wonder who will take over her project with the mice. She used to call them BFFs. Best Friends Forever." She shook her head. "Students are young enough to say 'forever' without irony."

"But what did she mean? The mice were her best friends?"

Aunt Sarah shook her head. "Black Footed Fieldies. Field mice."

"Still, it sounds like she took their plight personally."

"She did. Don't get me wrong, she was a rigorous scientist, a top-notch biologist. But she had a passionate streak that fueled her work."

* * *

Kate stood at the top of the hill and slid her skis back and forth to clear the kick zones. She wasn't looking at the pristine slope of fluff she'd seen the day before, but at snow trampled and flattened by snowshoes and pot-holed by boots. Despite the wind's attention, the surface was still a mess. The snowmobile had left its laddered tracks from the house down to a hole beside the oak tree.

Where the Dragon Lady had run out of fire.

Where death had reached out of the snow.

Kate pushed off and angled hard to the left to avoid the rucked-up area. The snow would be firmer today, and faster, but the trampled part of the hill wasn't safe. If a ski's kick zone landed on a pocket of boot-print air, she could lurch or even fall. Landing on the harder, rough area would be nasty—unlike her fall yesterday, which had been a comedy routine, floundering in soft snow, half-entangled with the eloquent Azul.

He'd be reeling now from the terrible news. She hoped he'd heard it from a gentle friend rather than being hit with a headline the way Uncle Pete had been.

Kate paused at the bottom of the hill, her back to the trampled snow and yellow tape. The morning was still cloudy but calm, a serene contrast to the storm and drama of the previous day. Ahead of her, wind had softened the edges of the crater she and Azul had made, but it hadn't yet been filled.

Sean drifted into her mind, the enigmatic FBI agent who'd saved her life in Maine and had come to see her in Pennsylvania a few weeks ago. That second time she'd seen him, he'd removed the tracking device he'd put on her truck, so he wouldn't know where she was now. She'd given him her number, invited him to phone her. She'd thought of him often in the days after he'd left, called away for an urgent assignment, but as time passed without any word he crossed her mind less often.

She was cold. She'd been standing, which sometimes resulted in snow sticking to her kickers. She picked up each ski and slapped it down, then gave it a firm back-and-forth. Each time she lifted a ski it threw a pink shadow as sunlight reflected up from the snow and hit the base. How pretty that was.

To her right, at the edge of the rosy aura, a golden object lay among the glitter. At first Kate thought it was an ornate earring.

No. It was furred like a fox, orange fading to tan. Unlike a fox, it had wings, shining cellophane wings she could see through, big and veined. The way the front legs tucked under its body reminded her of the way cats and dogs sleep. Its huge eyes were black, and the short antennae, also black, caught the sun and shone. The whole creature struck her as exotic, made of fur and lace, with feet that look clawed.

While it was a delight to look at, she was glad it wasn't alive and flying around. Because now that she understood what it was, the payload at its stern gave her chills: a bomb bay loaded with venom.

The bee was dead, of course, in this temperature. Wasn't it? She nudged it with the tip of a ski pole: no reaction. Good.

She pulled her fanny pack around to the front and found the case to her sunglasses. It was the hard-shelled kind, with a hinge that snapped shut good and tight, perfect for carrying the piece of fragile gold filigree she'd found. The insect charmed her with its intricacy, so much in contrast to the broad white swaths of snow and sky. She picked the bee up with a tissue, took one last look, and wrapped it loosely.

She'd been so involved in absorbing all the visual details that it wasn't until after she'd placed the biological ornament into her makeshift jewelry box and closed it gently that it occurred to her how odd it was to find a bee at the end of November, after a snowstorm. She mulled it over as she herringboned up the rise, unable to stop herself from glancing up at the crest, the image of Azul flying at her in his red jacket still vivid in her mind.

At the top, the field ahead of her was empty. Here and there a tuft of weeds held its head up, tall enough to have escaped being buried by the storm. Underneath the snow, the famous black-footed mice were no doubt nibbling and twitching and keeping a nervous lookout for predators, unaware they'd lost their human protector.

The bee must have escaped from some bee-keeper's care. Weren't hives sometimes moved? From some long-ago entomology unit in college, Kate remembered that bees winter in clusters, shivering their flight muscles to make heat and eating stored honey to fuel those muscles. The maverick she'd just stowed in her fanny pack had become confused and fatally cold away from the mass of his fellows.

Yes, active muscles make heat. She followed Azul's tracks, grateful for them because the snow was heavier today under the bright sun. Just a few minutes of kick and glide and she was hot, pulling off her headband and gloves, unzipping her anorak. The field narrowed after about a mile, an oak forest encroaching from the left and a chain-link fence appearing on the right.

The tracks took a sharp turn through a gap in the fence. Through some bushes along the back of the fence Kate saw a green clapboard house with a deck, two pairs of skis leaning against the wall outside a glass door.

Azul's place? How nice to be so close to the Reserve, like Aunt Sarah's house. Hers had the better view, but this green house had more privacy.

Kate carried on straight for another half-mile, then turned back, skiing in her own tracks and then in hers and Azul's. Much faster than untouched snow. She was back at the yellow tape before she was quite ready to be reminded of Dr. Chavez's accident.

* * *

"I don't understand what happened to her," Uncle Pete said, twisting in his seat to look over his shoulder as he backed down the driveway. The Volvo had come off an assembly line a decade before back-up cameras were common. "She was real outdoorsy, and she knew the Reserve inside and out. She must have whacked her head, or had a stroke, something like that. Fell down and froze to death. Damn." He shook his head and changed the subject. "Ready to visit the groves of academe?"

"You bet." The sun was making a mid-afternoon cameo appearance, sparkling in the icy branches of a blue spruce by the side of the road. The best kind of Christmas tree.

"Don't expect too much. The Otterlin campus isn't Harvard Yard." Then he grinned at her. "No ivy on the buildings, or on the professors, either. And our shirts aren't stuffed."

"I knew that," Kate said. "It's hard to stuff a flannel shirt." Uncle Pete usually walked to work, but taking the car would let him stash the box of his books in his office and then pick up groceries after seeing students.

"Check out the Student Union, which is a big glass-and-brick number right in the middle of campus," he said. "It has a cafeteria that's open early and late and in between, and you can usually find a quiet corner to read over your coffee. It also has a bookstore and conference rooms and a climbing wall and racquetball courts."

"Sounds like your students are a pretty athletic bunch."

"Yes, when Sarah goes to Northfield Mountain, half an hour from here, she says the place looks like the campus except everyone's on skis." His shoulders sagged. "She won't be going there this winter. But you'd enjoy a day there. Lots of groomed Nordic trails."

"Maybe when she's feeling better. I'm staying close until she perks up."

"I should tell you, Katie, the doc warned me not to expect her to bounce back. We're not dealing with an average break but a really nasty one. And she's not a spring chicken anymore. Of course, neither am I." He gave her a rueful smile. "Looks like you're the only chick in the coop."

"A temporary condition, Uncle Pete." She looked out the window. She was tempted to tell him about the dead hand in hers, how the raw shock of it had made her feel older, somehow, and sadder. How the hand looked so much like her own.

But no, he'd known the woman. It wouldn't be kind to talk about all that. And the moment had passed: he'd gone back to telling her about the campus.

"Across the street from the Union is the library, open until 2:00 a.m. when classes are in session. Are you a night-owl?" His heavy glasses swung toward Kate.

"I used to be, but lately I've been falling asleep at nine." Kate didn't tell him she'd been waking up at all hours. Insomnia was new to her; until recently she'd enjoyed sleeping like a hibernating bear. Could Prof. Chavez, someone she'd never met, be haunting her nights? Or was it the murders in Pennsylvania? She'd thought they were behind her.

"The student union and the library, those are the practical places. The real jewel of the campus, though, and Otterlin's claim to fame, is the aviary. It's a famous research site, not just for ornithologists but also for botanists and entomologists. The guy Camila was about to marry, for instance—he's from Brazil, tenure track, but we do a lot of collaborations with Germans and Swedes and Belgians who come over for a few weeks. You can't miss the place: it looks like a greenhouse the size of a city block. Well, almost."

"Awesome."

"Otterlin's different from other colleges its size. It was founded by a group of wealthy amateur ornithologists in 1835—funded by them, too. Money was never a problem until recently. The dean blames the board of trustees, and the trustees blame the dean." He shook his head. "Never mind that. From the beginning, Otterlin's had more of a research focus than most colleges—more like a university, even though it doesn't have graduate students."

"So is the aviary still in its original building?"

"No. The technology—glass, ventilation, heating, humidity, digital controls—all that stuff got so advanced we just couldn't update the building any further. We had to build a new one, as the founders had anticipated. It's only fifteen years old and doing great.

"It's a nice place to sit, too, but you can't eat anything. Crumbs would screw up the experiments." He slowed and made a left turn between stone pillars supporting a wrought-iron arch spelling out OTTERLIN COLLEGE. "Say, the aviary might be a great place to go to draw things. I go there to write sometimes."

"Great, I'll have a look." Hearing tropical birdsong in the middle of a Massachusetts winter might lighten her mood.

"Don't let those pillars scare you," he said as the Volvo passed under the arch. "I've always thought they looked like a cemetery entrance, but so far—" He caught himself and coughed, probably thinking of Prof. Chavez.

His next words confirmed Kate's guess. "Otterlin is small, but it's a locus of cutting-edge environmental research. Camila worked hard to make our reputation stay at the top, I'll give her that."

* * *

Still hungry from the morning's skiing despite the apple-and-cheddar sandwich she'd grilled for lunch, Kate decided on a snack of yogurt and coffee in the student union cafeteria on the second floor, a bright, pleasant place already strung with twinkling holiday lights. Its central area was busy with groups of students chatting and laughing, noisy as gulls on a beach. Quiet nooks along the walls offered refuge for couples or singles who wanted to read or simply sit and think.

She slipped into one of the alcoves. A cushioned chair that looked like a bowl tipped on its side invited her in, and once inside she felt silence spread over her like oil. The chair was behind a column and angled toward a window so

26

that all she saw was snow, and sky, and small conversations between white and gray.

Setting the empty yogurt container and coffee cup on the floor, she sat cross-legged, eyes closed, and let the peace of the place work its way into her tired mind. Falling asleep without meaning to, she dreamed of snarling dogs and small boys pointing guns at her.

She woke with a start. Slipping out of the chair, she stretched. The impromptu nap hadn't left her feeling rested, and the light was bluish. If she was going to get to know the Otterlin campus today, she'd better hurry. She bussed her cup and went down the stairs fast to wake herself up.

The ground floor of the building housed a bookstore on one side and a swimming pool and gym on the other. College bookstores carried more than books these days: Kate cruised the aisles, pleased to see a comprehensive art-supply section. Otterlin T-shirts and sweats took up a quarter of the floor space, and shelves of chips and cookies claimed a corner next to refrigerated cases featuring ice cream and soda. Oh, the metabolism of nineteen-year-olds, who could gobble down candy bars and pastries and not show an extra ounce of fat.

Until they did.

Kate went out into the cold, breath pluming around her face like a scarf. A flag hung limp at half-staff. The library could wait—she'd meant to ask her uncle if he could get her a card to check out books. But if the aviary was the college's jewel, she wanted to see it on this first visit.

She turned the corner. In the late light, the building looked like something out of a Disney movie: a glass cube the equivalent of four or five stories tall but without the usual infrastructure of floors and stairways. Foliage—trees and the vines that draped them—filled the space straight up to the domed roof. Lit like a casino, the aviary threw a green light. As she got closer, a long-tailed bird flared and swooped, disappearing into the emerald depths.

On the street a few students passed her in each direction, but none gave the building a second glance: the remarkable facility was, to them, ordinary campus furniture. She pushed the glass door open and found herself facing another set of glass doors with the sign DO NOT OPEN UNTIL OUTER DOORS ARE FULLY CLOSED. A simple method to make sure no birds zoomed to fatal freedom.

She'd expected them, of course, but the heat and humidity that enveloped her when she stepped through the second set of doors was a shock even so. A big yellow-and-aqua parrot leaned toward her from an overhead branch and shrieked; a neon-blue butterfly fluttered against her chest.

Despite the glass walls, the understory was dim, shaded by a bewildering assortment of trees, most of them unfamiliar to Kate: some with leaves that looked like umbrellas, others with broad, flat leaves like plates, still others with lime-green, feathery foliage. High above her the light was stronger, and small birds flickered and whistled.

Brick paths invited her farther in. She stopped to take off her fleece, then prowled deeper into the man-made jungle. Her shoulders brushed branches that overhung the walkways, and the hum of honeybees blundering their way into pink and white blossoms joined the twittering from the canopy. The air was heavy and sweet.

A person could get lost in here. The pathways wandered, curved and doubled back. An occasional bench looked promising for future drawing sessions, but on this first visit she was in scouting mode. It was hard, though, to keep an overview of the maze-like place in her head.

After a few more turns, she had to admit it: she wasn't sure which way to go to get back to the main entrance.

Rounding a corner, she came up behind someone leaning over a wooden filing cabinet, one in a long row, and holding an odd implement that looked like an upright teapot with a small bellows grafted along one side. Smoke drifted from the spout.

"Hello," Kate said. She didn't want to startle the person.

The strategy failed completely. The woman leaped and turned, a look of alarm on her face, and dropped the smoking device. When she saw Kate the alarm was replaced by anger.

Kate understood; she hated being startled, too. "I'm sorry," she said. "Didn't mean to make you jump." Why wasn't an aviary worker accustomed to visitors?

"It's all right." The woman's expression softened, and she picked up the smoker. She was tall and striking, with a sculptured face and blue eyes. Dressed like a student, in jeans and an Otterlin T-shirt, she had a couple of decades on the average undergraduate. "You might not want to spend too much time back here with the bees, though. They can be grouchy. Smoke is supposed to calm them, but I wouldn't count on it."

Hives, the boxes Kate had mistaken for two-drawer filing cabinets. Insects came and went through slots she'd mistaken for handles. "Thanks for the warning," she said, retreating. One bee didn't bother her, or two or three, but she found large numbers of them frightening, even repulsive. The hives were too busy for her liking, and as she turned away she marveled that the woman bee-keeper wasn't wearing protective clothing.

Kate worked at retracing her steps. Huge leaves beaded with water hung low over the paths, and below the knees her soaked jeans felt heavy. Orchids and hummingbirds brightened every turn. Yes, a fabulous place to draw. She couldn't imagine how Uncle Pete could write here, though, with all the distractions. Didn't writers need to withdraw, look inward, be protected by the hush of libraries or a snug studio at home? Wouldn't the parrots and bees and clouds of twittering songbirds pull his mind away from the page? Not to mention butterflies—another one flew erratically toward her and landed on the bright pink fleece over her arm. To butterfly eyes it must look like an enormous flower, disappointingly dry.

Well, there were all kinds of writers. Uncle Pete was an extrovert, hardly the Emily Dickinson type.

A small EXIT sign, almost hidden among exuberant ferns, told her she'd guessed right. Good thing: it was getting late. Her nap in the spherical chair at the union meant she'd have to see the library another day.

The butterfly riding on her fleece was a beauty. Its body was striped black and white, its wings orange underneath and black with white panes on top. It had those alien eyes, like the bee she'd found in the snowy Reserve. Ah, of course: this must be where the bee had come from— the aviary. It had gotten out somehow.

After silently thanking the butterfly for solving that mystery, she put her finger next to its head, hoping to inspire it to find a more natural perch. A foreleg—black, with a tiny pad on the end—touched her, but it was so wispy she didn't feel a thing. She looked into the huge eyes, wondering how she appeared to this creature. Its compound vision must break up her image into something closer to a late Picasso than to what she saw in her mirror.

Before she got too close to the glass door, she gave the butterfly the gentlest nudge she could manage, and it lofted up and away to the shelter of its unlikely paradise.

Back to the cold streets. Even as the first breath of dry air made her cough, Kate saluted the adaptability of the human body. We can live in jungles and deserts, she thought, in Greenland and in Alert, that city in Canada only five hundred miles from the North Pole. We're amazing.

But it was late, and Aunt Sarah needed dinner. Kate hurried through the campus, her wet legs chilled, her boots squeaking in blue snow. She tried to keep the aviary's soundtrack running in her head, but the squawks and songs of its tropical birds faded along with the winter light.

THREE

On Sunday afternoon, the bungalow on College Street became a busy place.

Aunt Sarah was a social person, member of half a dozen clubs, active both in civic groups and at the college. Kate knew it was hard for her aunt to be sequestered in her bedroom, tapping a cell phone awkwardly with her left hand to talk to friends. Of course the friends would rally around Aunt Sarah.

In person. With food and other offerings.

Odd, but newcomer Kate had already met two of the three early visitors. The first appeared as a tall blur through the frosted panes of the front door, resolving, when she opened it, into a sober version of the ebullient bearded man she'd met skiing in Topper Reserve.

"Azul," Kate said. "Come in."

"Thank you, my friend Houston." Despite the comical nickname, his face was grave.

"I heard about Camila. I'm so very sorry."

He nodded, his face strained. He took a paper package, stapled at the top, from an inside pocket and handed it to Kate, then hung his red jacket on the stand near the door and stamped the snow off his feet. Small cubes, dirty white, scattered over the black mat like blind dice: he had on ski boots. He took the small package back.

Before she shut the door Kate glanced onto the porch: yes, a pair of skis was propped against the railing. He'd come the back way, through the Reserve. Shorter than taking the road, faster than walking.

"Just let me tell Aunt Sarah you're here," she said, and ran up the stairs.

"Oh, I'm glad he's stopped in. Although I'm sure he's distraught," Aunt Sarah said. "Kate, dear, would you mind making a pot of coffee and bringing it up? Join us then, if you'd like."

Azul was already coming up the stairs, boots thumping. The paper was folded away from a bunch of freesias, which looked as small as jewels in his big fist. Kate stood aside at the top to give him room to get past her, snagging the yellow blossoms out of his hand. He looked like a sleep-walker, barely noticing she'd taken the flowers.

As the coffeemaker gurgled, she thought how socially adept Aunt Sarah was. Giving Kate a task allowed Azul time alone with his old friend, but didn't completely exclude Kate. Making such an arrangement on the spur of the moment might come easily to some people, but Kate couldn't have counted on coming up with it if she'd been in Aunt Sarah's shoes.

Okay, in Aunt Sarah's socks.

She took the stairs more slowly this time, carrying a tray loaded with mugs and a pot under a cozy printed with dark blue owls. She'd even found room for the freesias, in a small white vase. They put out a potent fragrance, almost too sweet.

Azul was in the stuffed chair by the window, sitting forward with elbows on knees, chin on hands. He looked up when she came in. "Hello, Houston." Tears sparkled in his beard.

"Houston?" Aunt Sarah asked.

"A nickname from our first meeting," Azul said. "We, ah, met the day before yesterday."

Ran into each other, he might have said. Kate set out the mugs and poured, letting the puzzled look Aunt Sarah gave her go unanswered.

"So I am baffled. The facts make no sense," Azul said, picking up a thread of conversation he must have dropped when Kate appeared. The sleep-walker had awakened: his voice was urgent. "She was fit, used to the conditions, dressed appropriately. We tent-camp in the winter for fun. It is absurd. As if—" he looked around for inspiration, his gaze sweeping past Kate without seeing her. "As if a NASCAR driver fell off a tricycle. She was a dragon, an unstoppable force. You might as well try to freeze fire."

"Is there something we don't know?" Aunt Sarah asked quietly. "Accidents happen. Did she have any medical conditions? Vertigo, seizures, anything that could have caused her to fall?"

"No, nothing like that. I have been over it all, in my head, a thousand times," he said. "Trying to imagine how she could have—how it could have happened." Light from the window heightened the dark circles under his eyes. He couldn't have slept much since he'd heard the news. "Her sister is coming, and I do not know what to tell her."

"Where's she coming from?" Aunt Sarah's eyes looked tired, too.

"Alaska. Rosa is not going to accept that Camila fell over in a couple of feet of snow and died of carbon monoxide build-up like an avalanche victim. Or lost herself to hypothermia."

"Have the police told you anything? They were all over the field out back," Kate said.

"Two of them came to the house yesterday," Azul said. "They questioned me and poked around the house, looking in the bedroom especially, but everywhere. The basement, the back porch, the car. Especially the car, after I told them Camila and I shared it."

Kate asked, "They don't suspect foul play, do they?"

He shrugged. "I do not know. They were pleasant but told me nothing. I suppose if you are a policeman it is your job to be suspicious, and the spouse is always number one on the list of suspects, is he not? In this case the almost-spouse." His shoulders sagged. "They wanted to know when I last talked to Camila, and where I was all night. You do not get crossed off the suspect list for being home alone, reading student papers and falling asleep over them."

"No," Sarah murmured. Her eyes shut.

Azul heaved himself to his feet. "Speaking of sleep, my dear Sarah, you are going there. As well you should. You must heal yourself."

Downstairs, at the door, the big man said, "Oh, my Houston, I am sad." Putting on his jacket, he paused with one arm in a sleeve, as if he'd run out of energy. As if finishing the task was beyond him. "Everybody says my Cammie was so hard to deal with, but that was only because they didn't know her well enough. I knew her best."

"Yes." She didn't know what else to say.

He got his other arm in its sleeve and zipped his jacket slowly.

She watched him drop his skis on the ground and step into them, kicking off between the porch and her camper to disappear around the corner of the house.

When she went upstairs to collect the cups and empty pot, Aunt Sarah was snoring. Gently, the way she did everything.

Washing up in the kitchen, Kate thought she heard the door. "Uncle Pete?" she called, but got no answer. Who else could it be? She started past the island. "Aunt Sarah's asleep, so let's try—"

A figure loomed in the doorway, arm raised, and Kate gave an involuntary cry as she dodged backwards, bumping into the counter behind her.

She caught her breath. She'd managed to avoid colliding with the tall woman carrying a plastic cake-holder aloft on one palm. The cake-holder tilted precariously and the woman shuffled a few quick steps to get back under it. Then she smiled at Kate. "Whew. That was a close one."

A familiar face. It took Kate a beat to place her as the worker in the college aviary.

The woman slid the cake onto the island. "Angel-food. No fat, no guilt. Fat angels can't fly." She stuck out a hand. "I'm Brenda, a friend of Sarah's."

"Kate." She was slow to take the hand because it wore a nylon glove, pale blue. Get over it, she told herself, but her handshake was brief.

Brenda's eyes searched hers. "I'm sorry I startled you." Kate's height, she had a graceful way of carrying herself that made her seem statuesque. And her eyes were the deepest blue possible.

Kate smiled. "We're even, then. I made you jump yesterday. By the bee hives."

"Oh, that's right." A luminous smile. "I knew I'd seen you somewhere."

"I'm Sarah's niece, here to help her out until her cast comes off."

"Nice niece," Brenda said. She pulled off her gloves, stuffed them in a pocket, and unwound the scarf around her neck, making it look like a dance move. Unzipping her parka, she looked down, and when her eyes came back to Kate's they were wet. "She's asleep? I really wanted to talk to her." She nodded at the cake. "I figured angel food was appropriate. She's certainly been an angel to me."

"I'll have a look," Kate said.

Aunt Sarah had slipped lower in the bed and pulled the blankets up. She wasn't snoring, but she didn't respond to her name spoken softly, twice.

Downstairs, Kate said, "I'm sorry. She's out like a light."

"I'll have to come back. I really need her." Brenda zipped her parka up. "I'm, I was, Camila Chavez's best friend. She, she—"

"I know," Kate said. "I heard. I'm terribly sorry about what happened." She didn't need to say she'd found the body. And she certainly couldn't recommend ditching gloves because they reminded her of this woman's best friend's dead hand.

Brenda looked at the floor. A tear fell to the linoleum, and she turned away. Birdsong floated behind her, as if she had a house finch in her pocket.

She did, more or less. She pulled out a cell phone, tapped it and held it to her ear. "Yes," she said. "I'll call you back." Slid the cell into her jacket and turned at the door. Her voice was still tight. "Thank you for taking care of your angel aunt."

Another pocket yielded a pair of oversized sunglasses. Wrap-around style, they concealed the amazing blue. Her eyes changed to those of a butterfly, or a bee.

* * *

The third visitor wasn't wearing a suit but he looked like he would be comfortable in one. Dark, crisp clothes: newish black jeans and a turtleneck sweater with a black windbreaker over it. Crisp haircut too: he might have been at the barber's an hour ago. Pleasant but alert. Energy coiled inside him like a prowling cat's. He might be a decade older than Kate but he looked as slim and fit as an undergrad. The difference was that undergrads could take their muscles for granted. This guy must be pushing forty, and he had to work for his.

He knew where to hang his jacket, too. Kate supposed it was obvious, but she felt superfluous. The door was unlocked during the day, and Aunt Sarah's friends could shed outerwear and climb stairs without any help from her.

"How she's doing?" His voice was low, his green eyes kind.

"Asleep the last time I looked, but I'll check on her now." She turned at the bottom of the stairs only to find him close behind her. "Are you her doctor?"

"Oh, sorry. I'm Mark. Mark Haley. Friend of hers from way back." He followed her up.

They peered through the half-open door together. The bedside lamp was on, and Aunt Sarah was reading a book called *Wolves at the Door.* She looked up and smiled.

"Come in, come in," she said. "Both of you," she added when Kate hesitated. "Mark, this is my niece Kate Corliss. From Danvers—the coastal branch of the family. Katie, this is my friend of many years who's one of Hunterville's finest."

"It's not really coastal. It's up a river."

"You're going to blow my cover right off the bat?" Mark asked Sarah. "I'm not in uniform anymore."

"Are you calling me a bat? My husband will be home soon. You'd better be careful."

"He'll be too hungry to care whether I've insulted his wife or not. You know how he is when he wants his dinner."

"Afraid I do," Sarah said. "But don't air all our dirty laundry, please. Katie just got here and she thinks we're nice."

"Oh, they're nice all right," Mark said to Kate. "And they're other things, too, like most people."

"That husband of mine promised to bring home pizza, Katie's made a spinach salad, and you should stay, Mark."

"Will you be joining us downstairs?"

"In a day or two."

He snorted. "You realize the pizza won't last more than ten minutes, don't you?"

"I'm counting on Katie to save me a piece or two. The doc said to take it easy, but I can't stand to stay perched up here in the rafters like a roosting hen for much longer."

As if they'd come to an implicit agreement, the smiles drained away and they dropped the banter. "The stairs in this house are steep," Mark said. "Be careful."

"Do you have any news about Camila?"

"No. We searched the scene thoroughly but didn't find anything out of the ordinary. Looks like simple hypothermia, but of course we'll wait for the ME to tell us cause of death." He looked at Kate. "Medical Examiner."

She nodded. In the past few months she'd come to know what ME stood for, through the experiences she'd rather not have had on her travels in Maine and upstate New York. We choose some aspects of our lives, she thought, and others come unbidden.

The front door banged open. Thumps and a shout. "Where's the old man?" Uncle Pete called. He must have recognized Mark's car.

"Mark turned forty-five a week ago," Sarah said to Kate. "He'll never hear the end of it."

"Until I turn forty-six," Mark said with a wink. "C'mon, Kate, let's go down there and gobble up all the pizza. Only to save your uncle from himself, of course."

Uncle Pete had set the salad out, and forks. Ice tinkled in a big pitcher as he carried it to the table. Kate took two slices of the pie up to Sarah, who shooed her downstairs.

"Thank you," she said. "Now scram. Enjoy the company. Mark's a dear."

At the table, the men were looking at each other as if one of them had just brought up something important. "Possible," the detective said.

"She made a lot of enemies," Uncle Pete said, "among political conservatives, oil company execs, ditto the mining crowd. Not just here in Massachusetts but all over the country. She stirred up more than her share of trouble, always badgering reporters to cover environmental issues. You could fill a book with her op-ed pieces. And not just the *Globe* or the *Worcester Telegram*, but the *Times* and the *Post*. She may have been pint-sized but she packed a gallon of trouble. And that's just politics."

"What do you mean, 'just politics'?" Kate asked. Her uncle was filling her in; Mark must know all this. "Politics can be intense."

"She was personally difficult, too. Fought with everybody in the biology department, everybody in the science building, everybody at the aviary. I'd bet she even fought with the parrots. And at faculty meetings? More than once I wanted to stuff her in a snowbank myself." He saw Kate's shocked expression. "A metaphorical snowbank."

"He doesn't mince words, does he?" Mark said, filling his glass with ice-water.

"Are you saying it wasn't an accident, Uncle Pete?"

"Just playing devil's advocate." He sat back in his chair and eyed the pizza, then reached for another piece. "A major pastime in academic circles."

"If I were looking for a criminal, which I assure you I'm not," Mark said to Kate, "I'd definitely start with local snowbank-stuffers, like Pete here. Not a mining exec in Utah who read something nasty Camila said about his company. Murder is home-brewed."

"Yikes," Kate said. "Should I lock my bedroom door?"

"Of course. And watch that man like a hawk," Mark said.

He and Kate looked across the table at Pete, who laughed so hard he had to hold onto his stomach.

* * *

Kate opened her glasses case and took out the tissue, then unfolded it carefully on the dinette table in her camper. The bee showed itself to be a collection of fine lines, legs and hair and transparent veined wings. It looked like a small but efficient gadget, ready to fly away at any moment. She thought of Paul Klee's whimsical *Twittering Machine,* one of her favorite drawings though nothing like her own realistic style.

She was almost afraid to breathe. This jewel of a creature—this buzzing machine—might fall apart. The winter air was dry, after all, and the insect's joints delicate. The electric space heater she was using in her makeshift studio meant the temperature fluctuated dramatically.

So she sprayed her uncomplaining model lightly with the permanent fixative she used on her finished artwork. The bee probably wouldn't hang together indefinitely, but she only needed a few days to draw it.

She sharpened her hardest pencils, enjoying the smell of graphite and wood, and started a sketch, then got out her recently acquired magnifying glass. It had been a great help when she'd examined photographs a month ago, in the Adirondacks, looking for clues in a murder case. Now she used it to investigate the intricate anatomy of the bee, its face with underslung mandible, its foreleg with hairs Kate remembered were used for cleaning antennae, the tiny claw at the tip. The rear legs were thicker. Wasn't that where the pollen baskets were? A biology major, she'd had a few weeks of entomology in college, but that was a long time ago.

She lost herself in work, her favorite state of mind.

FOUR

Uncle Pete was having a hissy fit. To his usual histrionic gestures he added stomping hard enough to make the house shake. Eclipse bailed from the window seat and scrabbled through the dining room to the refuge of the converted garage. Kate wished she could follow.

"Idiots! Dingbats!" He'd left for the college that morning only to come back within half an hour, closing the door so hard the glass rattled and thumping his briefcase on the floor. Kate had been pouring herself a cup of coffee, which she spilled when the door slammed. "The building is a mess, classrooms completely unusable. They ought to be fired, the lot of them!"

"You want to fire the classrooms?" Mopping the counter, Kate hoped for a laugh.

"No, I want to fire the morons who left the heat too low, so the pipes froze, and then the sun warmed them up and they burst and sprayed the plaster right off the walls and made us such a lovely wading pool right in the middle of Bascomb Hall!" He threw his arms around as if he were singing an aria instead of complaining. "The stairs are such pretty waterfalls. The pool was so deep I should have looked for mermaids!"

Then he sat down.

A wail floated down the stairs. "What's going on? Pete? Katie?"

Uncle Pete stood and trudged up the stairs, the energy of his anger spent. But he grumbled as he went. "Fish. I'm going to buy a dozen goldfish and give them to the dean."

A few minutes later, when he came back down, he was still muttering. "I'll get the head of B and G a pair of swimming trunks. The really skimpy kind. If they make them in his size." He sat at the table, pouting like a child.

"B and G?"

"Buildings and Grounds," Uncle Pete said. "Very flattering. He'll look like a sumo wrestler."

Kate couldn't help herself. She laughed.

Her uncle glared at her for a moment, then cracked a reluctant smile. "You wouldn't believe the scene over there. Faculty salaries are going to be cut in half to pay for repairing the place."

"You really won't be able to use the classrooms?"

"No, and I'm not the only one. Bascomb's mostly classrooms, with some faculty offices mixed in. My office on the fourth floor is okay, thank goodness. The pipes burst on the second and third. Wooden floors, wooden stairways. They'll be wrecked." He heaved a sigh. "I'm afraid at least one of my classes is going to have to meet here." He gestured at the table.

"Here? In the dining room?"

"Otterlin's a small college, so there wasn't a lot of classroom space going idle. Now there's a deficit, and I'm not the only prof who's going to be hosting classes. The library has a few meeting rooms, but those will go to instructors who live farther from campus. This house is a few minutes' walk for the students—I'm sunk." He paused. "So to speak."

Kate sat across from him. "Don't you like your students?"

"Oh, I like them fine. But they're students. And there are eight of them. They'll track mud on the rug and spill coffee and forget books and have to come back for them. They'll scare the cat and leave gum wrappers in the corners. We'll be lucky if they don't leave the gum, too, stuck under the table."

He'd already scared the cat himself. She'd spilled the coffee. "What's the class, and when does it meet?"

He was staring at the floor, perhaps seeing imaginary gum wrappers. "I don't like students knowing where I live. Of course they can look me up in the phone book—no, it's the Internet these days—and walk by and all that, but something changes when you let them inside. I feel invaded." He gave her a dark look. "What? Oh, a course for non-majors. Baby Botany. It's a half-semester course, seminar style, twice a week. First meeting tomorrow night at seven."

"You said only eight students? Wow, that's a small class."

"Yeah, we throw some small ones into the mix, to make the sciences a little friendlier. Looks great in the course catalogue." He brightened. "Say, would you like to join us?"

"Sure," she said. Startled, she responded to the eager expression on her uncle's face. Joining the class did make sense—it would be meeting right outside her bedroom, after all, and spending the time behind a closed door seemed unfriendly. It might be fun to watch Uncle Pete at work.

* * *

The old tracks were icy, gleaming in the sun. Kate went down the hill fast, hearing ice burr under her skis. Found a soft patch to make a turn left, came alongside the tracks she and Azul had made three days ago, widened and packed by others into a trail. On either side of it the snow was grainy, grippy: she stayed outside the icy trail and rabbit-hopped to the top of the rise, her skis juddering against the snowpack. Flat from here, out toward the green house where Azul's tracks had led. After she passed his gate she tried the trail again, since it was more shaded here and hadn't gone through the thaw-freeze effects of direct sunlight.

She pumped along, farther than she'd gone before, passing other openings in the chain-link fence that gave access to Azul's neighbors' houses. Why have a fence if there were so many breaks in it? Boundary marker, she supposed. Many of the yards had a row of evergreens along the fence, hemlock and cedar, their branches interwoven with the gray metal diamonds. Up high, birds twittered and flicked through the trees.

The trail curved to the left and dropped toward a pond, past a three-sided lean-to, its open side facing the water. Kate snowplowed to a stop and side-stepped to one end of the shelter to look through its small window. Her reflection looked back.

Its eyes blinked.

Holy cats! She jerked away, almost lost her balance, caught herself. Took a few strides toward the pond and skidded into a U-turn. A man stood just inside the lean-to. A slender man with dark brown skin, smiling.

"Sorry, didn't mean to surprise you."

"That's all right," Kate said, composing herself. She wished he weren't quite so amused. His face had blended with the lean-to's dark interior so she'd thought she was looking at her own eyes reflected. Until the blink.

"Are you here to count mice?" He skied out to meet her. Up close his face showed lines; he wasn't the young man she'd taken him for. Trim figure, hair military-short where it showed above a black headband.

"Mice? No." Maybe he was mistaking her for Dr. Chavez, the way Azul had.

"There's been some predation. See those tunnels?" He pointed with his pole to convex lines of pushed-up snow, a white version of what a mole would do to a summer lawn. "Those are left by ermines. White weasels. They follow mouse tunnels, but they're bigger and leave these lumpy lines. Which is a good thing, because it tells us they're here, and how much hunting they're doing. Sometimes if the snow is really deep, though, you don't see the tunnels."

Massachusetts. Everybody you tripped over was a PhD. "You must be with the college."

"I wear a couple of hats, but none of them is a mortarboard. I run a motel, and we get a lot of college business."

"Not too much at this time of year, I imagine."

"Right, spring's our big season. We're always booked up months in advance for graduation week. But there are other occasions, not as joyous. Crises of various sorts. I'm Brewster, by the way, but everybody calls me Brew."

"Kate."

"My other hat is running the campus bookstore."

"Oh, I checked that out. Liked it," Kate said.

"Are you with the college?"

"No, I'm visiting. My uncle teaches there, in biology."

"You must know all about this place, then." He waved an arm toward the pond, the woods around it. "Topper Reserve."

"I haven't been here long. What's there to know?"

"It would make a great golf course, wouldn't it? Especially the more open area near College Street, the direction you came from."

"Golf course? Are you kidding?"

"I wish I were." He leaned on his poles and sighed, still looking at the pond. "Do you know the name Don McCoy?"

"No, never heard of him."

"You sure are new to the area, then. He's a real estate developer, and he wants the college to sell this land to him so he can build a luxury condo complex with pools, spas, and a golf course."

"The college wouldn't do that, would it?"

"Don't be too sure. Otterlin's in a bit of a pickle, financially speaking."

She followed his gaze. The oak trees were holding on to their dried crisps of leaves, fawn-colored, rattling in the breeze. Snow had blown off one end of the pond to expose gray ice. Were fish sleeping below it, and frogs, a few turtles, their bodies sluggish with winter torpor? Above the water, beneath the oaks, mice and weasels carried on their warm-blooded lives in tunnels and nests. Owls would listen for them at night, and strike in deadly silence.

Prof. Chavez had spent her life studying black-footed field mice. Endangered creatures. Low on the food chain, they'd be hunted by foxes and house cats as well as by ermines and owls. In warm weather, snakes would join their list of enemies.

Building a golf course here would put humans on that list. Humans, the most powerful predator of all. Were the BFFs endangered, or doomed? She imagined backhoes and bulldozers ripping the forest apart, smoothing the contours. Native plants replaced by a monoculture of turf grass. The pond green with algae spawned by fertilizer run-off. Pests like chipmunks and woodchucks poisoned.

Pests like mice.

"I wouldn't be surprised if someone's knocked the old girl off," Brew said. "She would have done anything to stop the sale." He had an easy smile but his eyes were serious.

The old girl? "Who, Prof. Chavez?"

"Ah, you've heard what happened to her. You've been here at least a week."

Kate didn't tell him how accurate his guess was. "She was protecting the mice? Is that what you're saying?"

"Absolutely," Brew said. "She was ready to go to the wall for those five hundred mice. Five hundred furry roadblocks is how Don McCoy sees them."

"I hope the college doesn't sell."

"Tell your uncle to talk to the dean and to any trustees he knows. If Don becomes the owner of this land, the black-footed field mouse goes the way of the passenger pigeon, the sea mink, the Tasmanian tiger and all the others."

He'd said Don: he was on a first-name basis with the developer. "You know Don McCoy? Why don't you talk to him?"

"Oh, I've talked to him, believe me." The dark eyes left the pond and met her own. "He's my father."

* * *

Despite the missing back steps, the birdfeeder still needed filling. Leaving the Reserve, Kate stepped out of her skis behind the house and unscrewed the lid of the varmint-proof container. Two scoops of seed rattled into the feeder, and a blue jay jeered at her from a low branch. Was he alerting the troops that lunch was served?

Gosh, there were a lot of footprints here. With Aunt Sarah laid up, whose could they be? Kate had never seen Uncle Pete in the back yard, and she didn't think the police would have come this close to the house. Besides, the prints were fresh, the edges crisp.

She leaned over for a closer look. Yes, the bar at the front of the sole was clear. Cross-country ski boots.

Kate mentioned the tracks to Aunt Sarah.

"Oh? I don't know who would have been back there, unless it was the carpenter checking out the stairs. I hope that means he's going to show up soon and fix the darn things." She was sitting up, looking more alert than she had the day before. But the fingers that showed beyond the end of her cast were red and swollen.

Kate had brought up tea. She perched the cup and saucer on the small stack of books that had appeared on the bedside table along with a newspaper folded to a crossword puzzle. Her aunt was fighting cabin fever. Good. That meant she wasn't sleeping all day.

"I'm glad you met Brew," Aunt Sarah said. "He's quite active in the community, and his father owns the half of the Hunterville that the college doesn't."

"I hope the college doesn't sell Topper Reserve. It's such a beautiful place I'd hate to see it bulldozed for golf and condos."

"We'd all hate that. The whole faculty is begging the dean not to sell, but it's not up to him, it's the board of trustees that decides. I hear a lot of the board members like golf." Aunt Sarah blew across her teacup. "Some of us have a personal interest because our houses are right next to the Reserve."

"Like Azul?" Kate asked.

"Right. And two or three other faculty members. But even people who live farther out, or down in Amherst, are against McCoy's development. It would change the town dramatically."

Eclipse jumped onto the bed and rubbed his face against Aunt Sarah's cast. She winced and pulled him onto her lap with her left hand, awkwardly. "Cats," she said, in mock exasperation.

"My mother says 'men' in that same tone of voice," Kate said.

Her aunt laughed. "Men and cats. Creatures who do exactly what they want to do."

"And black-footed field mice," Kate said.

"They really are cute," Aunt Sarah said, but her face had gone serious. "Such large eyes, I guess so they can see at night."

"They're nocturnal?"

Her aunt nodded. "Camila studied them at night and taught during the day. I don't know when she slept. Some of her advanced students checked the cameras and counted tracks for her during the day, but she did most of the night work herself. Sometimes Azul helped, but he had his own work to do."

"What does he teach?"

"He's in entomology," Aunt Sarah said. "Bees and wasps. His main research project is breeding a less aggressive strain of honeybee." She smiled sadly. "He's a fine teacher, too, very popular. Camila used to tell him not to be so nice, so he'd have fewer students and more time for research."

"A dragon's advice?"

"Right. But I don't think she was serious. Her students adored her, feistiness and all. Pete says she poached some of his botany majors, converted them to ecologists and zoologists. Though he's pretty popular himself." Another small smile. "I heard one student recommend him to another. Called him a 'drama king' and said at least you

51

couldn't fall asleep in his class. They were talking about an intro course—neither one was majoring in a science."

"Faculty members take turns with the intro courses, right?"

"Right. It's a small place. So they all cover what they call service courses outside of their specialties. Pete's taught courses on herpetology and virology and ornithology."

"That's a lot of prep work," Kate said.

"It is. Faculty members here are pressed to their limits. Camila was the only one who seemed to have energy to burn. Teaching and research and activism are each demanding, and she excelled at all three."

* * *

Six students arrived together, boisterous, changing the air in the house from library-quiet to street-corner strident. Eclipse, poor kitty, scuttled into the former garage, where he'd gotten used to hanging out in peace with Kate as she read before sleep. The rack by the front door threatened to topple over, though, so coats and the accompanying litter of scarves and hats and gloves were piled on Kate's sofa-bed. Eclipse made a dash through the forest of legs and up the stairs to take refuge with Aunt Sarah.

The students sat at the table in the dining room, Uncle Pete at the head. Backpacks cluttered the floor and window seat. He asked the class to vote on whether it was acceptable for his visiting niece to sit in on the course, and hands went up in unanimous support.

"Thank you all," Kate said, and sat in the chair at the foot of the table.

"Before we begin, I'd like to offer my condolences to any of you who worked with Prof. Chavez, or knew her," Uncle Pete said. "The whole college is saddened by the sudden loss of a woman of great energy and vision."

He paused and looked around the table, but no one else spoke. "Please remember there's counseling available if you should need it, at all hours. Hotline and emergency numbers are given on the Otterlin website." Another pause.

Uncle Pete cleared his throat. "Some of you know each other, some of you don't. Let's start with everyone saying a little something about themselves. Phoebe," he said to the woman on his right, "why don't you go first?"

"I'm Phoebe, from Boston." Short bleached hair and metal studs in her eyebrows and nose. "I'm devastated by the news about Camila." She looked around the table, her face more angry than devastated. "She was my hero. She cared about everything important, and she didn't let the small stuff get in her way. Or big things, like greedy people and corporations."

"Yeah, she was awesome," the next student said, a boy with jet-black hair and a dark, angular face. "I'm Kareem. My parents are from Nigeria but I was born here, okay? I'm one hundred percent American. From D.C." He scowled. "I can talk street jive, dudes, but not here." His scowl vanished and he got a few smiles.

Next a small woman with a voice that barely carried the length of the table. She twirled the ends of her thin hair as she spoke. "Grace. I'm, like, Baptist? From Maine? Way down Maine." She smiled nervously at the notebook in front of her. "These guys have heard this story, but I'll tell you." She flicked her eyes at Kate. "Everybody laughs when I tell them how it blew me away when I got here that, like, the street lights get left on *all night.*" She gave a little shrug. "That's me."

Everyone smiled. A tolerant group. Or else Grace inspired tolerance.

Phoebe. Kareem. Grace. Kate wanted to remember the names in case she met her uncle's students on campus.

"I'm Zoe. Camila kind of blew me off, so I don't think she was so great. Impatient, always in a hurry. At least that's how she was with me."

Kareem stared at her, and Grace folded her hands as if she were praying. Phoebe looked furious.

"Okay, I'm sorry she fell down in the snow and froze," Zoe said. She was big, with big hair to match, wavy and auburn. The face had freckles and looked like it would enjoy laughing under other circumstances.

Knocks at the door, muffled by gloves or mittens. Uncle Pete looked at his class list, then around the table. "This must be Justin and Tim."

"If it's the same Justin who was in my English class last year," Phoebe said, "he's like a tree. Tall, strong, doesn't say a word."

"I know both of them," Kareem said. "They're older, that's why they hang out together."

"Justin told me his father does taxes for rich people and gangsters." The speaker, to Uncle Pete's left, hadn't introduced herself yet. "But he might have been making it up because it sounds cool, the gangster part."

"I hope so," the student beside Kate said. "I don't want to know anybody who knows criminals."

"Crime isn't contagious." Kareem had a point, Kate thought.

"But it might look bad, and I can't screw up my scholarship or I'm out of here."

The two late students came to the table, Uncle Pete urging them to be prompt next time. The sandy-haired one in a flannel shirt was blushing; the taller, lean one looked impassive.

"Let's continue," Uncle Pete said. "Kate?"

Not "Katie," thank goodness.

"I was in your shoes not so long ago," she said, looking at the young faces around the table and realizing that to them ten years would seem like a long time. "Graduated from UMass down the road, was a medical technician on an ambulance for a few years, then got into newspaper reporting. Fun job. Taking some time off for now, doing some traveling." Her art felt too private, at the moment, to share with this crowd of student strangers. She gave them a smile and turned to the girl on scholarship.

"So I'm Maddie, from Chicago, I don't know if I belong here, you guys are all so, you know, um, you have your own computers and stuff. Like I said, I'm on scholarship." Her hands were locked to each other on the table. "I thought Camila was amazing. I loved her. Didn't you, Pete?"

"She was a woman who had the courage of her convictions," he said soberly. "Otterlin College has suffered a great loss."

Kate wondered if she was the only one who noticed he hadn't answered the question.

The blushing late-comer went next, looking at the table in front of him. "Tim. I'm a handyman with the c-college— employees get a free course a year as a b-benefit, and I'm working on my degree. I don't know a thing about plants." He looked up, alarmed. "Except they're way c-cool."

"Suck-up," Kareem murmured.

"Justin," Tim's dark-haired friend said. "Couple of years in the army. Helicopters." His impassive face brightened. "Those birds are paying eighty percent of my expenses. Frankly, I wouldn't be here otherwise. This place isn't cheap."

"Crap," Maddie said. "My scholarship sucks. Guys get all the breaks."

"I earned it," Justin snapped. "Go enlist."

"Enough, both of you," Uncle Pete said. He looked at his list and turned to the last student. "Chaya."

Tall, somehow theatrical—was it the big earrings?—the student who'd mentioned Justin's claim his father had criminal clients tossed her long brown hair back and spoke directly to the professor. "Manhattan, Eleanor Roosevelt High, graduated a year early, here I am." The face she turned to the rest of the table was proud, perhaps condescending.

What was her name? Her uncle had just said it, but Kate had been distracted by the jabs between Justin and Maddie and hadn't added it to the written list she'd been keeping. Oh, hell, memorizing the names was only half the job. While her uncle passed out a syllabus and talked about his plans for the rest of the semester, Kate ran down the list, trying to link the names and faces in her mind. On the left: pierced Phoebe, black and mourning Kareem, religious Grace, big-haired Zoe. On the right: insecure Maddie, handyman Tim, chopper pilot Justin, and the superior one whose name she'd blanked on.

Uncle Pete had two other classes, each of them much bigger than this seminar. How did he keep all the students straight? Kate could never be a teacher. Although maybe the big classes were easier: if there were a hundred students nobody would expect the prof to know individual names.

She scanned the syllabus, which started with plant structure and the processes of photosynthesis, respiration, and transport. The most interesting material was at the end, as Kate had expected: population genetics and evolution, biomes and ecosystems. That's how courses had worked for her, building on basics and then flowering in the last weeks of a semester. She hoped even this half-semester course would work like that, not only for her but for the students gathered around the table. She'd bet Uncle Pete was an engaging instructor. The student Aunt Sarah had overheard was right, you couldn't fall asleep when a guy was waving his hands around the way he did. Would he miss his classroom's resources, a blackboard or whiteboard, a computer projection screen?

He was explaining that he hadn't liked any textbook enough to adopt it for the course, so he'd photocopied the best chapter on each subject from a number of different texts, augmenting them with research papers. "Readable ones," he promised. The course-pack was available at the bookstore. "A textbook has just come out that I'll use next time I teach this course, so tell your friends. And consider yourselves the last beneficiaries of an honored tradition." A flicker of a smile toward his niece.

A few groans came from the students when he told them a ten-page paper was required. Yikes, Kate was glad she didn't have to write that. Newspaper stories had come easily to her, but they were more like multiple-choice tests than term papers. Start filling in the Who? What? When? Where? Why? and the article wrote itself.

Luckily for her, the student whose name she'd missed asked Uncle Pete when the course-packs would be available: she'd checked the bookstore before coming to class, and they weren't on the shelf.

He frowned. "Should be there, Chaya," he answered. "Thanks, I'll check on it."

Kate added Chaya's name to her list and took another look around the table as the students began packing up. For this first meeting Uncle Pete hadn't taken the full two hours, and she had just another minute to nail down the name and face connections. It was unlikely the students would help her out by sitting in the same seats next time.

The group was less noisy going than coming, but Kate was more aware of the dynamics among the students. The two late-comers, Tim and Justin, made it to the door first because their coats were on top of the pile on Kate's sofa-bed, but Zoe pushed her way into the crowd to grab hers and headed for the door with one arm in a sleeve. "Hey, Justin, Tim, wait up."

But they didn't wait, or answer, or turn to look at her. Through the open door their footsteps changed from thuds on the porch to squeaks in the cold snow of the driveway.

Zoe looked at the floor as she finished putting on her coat. Kate felt sorry for her, remembering what it was like at that age to be interested in a boy. No incident was small; every word, every response was an omen.

No response at all was a disaster.

Phoebe brushed by Zoe. "Camila was a *saint,"* Phoebe said, holding the door for Chaya.

Zoe transformed from crestfallen to feisty in a heartbeat. "Not in my church, she wasn't." Kareem took Zoe's arm, but she kept glaring at Phoebe as he pulled her out the door.

Grace and Maddie, the two meekest students, were fittingly the last to leave.

Uncle Pete leaned against the closed door. "You see? I don't know what it is. They bring their loves and hates, their friendships and feuds to the classroom, too, but somehow it isn't as personal there. As personal to me." He looked around. "Maybe it's because the classrooms are bigger. I don't have enough room here for all that adolescent uproar."

"Yes," Kate said, thinking of Zoe's hurt, Chaya's hauteur, Maddie's insecurity. "I see what you mean."

In her room Kate found a mitten, a scarf and a small notebook, the forgotten items Uncle Pete had predicted. The scarf, green and blue with iridescent threads, was Zoe's, lost as the girl scrambled to catch up to Tim and Justin. Which one did she have a crush on?

The notebook was maroon, the mitten bright blue. Eclipse jumped onto the sofa bed, and she buried her fingers in his warm fur.

FIVE

Aunt Sarah made her first shaky excursion to what she called "the nether regions" of the first floor.

"The Netherlands?" Kate asked. "Are you saying I have a Dutch uncle?" She was two steps below her aunt, going down backwards, slowly.

"Pete can be critical, Katie, but he's rarely harsh. I wonder what real Dutch people think about that phrase." Aunt Sarah's left hand clutched Kate's shoulder. "I wish this staircase had a bannister, although I never gave one a thought before I broke my arm."

"You could have one installed." Kate felt behind herself with her toes for the next step. She was almost to the bottom.

"The back stairs had a handrail. Fat lot of good it did me." Aunt Sarah was bent forward over her cast; this was an awkward maneuver for both of them. "But you're right, one of these days we'll have a railing put in here. We're getting older, after all. Maybe after we get the back stairs repaired. Although I'd vote for getting the—"

Someone knocked on the front door. It opened, and Brenda stepped inside.

"—doorbell fixed first," Aunt Sarah finished, turning herself awkwardly into a chair at the dining room table. "This darn house is falling apart."

"Oh, Sarah," Brenda said. "I'm glad to see you're up. Are you feeling better?" She hung her parka and fluffed her hair, which didn't need fluffing. Even though her clothes were simple, jeans and a black sweater, she somehow struck Kate as elegant. The striking blue eyes, though, were bloodshot.

"Would you rather rest?" Kate whispered. Her aunt shook her head.

"We missed you at the Audubon meeting," the visitor said. "We had a great speaker last night. Costa Rican passerines, stunning photos. And trogons."

"Come, sit down," Aunt Sarah said. "You didn't come here to talk about birds."

"True." Brenda sat, apparently out of words. Her shoulders drooped.

"You poor thing. This is my first excursion downstairs, but I'm feeling well enough for us to have a chat. This is my niece Kate. She's here to help me, but I hope it will do her some good too. She's been through some trauma of her own recently."

"Hi again, Kate."

"The cake you brought was a real treat," Kate said. "We had it with frozen strawberries."

Her aunt's eyes were wide. "I thought you made that cake, Kate."

"Me? No way. Can't remember the last time I baked anything. I told you Brenda brought it, I'm sure I did."

"Oh, dear." Aunt Sarah looked at Brenda and blushed. "I'm sorry. I'm sure Kate did tell me and I forgot. I've been sleeping a lot, and losing track, maybe because of the pain meds. Otherwise I would have called to thank you. How are you doing?"

The answer was almost inaudible. "I wish I could sleep a lot. I can't sleep at all."

"Brenda and Camila were housemates," Aunt Sarah said to Kate. "Sweetie, could you make us some tea?"

Kate moved quickly to the kitchen and turned on the gas under the kettle. Her aunt's voice carried from the dining room, but Brenda's didn't. Like listening to someone on a phone, half a conversation.

"Yes, it shocked us all. But you especially, because she was part of your daily—"

"She was intense, yes. You poor dear."

"I know an excellent therapist. She helped me—"

"Talking with Azul? Excellent. For both of you. Camila's two closest—"

Kate stood at the window and let the muttering of the kettle block Aunt Sarah's voice as well. Chickadees flitted in the hedge by the street, black and white like commas and quotation marks snipped out of a book and come to life. The sky was busy with clouds, but they didn't look threatening. Cumulus, their white, round shapes like the balloons above cartoon characters. Except bigger, as if inviting the whole planet to speak.

What would it say?

It would say protozoa and polar bears, grasslands and glaciers.

It would mostly say oceans.

The kettle shrieked. Kate flipped off the burner and filled the pot. She could be such a daydreamer sometimes. She hooked a finger through the handles of two cups and took the tea to the table.

"Thank you, Katie. Oh, we need sugar. Would you get it? It's in the cabinet to the right of the island."

Kate went back to the kitchen. Neither Aunt Sarah nor Uncle Pete took sugar. Brenda must be a frequent visitor for her preferences to be known.

From this end of the kitchen she could hear both voices.

"The police went through Camila's room. It was so upsetting. They went through her desk, and the pockets in her clothes. Why? What were they looking for?"

"Nothing, Brenda. Calm yourself. They always look, when something like this happens. Just in case there's something unusual. But we all know there isn't."

Kate scanned the shelves. Where was the darn sugar? She didn't want to interrupt the conversation to ask.

"Azul came later that day. Asked me if he could sleep in her bed. I heard him sobbing. Off and on, all night."

"It's been a terrible shock, for him and for you. Please think about seeing the therapist. You'll need help to get through this."

"I couldn't."

Ah, there it was. The sugar bowl, behind a stack of cups, just out of reach. Kate pulled one of the barstools from the island to the counter and knelt on the seat. Success.

Aunt Sarah turned as Kate brought the sugar to the table. "Camila rented a room from Brenda, but they were more than housemates. They were good friends."

Brenda took a ragged breath. "It was temporary, when she first came to the college. Just while she looked for her own place. But then there was no reason to look. She had my guest room and the run of the house. I cooked for her, I cleaned, I helped her be what she was to the world."

"You did, sweetie," Aunt Sarah said. "You contributed to everything she did."

"She went to see two houses and then told the realtors that looking was a 'time sink.' And when they phoned to try to change her mind, she said houses were a pain in the ass and she had no interest in taking care of one." Brenda smiled weakly. "I felt so safe with her there." She put a hand over her mouth and closed her eyes. Tears spilled from under the lids.

"Safe? Do you feel unsafe now?" Kate couldn't help herself. She'd been in too many dangerous situations in the past several months to take anyone's security for granted.

Eyes still closed, Brenda was rocking slightly. "To think of her, out there in the snow, it's too horrible. I can't bear it."

Kate glanced at her aunt.

"I think she meant emotionally safe," Aunt Sarah said quietly. "Cared for."

Brenda clutched Sarah's left hand in both of her own.

Kate hesitated. She'd been drawn partway into the conversation, but she didn't know Brenda, who might prefer to talk to her friend alone. "If you don't need anything else, I'll go out to my studio." If Aunt Sarah asked her to stay it would mean she wanted the visit to be short; if she let Kate leave it meant she felt able to manage a longer talk.

"All right, dear," Aunt Sarah said. "Work well."

"Don't forget your doctor's appointment this afternoon."

"Oh, I'm so glad you reminded me." She shook her head. "I'm losing my marbles."

Kate thought how spaced out she herself had just been at the kitchen window. Well, she'd been trying to lose herself in thought, to avoid listening to a private conversation. She had an excuse. Aunt Sarah? She'd been thrown out of her normal routine, and her body was claiming most of her energy to heal itself. She had an excuse too, although she probably worried her forgetfulness was a sign of aging.

Before the door closed behind her, Kate heard a sob, and Brenda's voice. "I've lost my best friend."

* * *

64

"In my church we all try to take care of each other," Aunt Sarah said. "Brenda was already having a hard time, and losing Camila is just horrible."

Kate was making a simple lunch, heating tomato soup and buttering bread. She hadn't been able to concentrate in her camper-studio, knowing she wouldn't have much time, so she'd abandoned her sketchbook to read a novel Uncle Pete had taken out of the library at her request. *The Overstory* was so engrossing she knew she'd get lost in it, so she'd set a timer on her cell phone for an hour before her aunt's appointment.

"Brenda has such amazing eyes," Kate said. "But it's more than that. It's all of her. She has a presence. Like an athlete. Or a model."

"I know what you mean," her aunt said. "She's so beautiful she makes the air hum. But you know what? She isn't even aware of her effect on people." She hitched herself onto one of the barstools as Kate served the food. "With looks like that, how could she be insecure? But she is."

"Sometimes people take what they have, or what they are, for granted," Kate said, sitting across the island.

"Yes. And the hum effect does wear off after a while. I know her too well. The mind behind those stunning blue eyes is plagued with chronic depression."

"That's a shame."

"Anxiety, too. She's had a lot of family troubles."

The soup was too hot. They blew on their bowls, looked at each other through the steam. Aunt Sarah's face was lined, tired. "I hope you don't mind I told her about your sleuthing in Pennsylvania. I thought it might help her to realize she's not the only one who's faced a terrible situation."

Kate shrugged. "Can't do any harm, I guess."

"I thought you two might become friends. Heaven knows Brenda could use a friend or two." She tried the soup again and then stirred it. "I was actually closer to Camila than Brenda was," she said. "It surprised me when she said Camila made her feel safe, because she was treated a bit like a housemaid. On a scale of one to ten, Camila's interest in domestic chores was zero."

"Renting part of a house was perfect for her, then."

"And a godsend for Brenda. She inherited a lovely old house from her father, and it's more than she can manage but she won't give it up. She's been working part-time forever."

"The economy's in decent shape." Kate frowned. "Why can't she find something full-time?"

"Because she'll only consider openings at Otterlin. Period. Amherst scares her—she calls it the City, like it's a Manhattan or Chicago. She grew up here, and both of her parents were profs at the college. It's as if she thinks the school owes her a job."

"Stubborn."

"Very. Like Camila. When she first moved in I thought the two of them would fight like wildcats."

"Maybe she's scared as well as stubborn. If Hunterville is all she knows."

"That's true, Katie. I hadn't thought of that."

The soup had cooled enough to eat and they both dug in.

"Sounds like Camila knew a good deal when she saw it," Kate said. "Along with a couple of rooms she got a cleaning woman, a cook, and a fan."

"All she cared about was her work, and she was impatient with everything else. Until Azul came along. She's the one who started just walking in here, after the doorbell stopped working, and Brenda picked the habit up from her. And then Mark, and a few others from church. Sometimes it's like Grand Central Station around here."

"You're too well-liked for your own health," Kate said.

Her aunt rubbed her cast absently. "It's such a shame. Camila was about to blossom. Over the Christmas holiday she would have moved into Azul's house, and they planned to get married during spring break. She was already only half the dragon she used to be."

"I wish I'd known her," Kate said.

"You'd have loved the look on her face when she said his name. Azoool, she'd say. She called him her Brazilian baby." Aunt Sarah's laugh was fleeting. "They were like a couple out of a fairy tale. The Prince and the Dragon."

"I hope not," Kate said before she could stop herself. "I mean, don't princes slay dragons?"

But Aunt Sarah was looking blankly out the kitchen window, her lunch forgotten. "It shouldn't have ended like this."

* * *

"Because she's totally unqualified, that's why." Uncle Pete was pacing up and down in the dining room, cell phone to right ear, left hand alternately thrown in the air and clutching his head. "She's a fisherman. Fisherwoman. Whatever. She's hardly someone who'd know how to teach a class. You're not serious, are you?"

He paused, listening. "Yes, agreed. Let's talk in person." His voice was calmer. "I'll be there."

"The thorn in your side?" Aunt Sarah asked. She'd been downstairs since Brenda's visit, and the trip to the doctor loomed: Kate was worried her patient was overdoing it. "Arnold Thorne," she said to Kate. "Dean of faculty."

"Yes, that was my pal Arnie," Uncle Pete said. "How did you know?"

"There's a particular tone in your voice when you talk to him. Exasperation, but affection too."

He groaned. "The Thorne himself, also known as Arnie Palmer."

Kate looked puzzled.

"Oh, before your time?" Uncle Pete finished his coffee standing up. "He was a famous golfer who said 'The more I practice, the luckier I get.' My father was a fan of his. I heard that quote when I was ten and never forgot it."

"I don't know a thing about golf," Kate said. "Or golfers."

"I hate the sport," her uncle said. "It gobbles up land and promotes monocultures of non-native grasses. Massive amounts of polluting fertilizer. Literal tons of water. The appearance of perfection, in golf courses and many other man-made landscapes, is artificial and destructive."

"Listen to him," Aunt Sarah said. "Hates golf, loves to play it."

"You didn't have to tell her."

"Uncle Pete, a bag full of clubs lives in the front closet," Kate said. "I've been onto you for years."

"My father loved the game. And I loved being with him. It was before I knew any better. Now I'm in total conflict—a botanist who plays golf." He smacked his forehead.

"The sins of the fathers," Aunt Sarah said.

"But I only play once a year." He looked so sheepish Kate laughed.

"Yes, yes, once a year, and you keep telling the groundskeepers they're using too much fertilizer," his wife said as he picked up his briefcase from the chair next to hers. "You are forgiven. Now go talk some sense into Arnold Palmer, please."

"I'll do my best. About not selling Topper. And about finding someone to meet with Camila's classes for the rest of the term. Someone appropriate. Not her sister." He rolled his eyes.

"Her sister? Whose idea is that?" Aunt Sarah asked.

"Her sister's."

"Oh."

"She's coming to visit," Uncle Pete said, opening the door. "Get ready. The Dragon Lady is dead, long live the Dragon Lady."

"Not a chance." Aunt Sarah shook her head after the door closed. "There'll be no replacing Camila."

* * *

The mouse was beautiful, its pointed face topped with round ears, ears with fur inside them. Its brown coat had reddish highlights but the mouse was white underneath: the white part showed at its sides and on the chest, a bib that matched the snow. Kate smiled as she realized the large dark eyes and black whiskers did indeed remind her of Azul, who'd claimed mice were his rivals for Camila's affection.

Her smile faded. Not only were Camila's affections moot along with everything else about her, but there was something wrong with the mouse.

First of all, it was sitting in the open, on a leaf, as if it were in a cartoon about sledding mice. But there was nothing funny about a member of a prey species not staying hidden, and worse, not running for cover when a much larger creature approached.

Second, the mouse was visibly trembling.

Leaves had blown into the yard over the past few gusty days; even some oak leaves had let go. Kate had had to shovel the driveway again, not because of more snow falling but because of drifting. She didn't mind, and in fact enjoyed being outdoors and getting the exercise.

Going behind the house to check the bird feeder, she'd been happy at first to see the mouse. All wild lives thrilled her. She'd expected it to whirl and scamper into the undergrowth at the edge of the yard. But it sat, trembling.

She fished her cell phone out of her anorak's big front pocket and bent her knees to get a good close-up. Adorable, that tiny nose the color of her Pink Pearl erasers, those white paws that looked like hands.

Ah, good. It wasn't black-footed, so it wasn't one of Camila's orphans. It was an ordinary mouse. Not that it cared about the environmental status of its species. It cared only about its single, irreplaceable life.

Or it should.

Dropping her phone back into her pocket, she put on her mittens and scooped her hands together into the snow under the leaf the mouse sat on. It didn't react, staying crouched as she lifted the leaf and carried it a few steps. She put the shivering creature under a bush as far back as she could reach and backed away.

The mouse charmed Aunt Sarah, too, on Kate's next trip upstairs. "What a cutie," she said, looking at the cell screen. "And you're right, it's the common white-footed mouse. The black-footed are bigger, and darker all over, not just on their feet."

"Cute, but in trouble." She described the animal's behavior.

"That is odd," her aunt said, handing the phone back and sitting up higher. "But we'd better get started. This doc doesn't keep people waiting the way I've heard they do in Amherst." She threw back the blankets with her good arm.

After getting Aunt Sarah downstairs and her left arm into a coat sleeve, Kate draped the rest of the coat across her shoulders. Drove the Volvo as close to the house as she could get, snugged up behind her camper, and left the heat blasting while she helped her aunt down the porch steps. A station wagon isn't the coziest of cars.

While Aunt Sarah was being examined, Kate found herself staring at the tile floor in the waiting room, her mind going back to her own response to the older woman's Prince and Dragon comment. If the police turned up any evidence that Prof. Chavez's death wasn't accidental, Azul had to be considered a suspect—however charming he was, however much Kate liked him. She traced the zigzag lines between tiles, remembering Mark's comment over pizza that murder was "home-brewed." A spouse or fiancé was as close to home as it got.

The medical news wasn't good. X-rays showed one of the smaller bone fragments had shifted. Aunt Sarah had to wait almost an hour because the orthopedic specialist wanted to consult another doc and look at the X-rays with him. Kate worried the wait was tiring the patient.

On the way home, Aunt Sarah sounded distressed. "I hope I don't have to have another operation. One was enough." She huddled over the cast, and Kate left the car running with the heater set on high while she filled a new prescription in the pharmacy. A stronger antibiotic. She hoped the docs didn't suspect a bone infection.

She pulled the Volvo up to the back bumper of her camper and got her aunt inside the house, coat off, up the stairs.

"Oof," Aunt Sarah said, sitting on the bed. "I'm bushed. That's all she wrote." Kate got her shoes off and pulled the covers over her. Went back out to check on the mouse.

It was exactly where she'd left it, on the leaf under the bush. But it was on its back, front legs pulled against the white underbelly, unmoving. Nearby, two more mice were in the same condition.

Kate got disposable gloves from the cleaning supplies under the kitchen sink, threw the mice into a plastic grocery bag and tied a knot in the neck. Sang a troubled version of "Three Blind Mice" on her way to the trash can behind the house.

* * *

"Is there some kind of epidemic going on in the wild mouse population?" she asked Uncle Pete at dinner. She'd baked a chicken with red potatoes and put a frozen broccoli and carrot mix in the microwave. Uncle Pete, definitely a meat-and-potatoes guy, ignored the bowl of bright vegetables.

She was not an enthusiastic cook, but so far neither he nor Aunt Sarah had complained. Neither had they complimented her. They were apparently as easygoing about what they ate as she was, regarding food as a functional necessity rather than an end in itself. She ate to have the energy to do draw and hike and paddle. An occasional special meal was welcome, of course, but for Kate that meant a skilled friend or a restaurant. And hadn't Aunt Sarah mentioned she and Uncle Pete had gone to an inn in Amherst for their Thanksgiving dinner?

"No epidemic that I know of," Uncle Pete said, looking up from the *Journal of Plant Research.* He had an unsettling habit of reading while he ate. He'd respond if Kate started a conversation, but rarely began one himself.

"Of course, I'm not a rodent guy, or any kind of animal guy. Want me to ask somebody at school?"

Academics believe in specialization. "Sure," Kate said. "Because I found three dead mice out back. Three at once is a little strange, isn't it?"

"It is," he said, letting the magazine flip closed but keeping a finger in it to hold his place. He looked a little worried. "You still have them?"

"I bagged them and put them in the trash."

"Excellent," Uncle Pete said. "Why don't you get them out of there, and leave them on the porch? I'll take them in and talk to somebody, or a couple of somebodies, tomorrow." He opened the journal again. "I don't like sick animals. We're learning a lot about cross-species transmission now, how pathogens can mutate laterally." He frowned. "Cells can penetrate a body's defenses, and then the genes can shuffle themselves like playing cards. It's rare, but it happens."

A disturbing thought. Kate kept the dinner conversation to herself when she took a tray up to the guest bedroom. It was the second trip, since Aunt Sarah had been asleep the first time. Kate had stood for a moment then, studying the pale face, worried. Should her aunt be sleeping so much?

Awake, this time, she poked at the plate on the tray. "Chicken, is it? What's my Katie doing for protein? Are you suspending your vegetarian ways?"

"No, cheese and yogurt and chickpeas do it for me. And I've been eating the broccoli and green beans and spinach salads that seem to be invisible to Uncle Pete."

Aunt Sarah took a bite of chicken and gave Kate a sympathetic look. "I'll bet he gives you a hard time about that. He loves plants, but he doesn't think they're food."

Kate thought of the *Journal of Plant Research*. "You know, I don't think he notices what I eat."

Downstairs, she glanced into the living room: Uncle Pete was pinned on the sofa between two piles of paper, his hands busy on his laptop. The house was quiet.

Kate was happy to find Eclipse curled on her sleep-sofa.

She read for half an hour but had trouble concentrating. The alarm bells that had gone off in her mind with the first exposed, trembling mouse had only gotten louder after her later discovery. One sick mouse wasn't unusual, but three suggested something odd was happening.

Don't be a worry-wart, she told herself, and turned out the light. Stroked Eclipse and concentrated on the rhythm of his purr.

* * *

Skiing in a whiteout. Too fast. Flakes hit her face like needles, stung her hands. She wasn't wearing gloves, and her fingers were stiff and blue.

She was dreaming, but the fear was real. Panic clutched her chest.

Snow froze on her lashes and she couldn't see the ground, didn't know which direction was up and which down. She spun helplessly into a white abyss.

SIX

Kate woke, heart pounding.

Her phone said two o'clock. Staring into the darkness, she waited for her mind to settle.

It didn't. Instead it summoned the three mouse bodies she'd found, tails flung in graceful arcs, eyes squeezed shut.

Then the song "Three Blind Mice" started up in her head, and she gave up. No use lying in bed wide awake. It would be a kind of therapy, she supposed, like drawing the blue hand: she'd draw a darn mouse. The first one, the one she'd found sitting on a leaf. She had a reference photo on her phone. She'd draw the mouse and then maybe she could go to sleep. She'd draw it alive, its bright eyes wide open to the perilous world.

Snow squeaked under her shoes as she went outside and climbed into the camper. Her breath hung in wreaths, and she turned on the space heater.

And sat. She'd have to wait until the place warmed up before she could think about taking off her mittens and holding a pen or pencil. In the dark camper, she made an effort to turn her mind away from mice. She summoned the faces of the students.

She was ten years older than they, an important decade. Freshman and sophomores, they'd only recently been uprooted from their families—and were, in a few more years, fated to be uprooted again, leaving behind whatever friends they'd made, whatever recognition they'd won, the whole four-year adventure revealed as a device to house and engage and instruct them even as it propelled them into the next, less protected stage of their lives. College was a fantasy-land that evaporated one fine spring day, no more enduring than the balloons and champagne of commencement celebrations.

At least the disruption of graduation was foreseeable. Welcome to adulthood! An unpredictable country, where your partner could bring the curtain down after the first scene of what you'd thought was a three-act play. Where your employer could do the same. Both those things had happened to Kate just under a year ago.

Oh, the cynicism of the sleepless. Kate recognized it as a cousin of depression.

The students would enjoy their good fortune for a few more years, sheltered by a college designed to nurture them. Some—Chaya, perhaps—might look upon that luck as their due. Maddie wouldn't take it for granted, nor Justin, whose years in the military had likely been more demanding than his life at Otterlin. Kate hoped bewildered Grace would grow in the next few years, maturing and gaining confidence before she was on her own.

Sitting in her camper made her feel better. She hadn't turned on the light, hadn't touched a pencil or opened her sketchbook. Being in a classroom setting, she realized, had gotten on her nerves. Was her traveling lifestyle turning her into a hermit, unable to cope with even a small group of people?

The heater clicked and its orange light blinked off. The camper was warm. Kate was just about to stand up and flip on the light when she saw movement at the corner of the house.

Through the small window at the front of the camper, the one that connected to the truck cab, and out beyond the windshield: a low figure, dark against the snow. A dog?

No, a person. He stood, put a foot up on the end of the porch floor and pulled himself up and over the rail.

The back of her neck prickled. A student who'd left something behind would go up the front steps, not sneak onto the porch from the side. And it was two o'clock in the morning. Students were night-owls, but nobody would expect Uncle Pete to be up at this hour to return a mislaid cell phone or forgotten notebook.

The door was unlocked, her aunt and uncle asleep inside. A prowler on the porch. Time to call 911.

She felt her back pocket. Damn. She'd left the cell phone by her bed.

If she turned on a light, the man—probably a man—would run. But he might come back another night. She wanted to identify the creep, not just scare him off temporarily.

Kate eased open a drawer. The lowest of three, below the ones for silverware and then pencils and brushes. Her fingers recognized shapes: a box of wooden matches, pair of scissors, spare headlamp, packages of batteries, folding knife. She moved her hand deeper. This guy could be anyone from a drunk student to a voyeur to a burglar ready to steal anything he could put his hands on.

Ah, the metal cylinder of bear spray, cool to her touch.

She slipped out the camper's back door and left it ajar, held the spray in her right hand and a flashlight in her left, her finger on the button. Shining it in his face would give her the ID she wanted, and it might confuse him enough to give her a longer look.

Putting her feet down flat to minimize the squeak of cold snow, she moved quickly along the side of the truck.

Not fast enough. Footsteps thudded across the porch. The flashlight gave her only a glimpse of the dark figure vaulting over the railing. Kate ran for the corner of the house, slipped and fell to one knee, got herself up, slipped again. Took the corner wide, to make sure he wasn't waiting to ambush her.

Two loud clicks. Like a handgun being fired dry, unloaded. Like mousetraps snapping on empty air.

She ran along the side of the house, stopped when she had a full view of the back yard. The only upright figure was the birdfeeder on its shepherd's crook. Below it, two parallel tracks gleamed in the moonlight, stretching down the hill at the edge of Topper Reserve.

The noises had been the sound of ski boots clicking into bindings: the intruder was already at the bottom of the hill, moving fast, about to power up the next rise.

Kate went into the house and for the second time in a week called the police.

* * *

"He stole *what?*" The cop looked incredulous.

"A bag of frozen mice," Kate said, and laughed. She didn't feel much like laughing, but it did sound ridiculous. "Three of them."

"What, are you feeding a pet snake or something?"

"No, they were wild mice. And we don't know why they died."

She'd hoped not to wake her aunt and uncle, but the porch light went on and Uncle Pete opened the door, wearing a bathrobe and boots, his comb-over hanging in his eyes.

"What's happening out there, Katie?"

So she got to tell both the officer and her uncle at the same time. Efficient. She was also pleased with herself for taking a few photos of the intruder's ski tracks with her cell phone while she was waiting for the police. One showed a clear print of a kick zone where he'd clicked into his binding and stepped away, but she didn't know how helpful it would be. How distinctive were the patterns among different ski brands?

The cop flipped his notebook shut, and the three of them went wide around the side of the house, clear of the tracks the unknown man and Kate had left.

"He was moving pretty fast," the cop said, shining his flashlight onto the tracks. He glanced back at Kate's tracks, smudged where she'd slipped. "So were you." He took a picture with his phone, the flash strobing down the slope as far as the yellow crime scene tape, stretched and drooping after the wind of the past few days. "We'll get somebody out here in daylight to take some better pictures and follow the tracks."

"I'm going in," Uncle Pete said. "I'm cold."

Kate walked back to the cruiser with the cop.

"We normally wouldn't do much of an investigation over a bunch of frozen mice," he said. He couldn't help but crack another smile. "But I think the detectives will be interested in what's going on here because this house is so close to the scene of the—the unfortunate accident with that biology professor."

"Yes," Kate said. "She was practically in the back yard."

"Hunterville's a quiet city, and safer than most," the officer said as he got into his car. "A lot of people don't lock their doors, but you know what? If I were you I'd lock up after this. Something funny's going on around here." He wasn't smiling any more.

Uncle Pete was sitting in the dining room, drinking instant cocoa and looking haggard. "Help yourself," he said. "Water's still hot."

Kate flipped the deadbolt on the front door and repeated what the uniform had said about locking up. Hunched over his steaming drink, her uncle nodded dully. He wasn't used to being up at three in the morning.

She dumped cocoa powder into her cup and poured from the kettle. Too hot to drink, but the aroma was heavenly. Sweet and hot would feel good after standing out in the frigid darkness. She sat across from Uncle Pete and they looked at each other for a moment. Something was going on, and they both knew it. All three of them, counting the cop who'd just driven away.

"Is Aunt Sarah really good friends with that guy she knows on the police force?" Kate asked. "Mark?"

Her uncle was drooping now, staring into the cup loose in his hands. "They're great friends. He was married to a lovely woman who died a few years ago. Breast cancer. His wife and Sarah were as close as sisters, and Sarah took good care of her. All the way to the end. The four of us were good friends, but Mark and Sarah especially, now." He brought his gaze out of the cup of memories. "Why do you ask?"

"The cop who just left said the detectives would be interested in what happened tonight because this house is close to the scene of the—I could have sworn he was going to say 'the scene of the crime.' But he stumbled a little and said 'scene of the accident' instead. I was just wondering if the police know something they aren't talking about."

"I'm so glad Sarah slept through all this. She needs to heal." He gave a huge sigh and got up slowly. "In the morning, let's ask her to invite Mark over, see if he'll tell us anything."

It was already morning, of course. After her uncle trudged upstairs, Kate lay down on top of her bedspread and tried to coax her mind to sleep. Eclipse was no help, padding restlessly around her feet. She gave up. In the kitchen, she filled the coffeemaker and while it brewed she went into the front yard.

Tracks everywhere. She stayed outside of them, away from the ones the fleeing man had made, and circled the house. The ski tracks went down the slope and curved to the left, which would take him along that narrowing strip at the edge of the Reserve, out to the area where lucky landowners lived in houses that abutted the park.

Openings in the fence. Access to back yards, side yards, the street.

Such a good escape route. He could have parked a car along the street, driven off, been miles away last night by the time the cop got to the house.

Why did he take the mice? And why had they died in the first place?

Maybe those were two versions of the same question. Maybe the guy had come to steal the mice because he didn't want anyone to know how they'd died.

A small bottle lay at the edge of the porch, under the railing. The liquid in it looked like water. Kate didn't go near it, not wanting to disturb any evidence, but she examined the rest of the porch carefully.

She'd swept it both times she'd shoveled the driveway. Snow on painted wood was terribly slippery, and she'd been glad a rubber mat ran from the door to the top of the steps. Thinking of Aunt Sarah, she'd made sure she got every last snowflake off the porch and the three steps to the walk.

But the wind had blown some snow back onto the top step. A seam of white ran along the right angle where the tread met the riser.

No, it ran half the distance, and then stopped. That was weird.

She didn't touch that, either. Figuring the cops would show up pretty early, she went inside and took a cup of coffee to the back of her camper. Sat on the step and watched the sky brighten and trees get three-dimensional. Birdsong filled the gaps in their branches and unrolled invisible streamers above the snow-covered houses. Then the birds launched themselves in graceful arcs among their songs.

Kate itched to go skiing again, even though the snow was coarse and grainy. What Hunterville needed was another good snowstorm.

When the police arrived, both cars were unmarked: a tan sedan pulled into the driveway, behind Uncle Pete's Volvo and Kate's camper, and a black SUV parked on the street. The sedan's driver was Mark—good, maybe he'd have some information. He nodded at Kate, then waited while a man and a woman from the other vehicle opened its tailgate, pulled out a couple of soft cases, and joined him.

When he was done examining the lawn, Kate told the three about the bottle and the white powder she'd mistaken for snow. Mark nodded and gave her an appraising look.

"I didn't go off the mat," she said. "Didn't touch the bottle."

"Good. Thanks."

"There's a big pot of coffee inside, if you or these other folks want some. I put out extra cups," Kate said. "I'll be in my camper here if you need me for anything."

* * *

"Dead mice?" Marjorie's voice had been calm. As usual. A college friend, now raising two children and taking courses for a Master's degree in psychology, she was a soothing presence even by phone. Kate usually called on Sundays, but for some reason her hard-working friend had been on her mind. So she tapped the number; she could leave a cheery hello if she got voicemail.

They'd talked first about Aunt Sarah's slow recovery, and then about Marjorie's little boy's expanding vocabulary. When Kate heard a note of anxiety in her friend's voice, she wished she hadn't mentioned the darn mice.

"Do you think you might come home?"

"Home?" For a moment, Kate wasn't sure where that would be. "I can't leave Aunt Sarah. Not now. Even if her professor friend hadn't been found dead practically in her back yard. Uncle Pete's got his classes, and his book trips, and she needs help. I'm closer to her than I am to my mother."

"I don't mean right away—of course not. But once she's recovered, you might think about coming back to this part of the state," Marjorie said. After graduation from the University of Massachusetts, both of them had settled near Boston. "Where you know people, have friends. Where you'd be less likely to be ambushed by strange incidents."

"You're saying I should give up traveling in my truck camper?" Kate was startled; she looked forward to more time on the road. And Marjorie was usually so supportive of what people wanted to do with their lives, conventional or not.

"It's worth thinking about, isn't it?" For the first time since Kate had become a full-time RVer, her friend— usually upbeat and encouraging—sounded disheartened. "A dead professor, dead mice—I don't like the sound of it."

"Marjorie, what's going on? Are you okay?"

"I'm fine. It's just—I don't know. I'm feeling a little lonely these days."

Kate was stunned. Marjorie was the most rock-solid, capable, independent person she knew. And she never complained.

"You know I'd love to see you." Even though she sometimes vacillated about decisions for weeks, she came up with an instant plan. "Why don't I come out for a visit when Aunt Sarah's gotten her cast off?"

"I'd like that. I'd like that a lot." A smile was audible in her voice. "And Kate—"

"Yes?"

"In the meantime, don't have any more adventures, okay?"

SEVEN

With the chores she'd been doing and the time spent with her aunt, Kate hadn't thought she was getting much work done. But after only a week in Hunterville, her sketchbook was nearly filled. Landscapes near the pond in Topper Reserve, portraits of her aunt and uncle, sketches of Mark and Azul, of birds at the feeder in the back yard, of the front of the house and of the sky-blue Volvo. A cartoon of her camper. Only three blank pages left.

She walked along College Street toward the campus. No sense settling down to draw with three pages, because she never knew ahead of time how her work would go. Some days one page sufficed; other days she needed ten.

The air was cold and still; her breath plumed. After a stop at the bookstore for a sketchbook she'd look for new subjects around the college. There'd be plenty: she'd only made one visit to Otterlin. She'd meant to go back sooner than this, especially to the aviary, but taking care of Aunt Sarah and her visitors, drawing, and skiing had kept her busy. A full week had gone by.

Doors to buildings on both sides of the walkway opened and students streamed out, shrugging into coats and backpacks and brightening the snow-and-stone scene with their chatter. Kate spotted Maddie and Grace, but their heads were bent together in conversation and they didn't see her. Between groups, Chaya strode coatless, a stylish leather bookbag over one shoulder—no backpack for this sophisticated young woman. She saw Kate and gave a wave.

In the bookstore, Kate browsed the aisle of art supplies. Brew was busy unpacking a box in a corner of the store. He apparently had eyes in the back of his head like a teacher, because as soon as she went to the check-out counter he came right over. She'd chosen a couple of sketchbooks and half a dozen pens. She was always a sucker for pens.

"Hey, Kate," he said. "Why are aren't you out skiing on a beautiful day like this?"

"Heck, somebody's gotta fill my sketchbook."

"You're lucky to have the Reserve right in your back yard," he said. "It's wasted on Pete, of course. Does Sarah ski?"

"She does, but not now, with her arm in a sling."

"Right, I heard about that." He shook his head. "Bad luck."

"I don't need a bag," she said, putting her pack on the counter and unzipping it.

He saw the well-worn sketchbook and his face brightened. "Mind if I take a look?"

She looked around; a couple of students were browsing, but nobody was waiting behind her. She pulled out the notebook and let him prowl through it, his brow creased.

His expression must have meant concentration rather than disapproval, because he looked up with a smile. "Hey, do you sell your work? I'd like to have some of these for the store. I'd mat a couple of them for display, put the rest in the unframed bins. What do you say?"

"Glad you like them," Kate said. "And yes, take whichever ones you want." She hadn't thought of selling her drawings until recently, when a friend in Pennsylvania encouraged her to show some pieces at a county fair. She'd sold quite a few, gratified that strangers wanted to take her work home to be part of their lives.

Brew chose two Reserve landscapes, and the birds at Aunt Sarah's feeder. "College subjects would be a hit," he said. "Not that I'm telling you what to draw, but if scenes around the aviary or the library interest you, I bet they'd sell."

"I'll have a look," Kate said. "Thanks." His advice dovetailed with her own plan to spend time on campus.

She found a bench across the street from the aviary. Brew's praise energized her, and so did the pristine sketchbook. She flipped it open and decided to work in pencil instead of the new pens; afraid their ink would freeze, she tucked them in her anorak pocket. Working here would whet her appetite for later drawings inside. Tropical plants and birds in western Massachusetts—what a splendid resource.

Some of the big building's panes were opaque, gray with humidity frozen against the inside of the glass. Figures crossed the white street, one of them tossing a frisbee for an enthusiastic collie.

Every time she worked, she felt sweet relief.

Relief from what? The question hovered like a hummingbird in the back of her mind as her eyes took in the scene and passed it along to her hands, the right moving a pencil and the left holding a gum eraser at the ready as space and shapes were translated, sent from eyes to hands to paper.

Visual to graphic. Real to a different kind of real.

The process felt effortless. That wasn't true of every session. A few months ago, the effort to work at all had been agonizing. Over the previous decade she'd slowly lost touch with her talent, and reviving that part of herself meant abandoning the self she'd become. A huge change.

It had been a close call. If she hadn't been laid off from the newspaper, if an old friend hadn't then insisted she join her at an artists' colony, Kate wouldn't have approached the daunting task of recovering and nurturing her skills. And if she hadn't met a painter who encouraged and mentored her, she would most likely have failed.

And there was the answer to that hummingbird question. The relief she felt when she worked was relief from not working. Doing art had become imperative.

It was who she was.

* * *

"Who can tell me what factors affect the transpiration of leaves?" Uncle Pete asked.

The students hadn't been quite as noisy as they arrived at his house this time. The previous week they'd been as raucous as crows, and Kate had wondered if the racket would bother Aunt Sarah up in her aerie. Perhaps the students were quieter because the quarter was underway and they were immersed in massive amounts of reading, the college student's endless task.

Reading and assimilating. The first carefree days were gone.

They'd arrived in pairs, a Noah's ark procession of personalities. The two older students, Justin and Tim, were the first to arrive instead of the last. Right on their heels came Zoe and Kareem, Zoe chatting away but with her eyes on Justin instead of Kareem.

She's smitten, Kate thought, glad she wasn't nineteen herself anymore. Justin was attractive, tall and fit, with an air of disengagement that could be a social magnet, as if he knew something the others didn't. Which was probably true, since he'd been in the army for a couple of years after high school. Zoe, open and bubbly, didn't stand a chance with him.

Or maybe she did. Opposites can attract. Look at quiet, patient Aunt Sarah and her histrionic husband.

Grace and Maddie were next, probably the two least comfortable about being Otterlin students. Maddie must feel socially isolated, a scholarship student at a small elite school, without pocket money for concerts or movies. Grace would be uncomfortable culturally, her evangelical upbringing at odds with the liberal, secular atmosphere that prevailed on campus. Their conversation was muted; they stayed close together and sat next to each other.

Chaya and Phoebe arrived last, although they weren't late. Had they come with each other, or singly? Phoebe's facial piercings and short, bleached hair gave the impression she was her own person, never mind what other people thought. And Chaya, her long hair as lustrous as a shampoo ad on TV, had an air of confidence that bordered on superiority. Maybe their personalities did mesh, even if their outward styles didn't.

Uncle Pete had started too soon, his question lost in the small noises of students settling in: notebooks pulled from packs, pens found, greetings murmured.

He cleared his throat. "What affects the transpiration of leaves?" he asked again. "Anyone?"

"All the big environmental factors a tree has to deal with," Zoe volunteered. "Wind, humidity, light level."

"How so? What difference does wind make?" Uncle Pete looked around the table, inviting the others to make the conversation general.

Kate was surprised at her reaction. She would have enjoyed a lecture more; this Socratic conversation felt artificial, and she hated to admit she was bored. It had been fun to read the assigned chapters from Uncle Pete's books, which she'd borrowed when she saw how much the course-pack, the photocopied version, cost at the bookstore. And that had worked out well, because she'd noodled around the books and picked up interesting facts from chapters that weren't assigned.

"Air movement p-pulls water vapor away from the leaf faster," Tim said.

This conversation wasn't a conversation. The students had to provide answers that demonstrated they'd read the assignments and understood them. It was essentially a quiz. The class was unlikely to go further than the reading.

Rats.

Was Uncle Pete bored? His hands were doing their usual busybody routines, but his expression was focused. His role during class wasn't scientific, it was social. He was the moderator, the coach, the sheepdog herding the group toward the fold.

He was doing a good job. He'd called on Maddie to tell him why bright light would cause transpiration to increase, and her voice, faltering at first, grew more confident.

"The leaf pores open wider," she said, "for photosynthesis."

"And what are leaf pores called?"

"Stomata."

"Good job," Uncle Pete said. "Now what about humidity?"

* * *

One hour and fifty minutes, the academic version of a two-hour class, with the other ten left for students to get to their next commitment on the small campus. The time went slowly for Kate. She found herself contemplating her uncle's comb-over and trying to imagine what he would look like without it. Better, she thought. The few strands were intended to cross out his baldness, but instead they called attention to it. She gave him a mental crew-cut and then scolded herself for not paying attention.

But a moment later her thoughts drifted again, this time to the students' body language. Justin and Chaya were the most upright, he perhaps from army training turned habit, she from the poise of inherent hauteur. They took the fewest notes. Maddie leaned way back in her chair, hips slid forward, a position Kate nicknamed the scholarship slouch, while Grace somehow made herself small right in the middle of her chair. Like that trembling mouse on a leaf.

Kareem and Zoe leaned forward, intent on what Uncle Pete was saying, eager to contribute. Good students, they'd perfected the role. Zoe's big hair sent spirals out toward Kareem's dark figure on one side and Justin's khaki presence on the other. Of course she'd sat next to Justin, hoping for a crumb of attention, while Kareem sent waves of admiration pulsing toward her that she didn't notice. Or noticed but didn't value.

Tim was writing, eyes on his notebook: the carpenter who wanted to pursue some other goal. Kate hoped he had a plan: one free course a year meant he'd be retired by the time he had enough credits for a bachelor's degree. Phoebe was restless, playing with the metal hoop in her eyebrow.

"Yo!" a voice sang out, and everyone looked around. Uncle Pete paused, palms open, about to make a point. "Yo, girl, you way cool, way outta school," the voice chanted, "you so magic, don't be tragic—"

Phoebe dived under the table to her backpack and silenced the phone. "Sorry," she said, and Uncle Pete picked up where he'd left off without looking at her.

What Kate saw, when she considered them all together, was a gathering of young people simmering with passions of various sorts, some near the surface and others more hidden, perhaps even from themselves. Wants and needs practically vibrated in the air over the table. Vector arrows of emotion flew invisibly in many direction, some of them shot from Cupid's bow.

All in a day's work to Uncle Pete, but even he would like a little more distance. How long before the Bascomb Hall repairs were done?

The students laughed. He'd said something funny, which Kate had missed. Her smile was camouflage.

* * *

The students were all talking at once. No, only the talky ones: Zoe and Phoebe and Chaya. The quiet ones, Grace and Maddie, collected their belongings and slipped out the door, on the heels of the efficient Justin. Kareem had a question for Uncle Pete, whose deep voice played a bass line to the higher voices of the women students chatting.

A scream sliced through the room.

Startled into silence, Uncle Pete and the students blinked at each other.

As Kate hurried to the door she heard voices muffled by snow, and then male laughter. She stepped onto the porch. Justin was turning away from his classmates, a derisive smile on his face. Grace's face showed she'd done the screaming: she let go of Maddie's arm and stooped to pick up the tote bag she must have dropped in fear.

Maddie rolled her eyes at Kate. To Grace she said, "They're just mice. You're a lot bigger than they are, so they can't hurt you. Especially since they happen to be dead." Grace shuddered and almost dropped the bag again.

Half a dozen mice were scattered around the front steps, on their backs, paws tucked close to white bellies.

Kate went down the steps as Uncle Pete came onto the porch, the other students behind him. He surveyed the scattered rodents. "How odd," he said. More mice lay under the yew bushes.

Tim came up beside her. "Weird," he said, and moved on, jogging to catch up to Justin. Kareem and Zoe went past, too, and then Phoebe and Chaya, the post-class buzz dissipated. Subdued, the students trooped down the driveway and along College Street, dark figures silhouetted against the snow. The yellow streetlight gave the scene the look of an antique sepia print.

Uncle Pete came back out with a flashlight and shone it on a couple of the mice. "Oh, that's good. They're white-footed. Common as pigeons." He went up the steps.

"Wait, Uncle Pete," Kate said. "We have to figure out what's going on, don't we?" Maybe she was being oversensitive, but the mice made her uneasy. Not only because she had a sense of responsibility for the wild creatures around her, but also because in the recent past dead animals and birds had been used to threaten her.

"Sure we do, Katie, but not at night, in the cold, right after a class. Let's take a look at the situation in the morning."

"I'm going to pick them up. They might tempt predators." What if they'd been poisoned? She didn't want to wake up to dead or sickened predators—owls or neighborhood cats.

But she was talking to herself. Uncle Pete had gone inside.

In the sepia streetlight the snow was the color of sand, prompting Kate to think of the landscape near Tucson where she'd grown up. People in the East often thought the desert was an empty place, but she knew it was quick with life, with lizards and roadrunners, bobcats and coyotes. The litter of dead mice reminded her of what her father called the quail chicks that raced single file behind their mothers: popcorn for coyotes. She wanted to keep these mice from being popcorn for anything, at least until she knew what had happened to them. And in order to find that out she needed to keep them from being stolen like the first three.

She went inside for gloves and a trash bag. Uncle Pete was putting his notes in a folder, closing his books and stacking them. He looked exhausted. The electric energy of a roomful of young adults had drained him.

"Camila used to stop in sometimes, late, after her field work," he said. "Those were good times." He started up the stairs, moving slowly. "Good night, Katie."

"Good night."

On the lawn, she collected the mice around the porch steps and worked her way across the front yard. The last tiny body, farthest toward the road, was lit by the streetlight, and she paused before picking it up. Its front feet were curled close to its body, the fingers still pink. Not blue, as she'd expected, blue like the hand—

She corrected herself. She was looking at toes, not fingers. Mice don't have hands. And there was no connection between the mice and the human tragedy of Professor Chavez's death. She tied a knot in the trash bag and put it just inside the door of her camper. Locked the door. Before last night Uncle Pete would have wanted to take them to his biologist colleague for an opinion about the cause of death, but after last night's intruder the analysis became a job for the police.

EIGHT

She had plenty to work on. Nobody thought twice about cell phone snapshots these days, and Kate hoped her aunt and uncle didn't guess that she planned to make drawings from the reference photos she'd taken of them with her cell. She'd mentioned to Aunt Sarah that she wanted them to send to her mother. If the portraits came out well enough she'd have a couple of presents ready for Christmas.

It was hard concentrating. What was the white stuff on the porch? Was the liquid in the bottle just water? It might not be the prowler's at all. One of the students could have dropped it.

She closed her eyes. She wanted to visualize the wise, kind face of her mentor Farley, Farland McQuade, the man who'd helped her so much last August as she struggled to recover her connection to her art. It had been a battle she'd never have won without his help, and he'd emphasized how important momentum was. The habit of work was more important than the work itself, or at least that was how she'd learned to trick herself into working every day. If she thought about the quality of the work, she'd never start— she wanted it to be perfect, so nothing she produced would be good enough.

He'd taught her to make it simple: just show up.

Pick up the pencil.

She opened her eyes. She hadn't been able to conjure up his face clearly, and that made her sad. Thoughts of Farley were a potent mix of gratitude and pain. She'd found him at the bottom of a flight of stone stairs, dead from a fall that had turned out to be no accident.

A different face drifted into her thoughts: Sean. She wanted to get in touch with him but kept putting it off. Phone? Email? Text?

No, she was too distracted. This time it wasn't perfectionism or procrastination. Something was awry in the small world of Hunterville. Aunt Sarah and her friends, Uncle Pete and his students, Azul, Brenda, Brew, Brew's father the developer—Kate didn't know a lot of people here. But did she know enough to see a pattern? Her aunt's house did seem to be near the epicenter of the disturbance.

The next time she got in touch with Sean, she wanted to be upbeat, not mulling over the strange events in Hunterville, Massachusetts. The demands of his job had so far kept them from getting to know each other well; she didn't want to burden him, to be the equivalent of the pest who asks a doctor at a party for medical advice.

Only a week had passed since Kate arrived at Aunt Sarah's, but so much had happened it felt like a month. The disasters on campus fought for attention in her mind with the nocturnal intruder and the plague of dead mice at the bungalow on College Street. Touching Prof. Chavez's hand—finding her body—had rattled her, no doubt about it. But most likely the woman hadn't been murdered, and Kate assumed her own anxiety was due to the murders she'd encountered in the recent past.

Even without the disturbing events, the week still felt crammed full because Aunt Sarah's friends came to see her so often. When Kate had lived in one place in Massachusetts she'd stayed in touch with her friends by phone and text, seeing them in person every few weeks. Aunt Sarah saw her friends every few days, and sometimes Kate found the schedule overwhelming. Aunt Sarah said she hated missing church; maybe she had fewer visitors when she saw her friends at the social hour after the service.

And of course people visited more often when someone was ill or recovering from an accident like Aunt Sarah's. They wanted to help, to see if anything was needed, and keep the patient from feeling isolated and lonely.

Used to being by herself most of the time, Kate felt inundated.

She described her state of mind to Uncle Pete, and told him she'd prefer not to attend further meetings of his seminar. "I'm just not used to being around so many people so much of the time." He said he understood and offered his books so she could keep up with the course content, just for fun. That was fine. She enjoyed the reading, some of it familiar territory from her college days and some of it new.

She didn't say she found the classes dull. Uncle Pete did his best. His gestures were dramatic, and he was funny and often gentle with his students. He was firm, and fair, and he cared a lot about his work, both teaching and research.

Growing up, she'd spent much more time with Aunt Sarah than with Uncle Pete. Her mother's sister had married late, when Kate was twelve. Her father had disappeared the year before, and her mother had gotten even more difficult to be around, either irritable or withdrawn. Aunt Sarah had been a wise and patient friend, a surrogate mother when Kate desperately needed at least one attentive adult in her life.

After her marriage she had less time for Kate, and then Uncle Pete finished his PhD and the couple moved around the country to follow a series of academic jobs. Kate had to admit she'd resented her uncle for taking away her beloved aunt.

But that was adolescent thinking. A thing of the past. Uncle Pete was as much a part of her life now as Aunt Sarah. And downright lovable most of the time.

She stared at the pencil in her hand. No, she couldn't concentrate. Sliding the unfinished portraits back into the portfolio, she picked up the plastic jug. She'd fill it in the kitchen with water for the coffee machine on board her camper. Or maybe there'd be coffee in there: Uncle Pete sometimes made an extra pot after breakfast.

Outside, the policewoman from the SUV was taking pictures of footprints in the snow. The man was kneeling on the steps next to a black box with a hose attached to it ending in a nozzle. He ran it along the line of white powder, the box emitting a whine. The powder disappeared.

A mini-vacuum cleaner. Kate stood back until he'd finished and packed up his gear.

* * *

"I don't like this," Mark said as he settled at the dining room table, choosing the seat facing the door. "An intruder, and a substance of concern, so close to the place where Camila was found?" He shook his head. "I'm not closing her case. Nothing's clear yet, but let's say I have a suspicious mind. Occupational hazard."

Aunt Sarah had seen the detective from her window and had called down to him to come in. Before he did, he'd knocked on Kate's camper door—a relief, since even a dose of caffeine hadn't helped her work. She'd given him the bag of frozen mice, and they'd gone to his car together while he locked it in the trunk. By the time the two of them got inside Aunt Sarah was most of the way down the stairs. Kate wondered about that. Was the patient getting better or was her cabin fever getting worse?

For now, she got her aunt into the chair and sat beside her. She didn't look great. She should be putting her energy into healing, not getting upset about criminal cases.

"Suspicious?" Aunt Sarah sounded as if she'd never heard the word.

Kate put her hand on her aunt's.

"I mean we're not sure she wasn't murdered," he said, pursing his lips in apology as his old friend gasped.

"What did the autopsy say?" Kate asked.

"Hasn't been done yet." He didn't look happy. "Our ME is way behind. He's part-time, teaches at the college too, and there's been some kind of campus problem with pipes freezing that messed up his office. He's been dealing with that, says he lost a lot of work because his computer shorted out from water damage."

"Good thing Uncle Pete brings his laptop home," Kate said, glancing at Aunt Sarah, who was staring at Mark. "Otherwise he might be singing the same song."

"You wouldn't put it that way if you'd ever heard Pete sing." Mark's eyes stayed on Aunt Sarah, who didn't respond to his joke. "We'll find him," he said gently. "If it's murder, we'll find who did it."

Aunt Sarah blinked. "Yes." But her voice was faint.

The door flew open and Uncle Pete stomped inside. "Damnation!" he shouted. "The college is going to hell!"

"Peter," Aunt Sarah said, sounding stronger.

"Frozen parrots, motmots, toucans!" He was beside himself. "Toucans like popsicles, can you believe it?"

"What's happened, Uncle Pete?" Kate asked.

He was spent. He collapsed into the chair closest to the door, hands over his ears as if trying not to hear his own bad news. "The heat went off in the aviary. Some of the birds died. It was a nightmare. I helped with the count. Picking up beautiful, dead birds. Tossing them in trash bags." He looked exhausted.

"Oh, honey, that's awful." Aunt Sarah looked stricken by this second item of bad news in the span of five minutes.

The cold was taking a mighty toll, on human and animal communities alike. "Brenda must be a wreck," Kate said. "Did her bees survive?"

"Brenda?" Uncle Pete looked up and frowned. "She doesn't work at the aviary."

"No? I saw her there, the first day I checked out the campus, about a week ago."

He looked baffled.

"She's a floater," Aunt Sarah said. "I know her from church. She fills in for people who call in sick or go on vacation. You can run into her anywhere on campus." She shifted, her left arm cradling the big cast. "My friend Myra runs the aviary. I wonder if she's all right? I need to give her a call."

Everyone who worked at the small college seemed to be Aunt Sarah's friend.

"Otterlin will go broke at this rate," Uncle Pete said. "First the frozen pipes in Bascomb Hall, and now this. It's unreal."

"Is there any connection?" Kate asked. "Some kind of college-wide heating or electrical problem?"

"Arnie is looking into it. And the campus police," Uncle Pete said.

"They think somebody turned the heat off on purpose?" Aunt Sarah looked pale. "This is all too much."

Kate looked at Mark. His eyes were alert, and there was something in his face like appetite. He must be wondering what linked all the unusual events.

So was she. "Who hates Otterlin College?" she asked her uncle. "Two campus freeze-outs can't be a coincidence."

"My thought exactly," Mark said. "And I have a feeling the dean will be calling me. The way he does when he's in over his head."

"He doesn't have much manpower. The campus police force is only six people," Uncle Pete said. "And they handle everything—rowdy student parties, missing backpacks, parking tickets, troublesome townies, the whole shooting match." He looked startled. "Sorry, I didn't mean that. The whole, um—"

"Ball of wax?" Mark suggested as he stood.

"That's it. Beeswax." Uncle Pete recovered from his moment of discomfort.

The detective moved behind Aunt Sarah's chair and put a reassuring hand on her left shoulder. "I've got work to do."

He hadn't told them much. "What do you think the white stuff on the porch was?" Kate asked.

"Don't have a clue." Mark moved toward the door. "The techs bagged it, and the bottle. Should find out in a few days." His hand on the knob, he said, "Pete, you calm down. You're going to wear yourself out having those tantrums. The college will survive."

After the door closed, Aunt Sarah said, "Tantrums indeed. You're going to wear out your wife, you know." Her tone said she wasn't kidding.

Kate was startled. Aunt Sarah was hardly every critical. Recovering from her injury must be exhausting her.

"I'm sorry, Sarah," Uncle Pete said. "So much is happening at once. It's discombobulating being out of my office, and then every time I go to campus there's some new disaster." He heaved a sigh. "Let's try to have a peaceful weekend."

With a new crime scene in front of the house and an old one in the back? Kate didn't think peace was a likely prospect.

Aunt Sarah hesitated, then gave her husband the difficult news. "Before you got here, Mark was telling us Camila might have been murdered."

"God, really?" Her husband stared at her. "He could be wrong. The last time Hunterville had a murder was back in Colonial days, I'm pretty sure."

"The autopsy hasn't been done yet because the ME lost his office to the frozen pipes," Kate said.

"Oh, I know that guy. Teaches anatomy to doctor wannabes. Kind of stuck up, if you ask me."

Kate made a quick lunch, heating two cans of Snow's clam chowder on the stove and putting open-faced cheese sandwiches into the toaster oven. A subdued meal. Uncle Pete ate quickly and picked up his briefcase. "I'd better get some work done," he said, heading for the living room. He stopped to kiss the top of his wife's head. "I suppose Camila is just as dead murdered as she is if she died accidentally. I don't suppose it makes much difference in the long run."

"How can you say that? You're such a—such a—scientist!" Aunt Sarah spluttered. "It would make a huge difference to me if she's been murdered. What a nightmare. And I'd want the person responsible found and locked up for the rest of his life."

"Yes, I'm sorry. You're right, of course." He kissed her hair again. "Are you coming back to the master bedroom tonight?"

"I thought I might give the master a couple more nights to calm down."

"Ah. I see." He trudged into the living room, his voice floating back to them. "I'm working on it." The glass doors rattled shut.

After she helped Aunt Sarah up to the guest room, Kate went out to her camper. She was determined to focus, to work. Memories of her mentor's wisdom encouraged her, and she had more immediate examples: Mark and her uncle both found peace in their work.

"So do I," she said aloud. She seized a new pen, opened to a blank page and drew a series of lines, quickly, just to get to know the quality of the instrument. Then she saw what she'd begun, and she built it more carefully.

Forest by a pond, birches in the snow. Negative space made positive, a maze of white that drew the eye ever deeper.

The light in her tiny studio glowed late into the night.

* * *

The next day, a cold Saturday, she slept late and woke to the smell of coffee and Uncle Pete clattering in the kitchen. She helped herself to a cup and watched him whisk eggs and pour them into a frying pan. He did it dramatically, the way he did everything, energy beaming out of him like radiation. Maybe that was what had awakened her.

"For my wife, the invalid in the attic," he grumbled as he slid two glistening eggs onto a blue plate. He scrounged a bunch of parsley from the fridge and snipped a sprig for garnish. "The botanist's touch," he said, and lumbered up the stairs. "I don't eat the stuff, but she does."

Bright day, white sky, white road. More snow must have fallen overnight. Kate walked to the campus, past the

Union. Tim and Brew were shoveling the steps to the bookstore, and Kate's hello got a nod from the former and a warm hello from the latter. Tim had introduced himself to her uncle's class as a college handyman—clearing snow must be one of his jobs, and it was good of the store manager to help. No question, Brew was a great guy.

On to the aviary. If she hadn't witnessed her uncle's agitated bulletin the previous day, she wouldn't realize anything had gone wrong. Several large electrical heaters blowing at various angles were the only indications of trouble. True, the temperature and humidity were both somewhat lower than on her earlier visit, but not by enough—now—to freeze birds. Workers from Buildings and Grounds must have worked quickly.

Turning sideways on a bench, knees up, propping her sketchbook on her thighs, she settled in to work on drawings started earlier in the week. Another pass at the two Christmas portraits, and then the studies of the bee she'd found. The wild assortment of leaves around her, some of them huge, were also on her agenda. Thank goodness her concentration was back.

She scrolled through the photos on her phone until she got to the shots of the bee. Even sprayed with fixative, the thing looked fragile as a snowflake, so she hadn't wanted to carry it around with her. She studied the segmentation of its legs and the way the fur—was it fur?—whorled around the bulb-like area where the wing attached. The long body was segmented, too. In fact the more closely she looked, the more the creature's parts showed themselves to be composed of smaller parts. Some kind of strange bio-assembly process had made the bee.

That process is called evolution, she reminded herself.

It wasn't that she drew from the picture, exactly, but it helped her to look, and notice, and then focus exclusively on her drawing.

She was immersed in it, that no-mind state in which she felt god-like, a minor deity creating on paper a bee that would never clean its antennae with those combs on its forelegs, or look out of its compound eyes at cubist leaves, or fly—but Kate wanted it to appear real enough to do those things.

The contrast of her drawing lessened slightly, and it took her a moment to realize it was the effect of a shadow. Someone had stopped next to the bench. She looked up.

The woman was tall and round and energetic; even standing still she looked as if she were vibrating with strength and the intention to use it in the next moment. The way Kate wanted her bee to look. She swiveled her feet off the bench and sat up, smiling back.

"Hi," the mountain-woman said. She had on muddy rubber boots and a ratty T-shirt that said PICK FLOWERS NOT FIGHTS. "I'm Myra, and I love your bee." Glossy black hair spilled onto her shoulders.

"Thanks," Kate said. "I'm Kate. I recognize your name. My aunt said you were a friend of hers. You know Sarah Stewart?"

"Absolutely. She's a role model. She's in my church, and she takes care of everyone, never a bad word. Patient as sunlight."

"Then you've probably heard she needs some care-taking herself now. Fell and broke her right arm, and she's wearing a major-league cast. That's why I'm here."

"Yes, I heard. I'm an awful friend, just awful, not to get over to visit her," Myra said. She bounced on her feet, as if she were about to take flight. "I've been so busy here, I haven't talked to her in a couple of weeks. Beyond busy. We've had some real problems here. Especially yesterday."

"My Uncle Pete told us," Kate said. "I'm so sorry. Can I do anything to help?"

"Thank you, but I think we've got it under control. Counted the dead ones, did a census." She drooped for a second. "But back to Sarah. I'll make her a casserole or something. She's okay with visitors?"

"Yes, and a casserole would be awesome. I'm not a great cook, and neither is Uncle Pete."

Myra laughed. "Uncle Pete can't boil water." She sat down next to Kate. "May I have a closer look at this bee of yours?"

"Sure."

Her eyes went all over the drawing, as if she were reading it. "This is an Africanized bee, which is a silly name. It should be a Brazilian bee, because Brazil is where the hybrid was created." She turned the sketchbook and looked more closely. "You've got it perfectly. Better than a photo. I love it."

Kate felt herself blushing. Embarrassment or pride? Both.

Myra glanced at her watch, bounced to her feet. "Oh, gosh, I've got to get changed. I can't teach in this outfit. I'll come see your aunt. And you."

"Awesome," Kate said, but not fast enough. She was talking to Myra's back, to the swath of black hair floating behind her like a shadow.

NINE

Glorious to be out on skis again. She pushed her dark memories aside and enjoyed the sun sparkling on the snow as if it were water. Well, that's what it was, wet and heavy after the temperature had warmed above freezing. Kate slushed down the first slope and slogged up the second, then along the narrow stretch between the woods and the fence. The shortcut to Azul's house. Even on slow snow, it didn't take very long to get there.

This was the route the intruder had taken. So was Azul the guy who had sneaked onto the porch? Kate forced herself to keep an open mind. Just because the intruder had skied away in this direction didn't mean he was Azul. Plenty of houses were set along the edge of the Reserve: Kate had looked at the area online, and there were at least thirty houses on Topper Drive. And the guy wasn't necessarily a resident. He could have parked his car on the street and come from anywhere. Tracks leading *toward* Azul's house didn't prove a thing, and it was too late to look for tracks leading *to* his house. But surely the police had followed them as far as they could, the morning after the incident.

But whoever it was knew the city, or this part of it, well enough to plan an inconspicuous route to come at Aunt Sarah's house from the back. College Street, the usual approach, was a main street, after all, and well-lit. Plenty of houses along it. All it would have taken was one insomniac resident to notice the man, or his car, or both. Someone like Kate.

She should think about the big picture. Brew had talked about his father, the developer. If Prof. Chavez's death turned out to be murder, Don McCoy was somebody to consider. The biologist and her endangered mice were getting in the way of a high-end resort. Such a development would bring major profits to its builders, along with the much-touted jobs.

Kate hit the snow before she realized she was falling.

She laughed through the snow in her mouth. She hadn't been paying enough attention. Skiing on autopilot was not a good idea, especially when conditions changed. Going from the open field to the shaded area near the woods had meant the snow was icier, didn't give as much grip for her kicks, but she hadn't slowed down or shortened her stride. She'd done a classic face plant.

At least she was back in the real world instead of nominating people to be murderers when she wasn't even sure there'd been a murder.

She got to her feet and skied cautiously past the shelter and down to the pond. Birches bowed toward the water, ice in their crowns. The pond was pewter with a black rim, a bowl of winter.

She'd skied to an island once, across a lake near the New Hampshire cabin she'd rented with her then-partner Mike. It had been exhilarating to move away from shore, her skis biting into good snowpack above ice a yard thick. Where the wind had swept it clear of snow, the ice was transparent down to black water. Bubbles hung, trapped, like planets in space. Cracks and groans had resounded across the lake, but Mike reassured her the racket was harmless.

This early in the season Kate wouldn't trust any body of water to support such an adventure. But the trail that circled Topper Reserve's small pond offered birches and chickadees, plus one nuthatch circling a trunk, head down. They were more than enough to make her feel happy, connected to her fellow creatures on spaceship Earth.

* * *

There had been so many volunteers to take care of Aunt Sarah at Prof. Chavez's funeral that Kate didn't think she was needed, and since she hadn't known the woman she didn't need to attend. A few people would stop by the house afterwards, Aunt Sarah said, and supervised excavation of the party-sized coffee maker from the back of a cabinet under the kitchen counter. Kate had to remove a lot of seldom-used pots to get to it, and washing the big urn was awkward because it didn't fit in the sink. A sheet of paper stored inside gave instructions for making fifty cups.

Fifty? That was Aunt Sarah's idea of a few people? "Yikes," Kate said. "This thing's a monster."

Uncle Pete looked over her shoulder as she ran a wet sponge inside the aluminum cylinder. "Sarah underestimates. We invited everybody, so you can expect half the town to show up," he said. "And everyone at the college."

"It's a coffee dragon," Kate said. Then wished she hadn't, because of Azul's description of his late fiancée as the Dragon Lady.

But apparently Aunt Sarah didn't make the connection, her good nature in evidence despite the sadness of the day. "Yes, it will steam and snort and carry on. But it stays put.

It won't chase the cat or set the curtains on fire like a real dragon."

"Or it didn't last time," Uncle Pete said, jingling the car keys in his hand. "Ready?"

After the Volvo backed down the driveway, Kate relaxed in the quiet house, drawing the coleus plant on Aunt Sarah's desk next to the window, enjoying the contrast of the deep maroon leaves and their bright yellow-lime margins.

After an hour she turned on the coffee urn and then browsed through the assigned reading for Uncle Pete's next class. She'd lost herself in a section on the structure of pollen when car doors and voices outside brought her back to the present.

The number of cars in the driveway and along the street was daunting. Aunt Sarah was such a paradox, a quiet person with the vast social network of an extrovert. At least it seemed vast to Kate, who had perhaps five good friends. She blinked out the open door into the whiteness as it filled with people dressed in muted colors.

Myra helped Aunt Sarah out of the Volvo and brought her up the steps. Behind them Kate recognized Brenda, and Brew. Was that Mark? Yes. And some students, Phoebe and Kareem and Chaya. And many other people she didn't know. Azul at the back. She hoped she'd be able to talk to him, but there was quite a crowd.

Aunt Sarah made her way to the head of the dining room table and sat in the chair Uncle Pete ran his class from, while Kate collected coats at the door and dumped them on her bed in the converted garage. Myra went back to her car and got a huge tray of pastries—Danish and donuts and small squares of cinnamon cake that looked home-made—then made a second trip for two casseroles she put in the fridge.

Brew gave her a subdued smile, and Phoebe surprised Kate with a hug. Kate felt the cold metal of the girl's eyebrow ring against her cheek and wondered briefly how comfortable it could be to wear piercings in such cold weather. Then she thought of her own pierced ears and the studs she normally wore. Temperature wasn't a problem.

She had on her biggest earrings now, silver dangles. A black turtleneck and what she called her dress jeans, black and new enough not to be faded. Aunt Sarah had loaned her a stylish, flared jacket. She looked presentable enough, especially considering she was a nomad and the hanging locker in her camper was less than a foot wide.

A few people sat at the table but most milled and mingled, filling the kitchen and dining room and spilling into the living room. Uncle Pete had stashed his piles of paper somewhere, so the couch and coffee table were available for normal use. All the mugs Kate had been able to find were on the counter, most of them decorated with pictures of cats, and they'd been found and filled. People crowded around Azul, and hugs were frequent. The little house vibrated as the level of conversation rose.

Kate made her way toward Aunt Sarah, who looked distressed. "I don't know why Don McCoy had to go to the service," she was saying to Myra, who'd just come from the kitchen. "After all their fighting, in the paper and in person."

Myra had brought two cups. She set them down in front of Aunt Sarah and pulled a chair close to hers so she could hear over the hubbub. "Yes," she said. "I wish he'd stayed away."

"The demonstrators, too," Aunt Sarah said. "I think they were disrespectful." She looked up and saw her niece. "Katie, I'd like you to meet a wonderful friend—"

"Hi, Kate," Myra said.

"You've met? Good heavens, Katie worries she's turning into a hermit but she's met everybody important," Aunt Sarah said with a smile. "Without any help from me."

"I met Azul and Brew when I went skiing," Kate explained to Myra. "And you and Brenda at the aviary. I'm not exactly a party animal." She looked out at the crowded room. "This is more people than I've been around in ages."

"A lot of people will miss Camila," Myra said. "Her and her work."

"I'm sorry to hear demonstrators showed up at the funeral," Kate said. She couldn't find a chair, so she stood beside her aunt's chair. "What organization were they from, could you tell?"

"A pro-business, anti-environmentalist group that started having meetings around here last summer. I didn't recognize any of them today." If Aunt Sarah didn't know them, maybe they were from outside Hunterville. "Call themselves the HCDC, Hunter County Development Council."

"They really want Topper Reserve made into a golf course?" Kate asked.

"Yes, they were chanting 'Sell it, Sell it' as we went into the church."

"And 'We Want Jobs' as we came out," Myra said.

"Do you think that developer McCoy put them up to it?" Kate asked.

A new voice cut into the conversation. "I think my father's smarter than that." Brew spoke over someone's shoulder, then slid past it and joined the three women. "If he told those yahoos anything, he would have told them to make themselves scarce. Aggravating people who come together to grieve is not a winning strategy."

Myra hitched her chair back to make room for Brew so Aunt Sarah wouldn't have to twist her neck to talk to him.

"This is such a sad day," he said. "Don't tell my dad, but I contributed to Camila's black-footed field mouse preservation project. I thought she had years of conservation work ahead of her. Decades. Her passing is such a shame."

"I have to say this: I wasn't happy to see your father at the funeral," Myra said. "After all the lousy things Don McCoy has said about Camila, I wouldn't have thought he'd show his face."

"My father believes in doing the proper thing," Brew said. "But I know what you mean."

At the edge of the crowd, an elderly woman in a green shawl turned toward him. "Proper? You call that proper, showing up where he's not wanted?" Her voice was shrill, her face flushed. "I'd say he was there to gloat."

Brew looked taken aback, but he stood straighter. "I don't think so. But I'm not going to argue about it."

"Because you can't," the woman said. "To make it worse, he showed up with Dean Thorne. The two of them are a pair of weasels who are going to sell Hunterville to the highest bidder." She turned her back and pushed her way toward the kitchen.

Apt choice of metaphor, Kate thought, and wondered if the old woman knew weasels hunt black-footed mice.

"Politics can be difficult," Brew said, "but I assure you my father wasn't gloating. He's a decent human being, even if his conservative views are unpopular in this liberal place." He looked at Myra. "Unpopular even with his son." Then he turned to Aunt Sarah. "Thank you for opening your home to us all. I'm heading out, since I don't want to cause any further unpleasantness. I wish you well." He touched her hand and threaded his way toward the door.

"I like that man," Kate said. "He handled that—"

"Of course he thinks his father is decent," Myra interrupted. "Blood is thicker than water. Most of us think he's a slimy—"

"Myra," Aunt Sarah said.

After an uncomfortable pause, Kate asked, "Brew runs a motel as well as the bookstore? He's enterprising."

"I think the motel pays his bills, and the bookstore is a labor of love," Aunt Sarah said. "He invites novelists and poets to give readings that are free and open to the public. He's as good-hearted as they come."

"I've heard he writes poetry himself," Myra said.

Kate looked over her shoulder and spotted the green shawl, deep in the kitchen. "Who's the outspoken old woman?" Kate asked.

"Shannon Quigley," Myra said. "Has a chip on her shoulder about everything. Whatever the issue, she'll shout in your face about it."

"She gets my goat," Aunt Sarah said, the harshest criticism Kate had ever heard from her.

The door opened for a latecomer, a big man with red hair, wearing a coat with a fur collar. The conversation hit a lull and then started up again at a lower volume.

"Oh, Dean Thorne," Myra said. "I hope Shannon behaves herself." She looked like she hoped Shannon went wild. "Weasel is too good a word."

"He's an officer of the college," Aunt Sarah said, and Kate found herself irritated at the prim tone. Then her aunt sighed and said, "Unfortunately."

Good. Let rank and propriety not govern at all costs.

"He won't stay long," Myra said. "He's not taking off his coat."

"A courtesy visit," Aunt Sarah said. "Fine with me."

Thorne moved to the kitchen but didn't help himself to coffee. Was he looking for someone? People nodded at him but nobody started a conversation. The loneliness of power.

And then the dean looked pleased, and put out his hand, and gave another man a loose embrace.

Uncle Pete. Kate glanced at Aunt Sarah. Her head was down, and she played with her coffee cup. It said CATS ARE BETTER THAN PEOPLE. Then Kate watched everyone watch her uncle and Thorne talk. Beads of sweat ran down the sides of the dean's face. The crowd had heated the house and made the air stuffy, and he was paying the cost of the social signal of not taking off his coat.

Kate realized she was roasting, too. "I'm just going to step out on the porch for some air," she said. Aunt Sarah was still playing with her cup but Myra nodded.

The chilly air was as refreshing as a drink of ice water. Kate stepped onto the lawn and stretched her arms. As patient as cows waiting to get into a barn, parked cars stood in a line down the driveway behind her truck. Or maybe they were waiting to get into the converted garage. "Bad news, guys," she told them. "You're a decade too late."

Footsteps. Azul was on the porch, and Brenda behind him. Dr. Chavez's fiancé and her housemate. They'd known her best; that must be what drew them together so often.

"Houston, your aunt is a spider in a corner. She doesn't move or say much, but her web keeps the city from falling apart."

"I've thought that myself, Azul. She seems to be friends with everyone."

"There's a reason for that," Brenda said. She smiled, took a deep breath, and sang a few lines about Tupelo honey and angels, her mezzo soprano voice vibrant. *She's an angel of the first degree.* The song was visible in the cold air, a series of white plumes.

There was honey in the song, so of course there was a bee. The sadness on Azul's face lessened a fraction.

"Holy cats," Kate said to Brenda. "You're good."

"Not as good as your aunt," Brenda said. "At more important things than singing."

"Music's important," Azul said. "Especially at times like these. One of two refuges from life's miseries, according to Albert Schweitzer."

"That missionary guy who went to Africa?" Kate asked. "Okay, I'll bite. What's the other refuge?"

"Cats."

"Cats?" Brenda looked dubious.

Azul shrugged. "Just because he was a brilliant doctor and philanthropist doesn't mean he was right about everything. I would have voted for dogs."

"Maybe a tree full of songbirds," Kate suggested.

"Time to go, my melodious friend?" Azul went down the steps and turned, holding a hand out.

"Will you be able to get out?" Kate looked at the line of cars.

"Yes," he said. "My truck's at the end." He and Brenda stood close together. "Farewell, Houston," Azul said. "Perhaps we'll meet again on skis, but I promise I'll be more careful." His deep laughter started, then faltered. His face twisted in pain. Remembering their encounter in the Reserve must have taken him back to the morning his bride-to-be was found buried in snow. He turned away.

Kate watched the couple walk down the driveway, and a dreadful thought crossed her mind. What if Azul had decided he preferred Brenda's company to Camila's? What if he'd—oh, for heaven's sake, she told herself. Be real. A man who changes his mind about marrying just says so, he doesn't kill his fiancée.

She turned back to the house. A small group came out, elderly folks she didn't know. After they'd picked their way past her, nodding goodbyes, she took off Aunt Sarah's jacket and put it over her arm, ready for the overheated room.

Up the steps. When she opened the door Dean Thorne came out, followed by Kareem and Phoebe, both talking at once. Kate stood back as the three went down the steps.

"Sir, you were quoted earlier this term as saying the students don't care, but we do, we care very much, and—

"We have ways of getting the word out, and Otterlin's image—"

Phoebe and Kareem paused and looked at each other, then started talking at the same time again. Like two people in a doorway both dodging to one side and then the other, getting in each other's way.

"Do you read the student paper, sir?" Kareem's voice was polite but insistent. "Because the polls are eighty-nine percent against selling—"

"Otterlin's name will be mud on Facebook and Twitter and Instagram and Tumblr and any other platform I can think of," Phoebe said. "We're like, angry. And we're not going to go away just because you're ignoring us."

Sure enough, that's what he was doing. Thorne walked quickly down the driveway, putting his fur collar up. His car was parked on the street—he must have foreseen the need to make a quick getaway.

The students stopped. "Otterlin's name will be mud and your name, too, you stupid old—" Phoebe shouted after him.

Kareem grabbed her sleeve. "No insults. They backfire. Let him go, for now." He put an arm around her and turned her toward the porch.

"He's going to do it." Even with a consoling arm around her, Phoebe didn't relax. Her fists clenched. "I can't believe what a disaster this is. Everything she worked for is being trashed. And she's barely in the ground. It makes me so mad."

As they reached the steps Kareem's arm dropped away.

The door opened behind Kate. Shannon Quigley clutched her shawl to her throat, eyes darting at the three people in front of her and then past them. "Yoo hoo, Arnold!" she called.

At his blue BMW, Thorne turned. The resigned look on his face was comical.

"I need a ride home," Shannon said, scurrying between the students and down the driveway. Apparently the old woman took rides from weasels.

She'd left the door standing open. As Kate went inside with the students, it occurred to her the autopsy on Prof. Chavez must have been completed or the police wouldn't have released the body to the funeral home, a necessary step before the service. She looked around the dining room and kitchen for Mark, but didn't see him.

Chaya and Uncle Pete and another, older man were talking near the coffee urn when Kate got there. More people were leaving now and it was easier to move around.

"Katie, this is my colleague Dave Simmons. His office is next door to mine—or used to be, until the Great Ice Age came to Otterlin. Dave, my niece Katie."

"We're still neighbors in spirit. Nice to meet you, Katie."

"It's Kate, actually," she said. "Except to uncles."

"Dave is not the type to blow his own horn, but he's going to make medical history one of these days. He studies arthropods as disease vectors."

"An uplifting way to spend my days." Dave smiled. "Considering bad bugs and what they can do to humans."

"Bugs? And lobsters and shrimp and scorpions," Kate said.

Dave looked at her, and then at Uncle Pete, who shrugged and said, "I told you she was bright."

"Just your average former bio major," Kate said. "I'd better remember what an arthropod is."

"Bugs," Chaya said, and mimed a dramatic shiver. "Not my favorites."

"New Englanders who catch lobsters call them bugs, and call the traps bug crates," Dave said. "You like lobsters, don't you?"

"Only boiled and on a plate," Chaya said. "With plenty of melted butter."

"So what does a former biology student do these days?" Dave asked. "Although I object to 'former.' Once a bio major, always in the bio club."

"Never used my degree for a job, not unless you count being an ambulance tech for a couple of years," Kate said. "Right now I'm working as a free-lance artist. But I'm glad I majored in biology. What subject's more awesome than life itself?"

"Preaching to the choir," Dave said, and smiled again. "And since eighty percent of living species are arthropods, it's efficient to focus on them."

"Some people think they're creepy," Uncle Pete said, looking at Chaya. "Nobody says that about plants. And plants don't run away when you want to shake them down for data."

Dave glanced around. "Ever wonder what arthropods think of us? The species that invented war? Plenty of animals murder their own kind, but not in the massive numbers we do. Give me a bug any day." His smile had fled.

"Give me a plant," Uncle Pete said.

"Give me a cat," Chaya said, stooping. She came up with Eclipse, out of hiding now that most of the visitors had left. It was late; he must be hungry. His admirer tossed her hair back and cradled him in her arms. "Pussycats are the best. Long may they rule."

TEN

"I'm glad that's over," Aunt Sarah said the next day. "It's too bad Rosa didn't get here in time for the funeral." She was at the dining room table, where Kate had joined her after rinsing out the urn, putting it away, and loading the dishwasher. Uncle Pete had gone out to get the Sunday paper and some Danish.

"Rosa? Oh, that's Prof. Chavez's sister?"

"Yes. She's staying with Brenda."

"That must be strange. For both of them."

"I can't imagine what Brenda's going through. Rosa works on a fishing boat in Alaska, doesn't have much money. Took her a week to borrow enough from friends to buy the plane ticket. She wasn't clear about her schedule until the last minute, which is why the college and our minister went ahead and planned Camila's service without her."

"Nice of Brenda to put her up," Kate said. The dishwasher swooshed, a couple of plates rattling.

Aunt Sarah sighed. "I don't think I'm ready to go to church today."

"The funeral took too much out of you?"

"Yes. The service might be good for me, but getting there and talking with everyone before and after—it's too much."

"Yes. Save your strength."

"Although the HCDC probably won't demonstrate outside the church during an ordinary service," Aunt Sarah said. "That's what was the most upsetting, yesterday. I could hear their chanting even while we were inside."

"How many of them were there?"

She stared down at her cup. "Only about a dozen, more men than women. Most of them wore red jackets or hats. Red's their emblem—the opposite of environmental green."

"Hello, ladies," a voice said, and they both jumped.

Mark had slipped inside as quietly as Eclipse, and except for his face he was just as dark. Black jeans, black jacket.

"For heaven's sake, Mark," Aunt Sarah said. "You're not supposed to act like a cat burglar. You're supposed to *catch* cat burglars."

"Haven't you heard that police and criminals are cut from the same cloth?" he asked. "Adrenaline junkies who like to work independently and get immediate results?"

"That doesn't sound like you," she said. "You're calm and patient."

"Uncle Pete left the door unlocked. Old habits are hard to break," Kate said. "I'll get an extra cup."

The body language struck her as she came back from the kitchen: her aunt and Mark both leaning forward, eager to talk to each other. Good friends were better than music or cats, no matter what Albert Schweitzer had said.

The pleasure she felt on her aunt's behalf evaporated when she heard their conversation.

". . .more than hypothermia. She had an allergic reaction. Did she ever mention any kind of allergy to you?"

"No," Aunt Sarah said slowly. "She had strong likes and dislikes, as you know. Everything she did, she did with passion. But this isn't about hating licorice or shortbread cookies, is it?"

"No." Mark looked up as Kate set his coffee in front of him. "Thanks, Kate." He looked disappointed at what his old friend had said. "I put some pressure on the ME, who was a bit of a grouch about it. What was the big deal, he wanted to know, about an obvious victim of hypothermia during a record-breaking blizzard? A piece of pathological cake, right? Except it wasn't."

"So Dr. Chavez died of something besides exposure?" Kate asked, sliding into a chair across from him.

Uncle Pete huffed in the door. "Cold out there," he said. "Hello, Mark. What's the news? Besides this, of course." He thumped the Sunday newspaper on the table and put a white box tied with string beside it. The photo under the paper's masthead showed a crowd of mourners in black on the steps of a small stone church, while in the foreground a group of protestors carried signs that said JOBS FIRST and MICE DON'T PAY TAXES.

Aunt Sarah pulled the paper toward her with her left hand. After a moment she said, "You can't see their faces very well. A scarf here, a collar there—most of them have their backs turned."

Uncle Pete sat at the table with his coat on. "Maybe they didn't want to be recognized, and the paper went along with that."

"Mark, what about Prof. Chavez?" Kate asked.

"There was evidence of anaphylactic shock," he said, "an extreme allergic reaction that closed her airway, interfered with her breathing or stopped it completely. That could have been fatal by itself, or she could have collapsed from that and hypothermia finished her off."

Aunt Sarah put a hand over her mouth.

"It's not what we expected, but it still doesn't look like there was foul play involved."

"Was it something she'd eaten?" Kate asked.

"She certainly wasn't out there frying an egg in a snowstorm," Uncle Pete said, opening the box of donuts and taking a chocolate frosted. The sarcasm startled Kate. What was up with him?

"She hadn't eaten for at least four hours," Mark said. "Since about eight Friday night. The funny thing was that she had food with her, a sandwich in a little pack, but she hadn't eaten any of it."

"Nothing strange about that. She used to have a midnight snack after she got her work done," Aunt Sarah said. "Said she had to sing for her supper. Sometimes she ate it here, with me, but not always. It was a good thing Pete and I are such night owls."

Kate had to ask, although on the question sounded ridiculous. "Could the allergic reaction have been caused by a bee sting?"

Mark raised one eyebrow. "Theoretically, yes. But no bee would be flying around Topper Reserve in a blizzard."

"I found a dead bee near the scene. The next day."

He frowned. "That's—quite odd, Kate."

"Yes. Is there any possibility a bee got into her clothes, maybe in the aviary, and stayed alive because of her body heat and then stung her later?"

Mark looked skeptical. "I'll ask the ME if he saw any evidence of a bee sting," he said, "although that's something he shouldn't have missed." He looked at Aunt Sarah. "I'm not closing the file. The way things look now, it was a sad accident. But I'd like to know more about your night visitor."

"When do you think you'll know what that white stuff was on the front steps?" Kate asked.

"Couple of days," Mark said. "It might not have anything to do with what happened to the professor, of course."

Uncle Pete looked up from the newspaper, his attention apparently caught by the word professor. "I hope not. I don't want a murderer poking around my front porch." He hadn't listened very carefully to Mark.

"Of course. But somebody was up to something out there," the detective said. "I'm glad Kate noticed those white granules. They looked like snow, but they were heavier. The way they ran along the back of the steps and then just stopped, which means the guy must have been applying them."

"Some kind of poison?" Kate asked. "Considering all the dead mice we saw."

"Very likely." Mark stood and stretched. "Thanks for the coffee. Time for me to get back to work."

"On Sunday," Aunt Sarah said, shaking her head. It wasn't a question.

"It would be nice if crime took weekends off," Mark said, putting on his jacket. "I'll let you know as soon as the lab tells me what the white substance was."

"Is there some of it still out there?" Pete asked.

"No, the team got it all. Used one of those forensic devices that uses suction and deposits material right into an evidence bag. You're clean, Professor Pete."

"Thank goodness for that," Uncle Pete said without looking up.

Was Kate imagining it, or was he being sarcastic again? And Mark, too? Maybe they didn't like each other.

"What's going on in our little Hunterville?" Aunt Sarah asked the door Mark had shut behind him.

"A good question," Kate said. Sean came to mind, how helpful it would be to talk to him about the suspicious white powder. She pushed the thought firmly aside.

* * *

Since Marjorie had sounded lonely the last time they'd talked, Kate called her. "Just wanted to reassure you that all the deaths around here recently have been mice, not people," she said, and described the rodent massacre.

"That's not exactly reassuring, Kate," Marjorie said. "I'd rather hear there hadn't been any deaths at all. I mean, what's going on?" She was mollified by the autopsy results. "Now that's a big relief. A sad accident, but an accident. I don't have to worry about you getting tangled up with more murder and mayhem."

"Well, the mayhem part is out of my hands," Kate laughed. "The HCDC group is marching around downtown with signs, trying to get the college to sell the beautiful park behind my aunt's house so it can be turned into a golf course."

"My advice? Stay out of politics," Marjorie said. "It'll make you crazy."

"It's definitely crazy around here, with Topper Reserve on the line. What keeps me sane is drawing."

"For me it's my kids. I love watching them grow and learn." She laughed. "But the funny thing is, the high point of my day is when I put them to bed. Is it bad that I love them even more when they go to sleep?"

"I don't think so. Taking care of an infant and toddler is such a demanding job, I don't know how you do it. Your time isn't your own until they're asleep."

"It can be stressful, that's for sure, but I'm careful to give myself time off. A couple of other mothers in the neighborhood and I take turns with all the kids, which is a huge help. And I have a great sitter. I'd trust her with my life."

"Stress can sneak up on you," Kate said, thinking of herself as well as Marjorie.

"That professor who died sounds like she was overextended, taking on even more research than most and adding activism on top of it. She was probably undermining her health without realizing it."

"Yes," Kate said. "Maybe sacrificing it."

* * *

That night, even though Kate had bailed on Uncle Pete's botany class, she saw the students. They came to her.

She'd decided to get out of the house, since even with the pocket door between the garage and the dining room closed, she could hear Uncle Pete's voice and most of the students' as well, which made it impossible to read. Half an hour before the class she woke Eclipse, snoozing in her lap, and carried him up to Aunt Sarah in the guest room.

"I brought you a big furry present," Kate said, but of course when she put Eclipse on the bed he jumped to the floor and ran into the hall. His progress down the wooden stairs was a series of audible plunks.

"Cats," Kate said.

Aunt Sarah smiled. "Like herding students."

"Do you need anything?"

"Thank you, Katie, I'm fine. Feeling a little stronger."

"Good. Let me know when you want to move back to the master bedroom, and when you and Pete want your garage studies back."

"That'll be a while yet." She looked out the window, at the snowflakes whispering against the pane. "Keep your eyes open, Katie. I really don't like the thought of that guy on the porch and the mice he probably poisoned. We don't know what he's up to, and he may be back."

"I will, Aunt Sarah. And I'll make sure the door gets locked when I go to bed, even if Uncle Pete forgets."

"Good. He'll leave it open for the students on class night, and he's very likely to forget to lock it after they leave, since we just started doing that. I'm glad you're here, Katie dear."

"Glad to help," Kate said. Almost out the door, she turned back. "By the way, Brenda thinks you're an angel. She has a lovely singing voice."

Aunt Sarah laughed. "Impossible. In this old house my wings would get stuck in doorways."

Kate went down the stairs more quietly than Eclipse. "Have a good class, Uncle Pete," she called into the living room. Did she get a grunt in answer? She wasn't sure. She hoped he wasn't offended by her absence. "Please tell the students I enjoyed meeting them," she'd said when she'd begged off. "You could tell them I have my own work to do."

Which was true. She climbed into her camper, turned on the heater and the lights, and pulled the curtains closed. Paced the tiny cabin, three steps forward, three steps aft, waiting for her home-turned-studio to warm up. The news about Prof. Chavez was odd. An allergic reaction? To what? Whenever anaphylactic shock was mentioned, the most likely cause was a bee sting. And Kate had evidence right in her studio that a bee had been on the scene. But in a snowstorm, in freezing temperatures, it couldn't have been the culprit. Could it?

Voices. A knock at the door. Kate opened it to find Kareem's dark face and Phoebe's pale one looking up at her, their eyes blinking against the light snow.

"Could we please talk with you for a few minutes before class?" Kareem asked.

"Okay," Kate said. "Use this grab bar here and come on in." She flipped her sketchbook shut and slid it onto the bunk over the cab.

She wasn't used to having another person on board, let alone two. Good that they had only a few minutes before class.

"Have a seat," she said, sliding into one side of the dinette. "What's up?"

"Man, this camper is awesome!" Phoebe said, sitting across from her and peering around. "Pete said you spent the summer in Maine?"

Kareem nudged her to make space for him. He was all business. "We'd like to ask your advice," he said. "I'm on the Student Council and Phoebe writes for the campus newspaper, so we can see what's going on. Students are really upset about Prof. Chavez, and nobody believes she fell over in a snowbank and froze to death. She was way too smart and experienced for that to be the whole story."

"We all think she was murdered so she wouldn't fight the sale of Topper Reserve to the developers," Phoebe said. "Dean Thorne's behind it. He hired somebody to knock her off. You can tell just by looking at him."

Yikes. Full court press, evidence or not. "The police have been looking into Prof. Chavez's death," Kate said. "They're pretty sure it was accidental."

"Then the police are in the developer's pocket," Phoebe said, "just like the college." The look she gave Kate was full of mistrust, as if she might be an inhabitant of the same pocket.

"What kind of advice are you asking me for?" Kate asked, looking at Phoebe and then Kareem. He seemed calmer.

"The trustees meet in mid-January to vote on whether or not to sell the Reserve," he said. "We organized student postcard mail-ins to all ten members and to Dean Thorne, and got a huge response. We've contacted the Audubon Society, the Sierra Club and three local conservation organizations to urge them to contact the board members, too." He took a breath. "And we've held rallies outside the Hunterville city hall because we think everyone in the community hates this development plan as much as the students do."

"Last time, HCDC people showed up and held a counter-rally across the street from ours," Phoebe said. "But there were way more of us than there were of them."

"So we're wondering if there's anything else you can suggest," Kareem said. "I know it's short notice, since we just met you last week. But we thought—" he glanced at Phoebe—"a pair of fresh eyes might see something we didn't."

Kate was at a loss. "It sounds like you've done a great job," she said. "Alerting the Audubon Society and the Sierra Club was a great idea, since they have resources you don't."

"We don't know what they've done," Kareem said. "They haven't gotten back to us."

"Probably nothing," Phoebe said. She was playing with the ring in her eyebrow, taking it out and putting it back in.

"We're worried about the sabotage of college buildings," Kareem said, "and telling everyone to look out for people who don't belong on campus. Somebody's been sneaking around and turning off the heat."

"A lot of public buildings have little cages over the thermostats, with locks," Kate said. "Maybe Otterlin could do something like that."

"They're doing that," Kareem said. "The first one went up in the aviary. But it will take a while to cover the whole campus."

"It's probably the HCDC," Phoebe said. "The more damage the college has to pay to repair, the more it'll need the cash from selling the Reserve."

"Who are they?" Kate asked. "Who joins a county development council?"

"They're older, most of them, and work, but after five sometimes a bunch of them are at the front gate, wearing red, waving signs around. I don't know if they all live in Hunter County. They could be outsiders."

That the council members were "older" wasn't useful information, coming from someone Phoebe's age.

"The campus cops won't let them demonstrate on college grounds," Kareem said. "I only saw HCDC people on campus once, three big guys in red jackets, outside the bookstore. But the manager asked them to leave and got into kind of an argument. Finally two campus cops showed up and said they had to leave or be arrested, but it was ugly for a few minutes."

Brew. Kate thought of his small build and liked him even more for confronting three "big guys."

"How about appealing to the faculty to show up at the trustees' meeting and voice their opinions?" Kate suggested. "They can do that, can't they?" She hadn't paid that much attention to the structure of governance when she was an undergrad. "I'm not sure how it works, but you've already mobilized the students, which is great. Now get the faculty to commit to some actions as a body. In the eyes of the trustees, they probably have more clout than students."

"That's a good idea," Kareem said. "Lots of us have talked to individual professors, but I don't think anybody's asked them to organize."

"That would be a cinch if Camila were—oh, God, I miss her so much." Phoebe ran a hand across her hair, short enough to be a soldier's.

They left soon after that, grabbing their packs and scrambling to get to class on time. Just before she closed the door, Kareem looked up at her and said "By the way, we were freaked out by all those dead mice last week. Do you know what happened to them?"

"Not yet," Kate said. She didn't want to say the police were looking into it, or mention the white powder.

He waited for more, then looked disappointed, as if he guessed she knew more. Kareem was a smart guy. "Well, good night," he said. "Thanks for your input." She shut the door.

And had to laugh. They were both talking at the same time again, obviously unaware how well she could hear them.

"I told you she'd come up with something we could—" Kareem said.

"An accident," Phoebe said. "She thinks it was an *accident.*"

The small piece of the universe that Aunt Sarah's injury had called her to was in turmoil. Kate was happy to open her sketchbook and lose herself in her work. Two hours later, she barely noticed the students leaving.

Until she heard another knock. She glanced around her space. Had Kareem or Phoebe forgotten something?

No. It was Tim.

"Would you have a few minutes for m-me?" His look was earnest. He was holding his jacket and the botany reading packet in one hand and his daypack in the other. He must have rushed out of class.

"Okay," she said. "Give me your pack, so you'll have a hand free for the grab bar." She wasn't ready for how much the pack weighed and almost dropped it. "Wow, are you taking a geology course, too? Is this thing full of rocks?"

"Um, no, tools," he said as he climbed up. "The college makes us buy our own."

She put her work over the cab again and waved him to the dinette. He put his daypack and jacket on the seat. The course printout thumped onto the table.

He blushed and stumbled over his words at first, but finally got out his problem: Zoe liked Justin, but he, Tim, liked Zoe. "I thought you might give me a t-tip or two," he said. He was sweating now as well as blushing, though the camper wasn't overheated. "You know, an older woman? Wait, that d-doesn't sound right—"

She wanted to laugh. Not at him, but at herself, asked for political and now romantic advice. She was expert at neither, and thought the situation hilarious. If she was the students' idea of a counselor, they were in big trouble.

"Oooh, Tim," she said. "I'm not exactly a role model. I've only had one relationship that lasted more than a month." She stopped herself from adding that it had crashed and burned a year earlier, and she still wasn't sure why.

"B-but you've had that," he said. "One is more than none, which is what I've had."

Kate sat back. What would her younger self have wanted to hear? She tried to make contact with that self, but her memories were of confusion and self-doubt. Decisions made, reversed, re-made.

"All I can suggest is that you talk to her," she said. "Not a lot, don't be a chatterbox or a pest, but maybe two separate times each class meeting, say something. Even if it's just to ask her how she's doing. Or say something about the course, or a campus event. Make it positive; don't complain."

"Okay." He was looking at the floor and seemed to be talking to himself. "Twice, not a pest, d-don't complain." Then he made eye contact. "Okay. G-got it." He wiped his forehead with a forearm, the flannel sleeve coming down wet.

"I hope it helps," she said. "I'm not much of a resource when it comes to this sort of thing."

"No, really, this has helped," Tim said. He reached for his pack and unzipped it to stow the thick course-pack. There wasn't much room left. "Your uncle's a good t-teacher."

"Thanks," Kate said. She remembered Kareem muttering "suck-up" when Tim had enthused about botany at the first class. She'd take the compliment to Uncle Pete as innocent flattery.

"Did you ever figure out why there were all those d-dead mice last week?" The stack of paper was uneven, and the pages that stuck out were getting crumpled as he tried to jam it into the pack.

"No, the police haven't gotten back to us."

He looked up quickly "Police? The p-police are investigating *mice?*"

"Oh—" She'd remembered not to tell Kareem and Zoe, but distracted by Tim's awkwardness she'd spilled the beans. Not that it really mattered, but the less the house figured in campus rumors the better. "Not exactly. It's a long story." She wasn't going to mention the white powder or midnight prowler.

He'd finally gotten the papers stuffed into the pack, tearing a few of them. She'd bet his dorm room was a mess. He stood and grabbed his jacket, put the pack over one shoulder. "Thanks," he said, but his face was full of questions and he didn't move toward the door. "You should have seen G-Grace walking up the driveway before class tonight. Like one of those big wading b-birds, you know? Picking her feet up, looking everywhere for more mice." He laughed. "I asked about them because I thought it would calm her down to know why they died."

Inspiration struck. "Ask Uncle P—" Kate said. "Ask Prof. Stewart."

Delegation. According to Uncle Pete, an honored tradition in academia. She'd let him deal with the mice during his office hours. She, after all, didn't have office hours—but the students apparently thought she did. They'd made her an unofficial and unaccredited professor.

After Tim left, Kate wondered why she was getting such attention from students. Surely professional counselors were available on the Otterlin campus, people trained to understand the dramatic transition college represented as fledgling adults spread their wings. Even in the best of circumstances it was a major shift; for some students, probably including Grace and Maddie, it could be fraught with difficulties. She winced as she thought of her advice to Tim. Of the three students who'd knocked on her door that night, he was the biggest surprise. Wouldn't a guy want advice from a guy?

Maybe the question only illustrated how little she understood the male of her species, especially ones Tim's age.

No, there was something fishy about his visit, she was convinced.

If asking her advice about Zoe was an excuse, why had he really come? To flatter her uncle through her, in hopes of getting a good grade? That didn't make sense, since he couldn't be sure she'd pass along the compliment.

Whatever he'd come for could be as innocent as wanting to see the inside of a camper. Or it could be—

Another knock. Kate couldn't believe it. Were they waiting in line out there? If it was another student, she was going to post hours on her door and tell Uncle Pete she needed to be put on salary.

Zoe. She'd been crying, and Kate relented.

"It's like I'm invisible," Zoe said. "The only time he looks at me is when I say something in class, and sometimes not even then."

"Justin?"

A tearful nod. "He talks to Tim all the time. They're best buddies. But I know they aren't gay, because I heard him talking to Tim about a girlfriend he had in the army, another chopper pilot, how cute she was." She hiccupped once, twice. "Could I have some water?"

"Sure," Kate said. The camper was winterized, tanks empty, but she had a jug of water handy in case she wanted to make coffee. She poured a cup. "Let's sit," she said.

Zoe hiccupped again, then took a long drink and held her breath. When she spoke again, her voice was calmer but still pained. "I know Tim is a few years older than the rest of us, but he's such a puppy," she said. "The only thing I don't like about Justin is how much attention he pays to that—that child."

Kate didn't have a clue how to help her visitor feel better. "Men mature more slowly than women," she said. It was a fact she'd heard more than once from Marjorie, but it seemed completely irrelevant to Zoe's situation. And individual variation was illustrated by Tim and Justin, both a couple of years older than the other students but with emotional ages that appeared dramatically different from each other.

Apparently Zoe found the sociological fact irrelevant, too, because she ignored it. "He's all I want," she said. Her eyes were filling again. "I don't care about anything else. Grades, friends, the debate team—I used to be interested in that stuff, but who cares? They're not important any more."

Oh, brother. She had it bad.

"Zoe," Kate said. "That's self-destructive, not to care about grades or friends. You can't stop living your life because one guy doesn't look your way."

"He's all I care about. Nothing else matters."

Kate got up and found a box of tissues in a cabinet. Put it on the table. Sat and waited for Zoe to blow her nose and wipe her eyes. It took four tissues before the waterworks abated and she looked calmer.

"This is serious." Kate sat down and leaned forward, talking slowly for emphasis. "You really need to talk to someone trained to help you."

"You could help me." Her tone was edged with resentment.

"I like you, Zoe, but I don't know how to help you steer your life. I can draw, I can write a pretty good newspaper story, and I know what to do with a sprained ankle or a nasty cut on someone's arm. But I'm not a counselor, and what you're hurting from I don't know how to fix."

"But you've been traveling all over the country," Zoe said. "Your uncle said so. You've met like all kinds of people, and been in crazy situations. I bet you know a lot."

Oh, so that was it. The fact that she'd lived in her truck camper was what impressed the students. Kate was annoyed with Uncle Pete for letting them in on her life. She had indeed faced some crazy situations—murderous ones, in fact—but he shouldn't have passed that on. She wondered how much he'd let Zoe and the other students know.

"Please tell me you'll see a counselor," Kate said. "You've worked hard to get where you are, and if you throw it all away now you'll be making huge difficulties for yourself in the future. And not the distant future. The future that's practically here."

Was she getting through? She couldn't ask Zoe to absolutely promise to see a counselor; she didn't have enough leverage to demand that.

Zoe didn't answer. She had another little cry—only two tissues for this one—and then pulled herself together and left. Kate had no idea if she'd done any good at all.

* * *

A cloudy morning. She'd worked on her Christmas portraits, and then another of Azul. She didn't have a photo of him, so she worked from memory. He had a distinctive face, with thick eyebrows and full lips. Plus that magnificent beard. She was having trouble with the eyes, though, with their expression. They should be lit with intelligence, but they looked unbearably sad.

Voices roused her. People coming up the driveway. A low voice like distant thunder, and a higher one.

Azul. Had she conjured him? And a woman. Brenda? Kate put down her pencil. She'd have to help Aunt Sarah get downstairs, or at least check to see if she was sleeping before she took Azul and his friend up to the guest bedroom. And she'd make coffee, which is what her aunt would do if she could. Kate was the hostess replacement for the one-armed bandit.

The term had popped into her head when she'd found Aunt Sarah earlier that day putting coffee into the machine, holding the scoop in her left hand. The exercise hadn't gone well, ending with grounds scattered across the counter. Retreating to the dining room, the older woman had said that's what she got for trying to pretend things were normal. Kate had called her a Pollyanna, and then a one-armed bandit. She'd never gambled, only been in a casino once, because it was right inside the airport in Las Vegas when she was making a connection. The slot machines were noisy and the lighting garish. She'd been disoriented to find herself in such a place on the way to an airline gate.

Aunt Sarah had tried to sling a dinner napkin around her face, bandit-style, which had worked out about as well as her filling the coffeemaker.

"You make a terrible bandit," Kate said.

"I need accomplices."

"Okay. I'm in. You and me."

"That's not much of a gang."

"You, me, and a whole crowd of raccoons? They wear masks."

Now, as she got out of the camper, Azul was at the door, rattling the knob, sounding confused. "What, it's locked? But they don't—"

"Hang on, Azul. I've got the key."

He turned, the lost look on his face clearing, but not completely. "Houston. Always the one with the answer."

The woman turned too, short and powerful-looking in a yellow slicker. Kate got the door open and they all trooped in. "I'll see what Aunt Sarah wants, if she's awake—upstairs or down."

"Ah, Houston, you underestimate us. We have called, we are cleared for landing. Upstairs." He took the woman's coat and hung it with his own on the stand. "This is my new friend Rosa. Who is—" He swallowed hard. "Camila's sister. Rosa, this is Kate."

Rosa looked like a cross between a fire hydrant and a pit bull. She wore a blue jersey that didn't disguise the muscles of her shoulders and arms. She put out her hand. "Hi, Kate Houston. Rosa Chavez."

"Kate Corliss." She left Azul to explain his nickname for her as she scooted up the stairs to check in with Mission Control herself.

"It's fine, Katie," Aunt Sarah said. "I'm excited to meet Camila's sister, although I'm sure she's not at her best. If you wouldn't mind—?"

"I'll fire up the coffeemaker."

Downstairs, Kate waved the visitors up, then went to the kitchen. Thank goodness she'd put away the coffee dragon and had her friend the ten-cupper back.

Darn, she hated missing the beginning of most conversations when people came to see Aunt Sarah. She looked out the window while the machine chugged and snuffled. Snow was piling up. Looked like two inches in the driveway, and she'd shoveled once already today, around noon. Uncle Pete's footprints had vanished, filled with falling snow.

A few months ago she'd thought she might be spending December someplace warm like Texas. Or if she'd chosen a leisurely route to Tucson, maybe Tennessee or even the Florida panhandle. Living in her truck camper meant she could go anywhere in the country. She wasn't sorry to be where she was, though: Aunt Sarah was one of her favorite people, and Kate was happy to help. Plus the cold weather was invigorating. Skiing and keeping the driveway clear were great exercise.

Not to mention going up and down the stairs. Climbing them again, Kate put the tray down on the foot of the bed, poured three cups and handed them around. No more chairs, so she sat on the corner of the bed.

It was quiet. Had she interrupted the conversation? Should she leave? Then Azul said, "Rosa's been telling us she doesn't believe Camila died accidentally."

"I can feel her," Rosa said. Her voice was husky. "We weren't twins, but she was only a year older. We did everything together growing up. Saved each other's lives." She shrugged. "Thin ice is just a saying here. Up there, it's for real. And when we say something's a bear, we mean that, too."

"You grew up in Alaska?" Kate asked. Had her uncle told her that?

"Our parents moved there from New Mexico when I was five. We all knew how to handle snow, and cold. The real thing. This should not have been the end of her."

Azul put a big hand on her shoulder, gave it a squeeze.

Rosa looked out the window. "It's not your fault. You're Outsiders and don't know the difference. But what's happening out there? It's not a storm. It's only decoration for your Christmas." She turned back. "I can hear my sister. She says this city is full of danger, and lies."

Another long pause while the three Outsiders absorbed Rosa's words.

"How long will you stay?" Aunt Sarah asked.

"As long as it takes."

ELEVEN

Kate had been in Hunterville for almost two weeks, and Aunt Sarah was somewhat better, although her progress was erratic. On good days she spent time downstairs, reading and doing crossword puzzles, sometimes falling asleep over them, while on bad days she stayed in the guest room and dozed. Bad days still outnumbered good. She hadn't asked to be moved back into the master bedroom, which surprised Kate. Her arm must hurt but she never said so; her only complaint was that the carpenter hadn't fixed the back stairs. Kate wondered if it was symbolic, if Aunt Sarah might be encouraged to heal faster once the wrecked stairs were restored.

She seemed happy enough to let her niece have the night off. It was Thursday, so by accepting Brenda's dinner invitation Kate would be out of the house entirely during Uncle Pete's seminar.

Brenda, Azul, Rosa. Three people devastated by the unexpected loss of a larger-than-life housemate, fiancée, sister. Kate might as well be going to another funeral, although an informal one. For someone she'd never met.

"Of course you should go," Aunt Sarah said, "although I wouldn't expect to have a fun time. Your dinner companions are going to be depressed, to put it mildly." She shrugged. "At least Brenda's a good cook."

Uncle Pete had moved his Volvo to the extra space Kate had been keeping clear at the street end of the driveway. She unplugged her camper and backed it down the drive. Along College Street and through the campus, she drove slowly, the slush loud as the tires kicked it against the wheel wells. The cab floor vibrated. She hoped the road wouldn't be frozen ruts on her way home.

It felt good to be moving in her truck, even for a few minutes. She felt disloyal, both to Aunt Sarah and to the students who would see her camper gone. But she had a touch of cabin fever herself.

She followed the turns on her GPS. It wasn't far, on the other side of campus. She crossed a one-lane bridge just after a small sign for Pauchaug Brook and climbed a low hill on the other side. A pretty area, secluded houses nestled in hollows and among pines. When she got to the address she saw a familiar pond below it: Brenda's house abutted Topper Reserve.

A circular driveway big enough to qualify as a roundabout made it easy for Kate to park pointed out. She'd never understood why drivers of pickups did that until she'd gotten one herself. Starting out in reverse without good visibility to the rear was an exercise in anxiety.

She parked next to a fellow pickup and an aging Jeep. As she turned off the engine she wondered again what this crew of mourners wanted of her. Were they looking for advice, like the three students who'd visited her camper Tuesday night? What sort of advice could they possibly need? She'd lost a dear friend last summer, but the experience didn't qualify her to help anyone else with such a loss. Accepting a death was a long, lonely trip. She bowed her head as a wave of sorrow for her mentor washed over her.

Shaking it off, she dropped out of the truck. The moon was waxing behind thin clouds, and its light helped her follow a flagstone path, shoveled and sanded, to the front door. Azul opened it and gave her a hug, quick but firm. Brenda, behind him, welcomed Kate in that rich voice of hers. Inside, Rosa sat in an overstuffed chair with arms so high it made her look small. She raised a hand in greeting.

The curtains were open. Light from one floor lamp joined the snow-light from the window.

Brenda swept her hand toward a lounge chair, and Kate took it. Azul and Brenda sat on the couch. The aroma of pizza filled the room, and Kate realized how hungry she was.

The silence lengthened.

"This chair," Rosa said, "was hers. Right?"

"Absolutely," Brenda said. She looked at Kate. "I was skeptical at first, but she does seem to know things she couldn't know."

Rosa shrugged. "I feel her here."

Kate didn't scoff at people's beliefs. She didn't necessarily accept them, either. If Camila's spirit was communicating with her sister, fine. How could Kate possibly judge whether that was happening or not?

"So what's up?" Kate asked. She looked at Azul. She didn't know anyone here very well, but he was her best shot.

"Ah, Houston." He sighed, and gathered himself. "We needed to talk to you away from your aunt and uncle." Leaned forward, elbows on knees. "Rosa's convinced—and she's half-convinced Brenda and me—that somebody murdered Camila. We suspect the HCDC, or else the developer Don McCoy or somebody from his camp, with or without his knowledge. So we were hoping you'd join forces with us."

"To do what? And why can't my aunt and uncle know?"

"We're not quite sure where Pete stands. He says all the right things, but he's awfully friendly with Dean Thorne, who in turn is friendly with McCoy. And Sarah is a sweet woman, but she's his wife." He looked uncomfortable. "Whatever she knows, he knows. Or so we must assume. And we do not wish to distress her while she heals."

Kate gave each of the two women a glance, then asked Azul, "What's your plan?"

"Rosa's hoping you'll go with her to an HCDC meeting. Brenda and I can't go—anybody who knows anything about Camila knows that I'm—that we were engaged, and that she lived with Brenda. We're both known, locally. You and Rosa, you're new faces."

"I want to get close to people there, see if I can feel their vibes," Rosa said. "The meeting's a call for volunteers, for new people, which is perfect. We won't stand out. The people running the show—they're the ones I want to get close to, the ones who might have killed my sister."

Hadn't Rosa been given the autopsy results, being Camila's next of kin? "You probably know the police believe Camila had an allergic reaction," Kate said. "That doesn't sound like murder."

The other three looked surprised, and Brenda sat up. "How do you know that?"

Maybe she shouldn't have given out the information, but Mark hadn't said it was confidential, and Kate didn't see what harm it could do. "My aunt has a detective friend who told us."

"Doesn't matter what they think," Rosa said. "I still want to go to the meeting. Something's not right."

Brenda fell back and stared at the ceiling.

Kate was imagining herself in a room full of anti-environmentalists. They would be saying things she'd disagree with, things that might even make her angry. She could keep her mouth shut—that was easy. But over the years many friends had told her that she had the opposite of a poker face. Way too open and readable.

"When you say you want to get close to these people, do you mean you want to have conversations and get to know them? Or are you talking about physical closeness?" Kate asked. She could keep a lid on her face for an hour, couldn't she?

Rosa shrugged. "I just need to be near them for a couple of minutes. Look into their eyes, taste the air around them."

Kate blinked, distracted by thoughts of arthropods using their antennae exactly like that, to taste air or water for pheromones, chemical signals of enemies or mates.

Azul's deep voice filled the pause. "Let's eat, and give Kate some time to think about it."

Over the pizza Kate learned he'd been in the U.S. for fourteen years, first in a Ph.D. program at CalTech and then teaching at small colleges in Iowa and Maryland before getting the tenure-track job at Otterlin. "I'm a recovering academic gypsy," he said. "May my years of peripatetic assistant professoring be over."

A familiar story. "My uncle went through that," Kate said. "Moving every few years is exhausting." She remembered Aunt Sarah's stories, mountains of boxes and epic drives in U-Hauls.

Brenda apparently hadn't been up to cooking, but she'd put together a kale salad with chopped-up dates and green olives to go with the pizza. She didn't talk much, only asking how Sarah's recovery was going and how long Kate planned on staying in Hunterville.

At one point Brenda's cell phone barked like a dog, and she picked it up from the coffee table and held it in front of her to look at the caller ID. Smiled and shook her head and touched the screen. The cell made a clicking sound, and Brenda looked over the top of it at Kate. "Telemarketers," she said. "Such a nuisance."

Rosa didn't say much until just before Kate left; she didn't know whether this was the woman's normal style or whether it was a sign of bereavement. As much as Kate was curious about what life was like in Alaska, especially for someone who went out on fishing boats, it hadn't been the time to ask.

She invited Rosa to ski at Topper Reserve the next day, partly to distract her, partly to get to know her better—especially since they were going to infiltrate the HCDC meeting the day after that. Aunt Sarah's skis and boots should fit Rosa, since they were both small women, but if not she and Kate could snowshoe instead.

Brenda stacked the plates and took them to the small kitchen, urging the others not to help. "Let's get together again," she said when she came back. "Not to plan mischief, but to enjoy each other's company. How about a ski party? I don't ski myself, but everyone who does says Topper is a great place for it. If the snow's good, we could do it when the moon's full."

Kate was surprised, but then it made sense. Brenda must be trying to fill the void her housemate had left.

"Topper's pretty at night," Azul said sadly.

"Fine with me." Rosa wiped her hands on her jeans and stood. To Kate she said, "Before you go, I'd like to show you Camila's room."

It was good-sized, probably four times as big as Aunt Sarah's cramped guest room, with a double bed and a large table in front of a window overlooking the pond. One wall held shelves crammed with books and stacks of paper. Rosa had set out candles, the small kind in tins like those in churches, on the table, the windowsill and the bedside stand. The place looked like a firetrap to Kate. A stick of incense was burning somewhere, sandalwood scent thickening the air.

"It was her place," Rosa said. "A part of her is still here." She moved to the closet, opened it. "The police gave me her things back, but I haven't looked yet." She pointed with her foot to a big white bag with PERSONAL BELONGINGS across it in black on the floor of the closet. "Once I look, it is really the end."

"I'm sorry," Kate said. "I wish I'd known her, but we never met."

"Perhaps you will meet her someday," Rosa said. She shut the closet door. "I think she's going to like you."

The hair on Kate's forearms stood up.

* * *

The slush had in fact frozen, and it was snowing again. She drove slowly, mulling her decision to go to the HCDC meeting with Rosa on Saturday. She liked the tough woman from Alaska, despite her far-out ideas about sensing the spirits of the dead and the living. It couldn't do any harm to go to the meeting, and maybe it would help Rosa deal with her grief.

Azul had stepped outside with Kate as she left, and thanked her for agreeing to the plan. He delivered a brief bear-hug. "I doubt my Camila was murdered," he said quietly, glancing over his shoulder, "but if she was, I want to know. I must know." His host-like goodbye suggested he felt at home in Brenda's house. Perhaps he'd spent a lot of time there in the early stages of courting Camila.

* * *

Kate went back the next day to ski with Rosa. In the daylight the house looked like it needed work: a few shakes were missing from the siding, and a cascade of ice along a downspout showed it had come loose from the gutter. She was glad she had only her truck and camper to worry about. A nicely designed house in an exclusive neighborhood like this called for a good amount of maintenance to both house and, in the snow-free months, landscaping.

Aunt Sarah's skis and boots fit the Alaskan. Kate had brought an extra pair of socks to fill out the boots if they were too big, but Rosa was happy with thin liners and one pair of wool, which was what Kate wore. They put on the boots at Brenda's house and carried the skis to the edge of the circular drive above the pond to clip in.

The inch of snow that had fallen during the night made things tricky. Powder over the earlier snowpack meant fast skiing, but the new snow hid occasional stretches where ice had formed. Kate fell first, and before she'd gotten up Rosa took a spill.

As Kate got her skis back under her, she found herself smiling. The speed, the cold air, the irascible chitter of a red squirrel were all exhilarating. She loved cross-country skiing, far from crowds and lifts and tickets. A sport where falls were almost always of no consequence, the snow a cushion as well as a medium of propulsion. Far more pleasant to fall here than while ice skating, say, or riding a horse.

Rosa didn't come up smiling, but she brushed snow off her pants with no comment and was ready to go in seconds. They skied past the pond, then turned right along the narrow stretch between houses and woods. All the way to the house on College Street, where they rested on their poles for a few minutes. Then back in their own tracks, fast and bright and fun.

They skied the length of Topper, all the way to the top of the hill below Aunt Sarah's house, then back in their own tracks. Past Azul's house, to the shelter where Kate had met Brew. A bench on the side with the pond view was a nice touch: they could sit and have a rest and a snack without taking off their skis.

"Her mice are here," Rosa said. "The black-footed ones."

"Yes." Kate looked around. Was Rosa seeing them or sensing them? The mice were nocturnal, and had plenty of snow cover for their daytime snoozes. Kate didn't see any of the weasel tunnels Brew had pointed out, and she was glad. She didn't have to bring Rosa's attention to the enemies of her sister's mice.

"Today I decided to celebrate Camila by wearing her clothes," Rosa said. "The ones from the bag the police gave me. To give me strength for what is coming."

Honestly, this woman gave Kate the creeps. Her dead sister's skiwear? She'd thought the clothes didn't fit very well—pant legs rolled up, sleeves likewise—but she'd figured Rosa was making do with something she'd been given or bought at a Goodwill store. No, she was paying homage.

Well, whatever helped.

They sat and took in the wintery landscape, pluming their white breaths toward a white sky. Kate loved birch trees in snow: white on white, like some kind of confection. Every now and then an upper branch sprang free, its coating of snow falling away as the day warmed.

"We call that dog hair," Rosa said, nodding at the woods.

"What?"

"See that patch of saplings so close together you couldn't walk through them easily? That's dog hair."

"Neat phrase," Kate said. "The trail around the lake goes through that patch, but off-trail you wouldn't get very far. Like being tied up by trees."

"Dog hair," Rosa said again. "The next time you use that trail you can pretend you're a tick."

The woman's imagination took her strange places. "Would you like a food bar?" Kate asked. "I've got extras."

"No, thanks, I'm fine. Let me see what's in here," Rosa said, pulling her fanny-pack around to her lap and unzipping it.

"Nice of Brenda to offer you a place to stay," Kate said. If you don't burn her house down with those votive candles, she didn't add. "And she packed a lunch for you, too? Quite the hostess."

"No, I took this pack out of the bag the police gave me. Whatever's in here was what she packed for Camila."

"That would be, what, two weeks ago?" Kate asked. "The Friday before last."

"That's right," Rosa said, unwrapping a sandwich. "Oh, peanut butter and honey. A standby of hers."

"The bread must be stale."

Rosa took a bite. "Sort of, but the honey soaked through so it's soggy, too. It's fine."

Another form of homage, eating food meant for Camila. It wasn't how Kate would mourn: she'd be at home, having crying spells. Pacing. Sleeping. Trying to work.

She wondered if she'd be able to work if she'd lost someone close.

And then remembered last summer. The answer was yes. But it had been hard, hard, hard.

"I wonder what was in here," Rosa said. "It feels empty." She was unscrewing the top of a dark green plastic bottle with the Otterlin logo on it in white. The cap off, she sniffed the opening and tilted the bottle toward the light to see inside. "What's this?" Pulled out a crumpled piece of paper and flattened it against her knee. "From the Hunterville newspaper," she said. "Just a piece of the classified ads. Want to buy a guitar?"

"Odd thing to find in a bottle," Kate said. "What's that stuff on the cap?"

Rosa poked at the yellow blob. "I don't know," she said. "It's sticky. Maybe some powder for a drink that didn't finish dissolving." She shrugged and stuffed the paper back inside and screwed the cap on.

"Here, have some water," Kate said, handing the Alaskan one of her two containers. The other was a small thermos with coffee in it. She loved drinking coffee outdoors, especially in cold weather.

The chickadees were active, flitting through the birches and adding to their calls the *ticks* of beaks against bark. They'd be hunting for dormant insects as well as recovering the seeds they'd hidden in the past few months. The spatial-memory parts of their brains enlarged during the fall.

"I never met your sister, but even so I know you're very different from her," Kate said. "You both worked hard, but your work is much more physical than hers. It's a long way from the deck of a fishing boat to a college classroom. How did you come to choose such different lifestyles?"

"Yes, people always said that about us. How could we be sisters?" She looked at the sky and smiled. "Oh, but we were one. Yin and yang. Mind and body. She said we were two sides to the same coin. She was way better in school, but she told me not to mind. So I didn't. I don't. She said we were the same in spirit, and that was what mattered. And we could feel it, our connection. I still feel it.

"And something she always used to say? 'Death is coming.' She'd say it with a grin. It was her way of urging herself on, of reminding herself that our time on this earth isn't endless."

"'Death is coming'? Do you think she knew—"

"That it would be this soon? No. I'm sure she didn't, because if she knew I'd know too."

That was the most talking Rosa had done since she'd arrived. Now she stared into the woods, but she was probably seeing not trees but memories.

"Can you, ah, read me, Rosa? My mind?"

She blinked a couple of times, returning from somewhere Kate was pretty sure she couldn't go.

"No, I can't. Camila and I couldn't read each other, exactly, but we felt each other's closeness." A touch of a smile passed across her face. "We had three brothers, and we could read them like playing cards."

"So you can only read men?"

"Men are a lot clearer than women. I wanted to meet Azul to see if I should suspect him, but he's not hiding anything."

"Glad to hear that. I like him." Kate wasn't going to cross him off her list, though. Not based on a psychic's opinion.

"I wanted to like him, and now I do."

Thinking of their plans for the next day, Kate said, "You know, I think we shouldn't say much at the HCDC meeting. Just kind of go along with whatever happens."

"Don't worry, I won't let them know what a raving left-wing kook I am," Rosa said. "I know how to lie like a bearskin rug. Jobs Rule! Move Over, Mice! People First!"

Kate gave her a rueful smile. Rosa had read her mind after all.

* * *

They pulled into the school parking lot Saturday afternoon, five minutes before the meeting. She hadn't wanted to be conspicuous by being early; she'd wanted a crowd to get lost in, and she'd gotten her wish. About twenty vehicles, half of them pickup trucks, were already there, and a few men were going in the door. She and Rosa hopped out.

Rosa had on a red flannel shirt that had been washed so many times it had faded almost to pink, along with an enthusiastically red Bass Pro Shops baseball cap worn backwards. Kate felt underwhelming in a red bandanna she'd tied around her head. Their jeans and hiking boots were pretty much the same as the ones worn by other people heading for the door, most of them men.

Kate wasn't worried about being discovered. Still, it didn't hurt to be careful. She'd suggested to Rosa that they not call each other by name, and she'd parked away from the building, facing out. Politics sometimes makes people aggressive.

"If I get a good feeling—I mean, not a good feeling but if I get what I need—then I'll just leave, okay?" Rosa said. "And you just follow me? We don't have to stay for the whole thing."

Two men were standing outside, one on each side of the double doors, leaning against the wall, arms folded. One of them came off the wall as Kate and Rosa mounted the steps. "How're you girls doing?" His red jacket looked new, but his jeans were worn and dirty and he'd needed a haircut a month ago.

"We're fine," Kate said. "Looking for the Hunter County Development Council meeting. This the place?"

"You got it, girl."

Inside, signs pointed the way through a foyer and left to a classroom. The seats were full and a few people stood along the back wall. A beefy man stepped up to a podium, his voice sharp and thin through a small speaker on the floor. Kate and Rosa found spaces against the wall.

"Thank you all for coming out on this cold day," the man said. "Days like this tell us what to think about global warming, don't they?" A few people in the audience hissed. "Okay, okay, I got told I gotta stay in line, gotta stay local. No global anything. So okay, let's hear it for our own black-footed field mouse!"

Hoots of laughter and a chorus of boos erupted from the audience. The guy up front was laughing. Kate felt the heat in her face, and she didn't dare look at Rosa.

"Another local phenom is our very own Don McCoy. He's the real thing. Realer than Coca-Cola. Real as real estate." The guy got some laughs; this crowd was of one mind. "Give him a big welcome, y'all." The applause was enthusiastic. Kate slapped a smile on her face and clapped with the crowd.

A draft cooled her face as the door opened and closed for a couple of latecomers. Two men passed Kate and stood farther along the wall, while a woman in a bright green shawl scuttled straight down the aisle. Halfway down, three people stood to let her get to the empty seat she'd spotted. Shannon Quigley.

The woman got around. Which side was she on? She'd called McCoy a weasel, but here she was. Wearing green made her stand out in this crowd. Maybe she was doing the same thing as Kate and Rosa: scouting.

Don McCoy had the air of a politician. In a dark suit and red tie, he looked like he was ready for a TV interview. He took the microphone off its stand and came out from the behind the podium, an old hand at public speaking. He tapped the mike with a finger, and two dull thumps filled the room.

"Opportunity knocks," he said, and smiled until the laughter abated. "The city of Hunterville is about to put itself on the recreational map big-time. A Masters-level golf course next to luxury condominiums is just the beginning. Sports is money, and if we build the right kind of facilities we can draw not only golf tournaments but tennis, swimming, skiing. Think out of the box. Think polo, cricket. Think jobs, folks, jobs!"

Shouts of approval mixed with the burst of applause. Then the group chanted *jobs, jobs, jobs,* clapping in time. Kate clapped, and glanced at Rosa.

Beyond her, one of the men who'd come in late was staring at Kate. "What are you doing here?" he said. "You're not one of us."

The guy who'd come in with him leaned forward to have a look. Not as big, but big enough. And he had an evil look on his face. "Yeah," he said. "You and your uncle Pete, you're about as red as grass."

"What are you doing, spying on us?" the first one asked.

The men's voices weren't quiet, and the chant was ebbing. Other faces turned, and heads in the back row swiveled.

Rosa flung herself toward the door, yanking Kate's sleeve on the way.

"What's going on back there?" McCoy's voice crackled from the speakers. Kate dived into the hall, linoleum hard under her boots. Through the outer doors, down the two concrete steps and onto snowy asphalt. She felt like she was playing tag as a kid, and she laughed.

Rosa was almost at the truck. Kate pulled out her keys and punched the button to unlock the doors. The horn beeped and taillights flashed, responses that were even more comforting than usual.

The Alaskan was half in the passenger door, standing on the running board. She looked back and shouted at Kate.

"Hurry!" Then somebody passed Kate, threw an arm around Rosa's neck and hauled her to the ground.

Kate looked over her shoulder. The front doors of the school were closing behind another guy who jumped from the top step to the pavement and ran toward her.

She wasn't laughing any more.

TWELVE

"Kate, drive! I've got this guy!" Rosa said. Her attacker was face down in the snow, his hands behind him, her knee in his back. "Quick!"

Kate skittered around the back bumper and jumped behind the wheel. Keys in the ignition, twist, engine roar. But she couldn't get her door shut. She yanked on it again.

It wouldn't shut because of the arm reaching past her left elbow, the hand groping for the steering wheel, finding and gripping it. A big hand, tendons standing out with strain, the knuckles hairy.

"Go, go, go!" Rosa shouted as she jumped in. She couldn't shut her door either, but she had both hands free to deal with the invading arm, holding the wrist and bending the fingers backwards, hard.

Kate dropped into gear and the truck lurched forward, but she couldn't steer with that other hand gripping the wheel. The guy was either running alongside or being dragged. She fought to turn toward the exit, and then Rosa reached in front of her and there was a yelp of pain. The wheel came free. Relieved, Kate stepped on the gas, seeing raised fists and angry faces in the side mirrors as she skidded into the road. The truck fishtailed once and then settled down to business. With her left hand she opened her door wide and slammed it.

She let out a huge breath and laughed in relief. That hadn't been a kid's game of tag. "What the hell just happened?"

Rosa's baseball cap was gone. Her hair was a mess. She had snow in her ear and a trickle of blood at the corner of her mouth.

But she was grinning. Then she was laughing. Then the two of them were howling with laughter and tears came into Kate's eyes so she could hardly see the road.

She sobered up enough to take some lefts and rights so the truck wouldn't be easy to find, steaming down the main road like a train on a track. Bad enough that the camper was so recognizable. Not your average Ford or Toyota pickup.

"Damn," she said. "I'm confused. Who the hell were those guys? They sounded like they knew who I was."

"What, you don't know them?"

"Never saw them before in my life." She shook her head. "Neither one."

"That's funny," Rosa said. "They were pretty good fighters, for being from Massachusetts. Good thing I had my knife."

"Your *knife?* You *stabbed* him?"

"Just a little poke," Rosa said. "Don't worry, he won't report it."

"How do you know that? Crap! I'll take you to the police station. You should turn yourself in. It's the best thing to do."

"Kate, Kate, it was a flesh wound. That macho dude is not going to go whining to the police that some girl whipped his ass. Trust me." She laughed. "Besides, you've got blood on your hands, too."

"I do?" She looked at her hands. Rosa was right. Blood on her hands, the wheel sticky. "How did that happen?"

"That guy who had a couple of fingers wrapped around the wheel and was trying to pry your door open? I had to poke him, too. Sorry about the blood on your jeans."

A dark patch above her knee. Now that she'd noticed it, Kate felt the wetness. "A hand is a bad place to get cut—all those tendons and little bones. I suppose you're going to say that guy isn't going to go to the cops, either."

"Absolutely. If he goes anywhere, it'll be the ER. He'll say his power drill slipped." Rosa wiped her mouth. "Damn. I bit my tongue."

Kate decided to believe Rosa. She apparently had some street-fighting experience, a category that had appeared on Kate's resume only in the past ten minutes. Her new friend sure was a gutsy woman.

The truck whispered along snowy back streets. No vehicles were chasing them. Nobody had gotten a close look at her or Rosa, probably, except the two men who'd spoken.

Who were they?

Kate pulled over and got her GPS out of the glove compartment. Tapped Brenda's address into it. "I'm so bad at directions," she said. "I should have had one of these devices implanted at birth. Uh-oh," she said, glancing at Rosa and doing a double-take. "You're about to have one heck of a black eye."

"Won't be the first one."

Back onto the road. "So," Kate said. "We almost got beaten up by a mob of right-wing fanatics. Did we get anything for our trouble?" She looked at Rosa. "I know what my answer is. I got nothing this afternoon but scared silly. Did you get the vibes you were looking for? Mission accomplished?"

"I had a bad feeling the whole time," Rosa said. "First from the guys outside the doors, then in waves from the whole audience. Then the bad feeling went through the roof when those two guys came in. I wish you knew who they were."

"It's kind of scary," Kate said. "I've been here what, two weeks? Nobody should know who I am. Or that Uncle Pete's my uncle."

"Let's go back," Rosa said.

Kate's head snapped around. "Are you nuts?"

"Pulling your chain." She sounded strangely cheerful. The encounter must have felt good to someone as active as she was, used to hauling nets and slinging big fish around.

Kate sighed. "Rats. I might have to talk to Uncle Pete about this. I'll try to leave Aunt Sarah out of it. She might be freaked."

"Like you were?"

"Still am."

"An occasional fight does a person good. Especially us women. We don't get enough opportunities."

* * *

But there never seemed to be a good time to talk to Uncle Pete about her adventure.

For one thing, when she got back to the house after dropping Rosa at Brenda's, a cruiser was parked on the street. Mark sat at the dining room table with Aunt Sarah. Kate didn't join them right away, but slipped quickly into her room and changed her jeans. No sense in letting Aunt Sarah get upset by seeing the blood.

Mark turned when she came in. "Kate," he said. "I've got news."

"Great. About the white stuff on the porch?"

"A very simple test," he said. "I stopped by the lab at the right time and one of the technicians let me watch the stuff turn blue."

"And that means—?"

"It shows the presence of nitrates," he said. "Potassium nitrate, that's what the tech told me. It has a bunch of applications." Mark pulled a notepad out of his pocket and flipped it open. "It's used in fertilizer and gunpowder and—can you believe this?—as a food preservative."

"Ick," Kate said. "I'll be more careful reading labels. Gunpowder doesn't sound appetizing. Or fertilizer."

"Is it used for anything else?" Aunt Sarah asked.

Mark pretended to consult his notebook, but he was already smiling. "Rodenticide? You think that's important?" His smile broadened.

"Ah," Aunt Sarah said. "Hence the mouse massacre."

"Indeed. The dry powder isn't active, so our sneaky visitor brought a bottle of water to splash on it. The solution's less visible than the powder. Nobody might have noticed it if Kate hadn't interrupted him before he finished the job."

"But why would the mice drink that stuff?" Kate asked.

"In winter weather, mice have trouble finding liquid water sources," Mark said. "The solution freezes at a lower temperature than plain water, so it's available. And they must not think it tastes bad, or it would be a lousy rodenticide." He looked satisfied, briefly. "So we know a lot, now. But we don't know the why of it."

"Exactly," Kate said. She sat down on the other side of Aunt Sarah.

Mark looked from Kate to her aunt and back again. "I'm telling you, the family resemblance is downright eerie. You two look like the same person at different ages." He shook his head as if to clear it. "I'm assuming you didn't put out the potassium nitrate yourself to get rid of house mice, Sarah? You or Pete?"

"Heavens, no. I didn't know they were living under or around the house, and even if I'd known I wouldn't have poisoned them. I would have used those live traps. Or just left them alone."

A knock on the door pushed it open: Kate hadn't locked it. A thin guy with wispy hair stepped inside, his smile revealing a missing front tooth.

"Frankie," Aunt Sarah said, "I'm so glad you're here." To Kate and Mark she said, "The carpenter."

Such a gentle soul, her aunt. What she'd just said was her version of What the heck took you so long, Frankie?

"I'll be working on the stairs out back," Frankie said. He was wearing sneakers, and his jeans were frayed through at the knees, white strands of denim hanging. Wasn't he cold? "Didn't want to alarm you by starting up the saw without saying hello first. Other than the saw and the drill and a little hammering I'll be quiet as a mouse."

Kate looked at Aunt Sarah and Mark. "Right," she said. "The mice around here are pretty darn quiet these days."

* * *

After Mark left, Kate rinsed the blood out of her jeans and hung them over the shower curtain, then put on long underwear and ski pants. Let the snow wash her mind clean.

Clipping into her skis, she felt guilty about her encounter with the HCDC. Going to the meeting had been a crazy thing to do, or so it seemed to her now. But how could those men have known she wasn't a McCoy supporter? There had been more men than women in the audience, but enough women that Kate didn't think her gender was the tip-off. And she hadn't been on campus often.

Of course, people who didn't look like HCDC members could probably prowl all over campus without being noticed. Drop the the red clothing and the JOBS ARE US buttons and they could pass for professors, who all seemed to wear jeans and boots, too.

Her only contact with the college, aside from a few visits to the student union, the bookstore, and the aviary, was Uncle Pete's class. But didn't his students support keeping the Reserve as it was? A few of them hadn't been fans of Prof. Chavez, but surely they didn't belong to the HCDC.

Kareem and Phoebe had sought her out. They were definitely tree-huggers and field mouse fans. Unless they were extraordinary actors.

No, she trusted them both. Phoebe might be high-strung, ready to jump to conclusions, but her heart was definitely on the side of the black-footed field mice.

What about the two older students? Justin was ex-military, so it was possible he was a lot more conservative than the others. With his stammering and clumsiness, Tim didn't act as old as Justin, and he was a handyman. Weren't tradesmen traditionally left-leaning union supporters?

She was swimming in stereotypes. Even if tradesmen as a group were lefties, that didn't say a thing about Tim.

What exactly was she suspicious of these kids for, anyway? Taking a picture of her and showing it to some HCDC members so they could identify her? None of the students could have known she was going to the meeting.

Still, Justin was on her mind, probably because he was so quiet. She didn't know where he was coming from.

So far she'd accounted for four of them. What about the others? She imagined herself at the table in the dining room, Uncle Pete at its head, in order to recall the rest of the group.

The religious student Grace. She seemed too timid to cause trouble, but her family would very likely be conservative. Chaya seemed more confident and mature than the others, and could well have strong opinions. Maddie, the scholarship student from Chicago who was uncomfortable at Otterlin, wouldn't be likely to side with wealthy developers.

Zoe, love-sick over the silent, enigmatic Justin? No, Zoe was so outspoken she wouldn't sneak a picture of Kate to the HCDC. If she was on their side, she'd say as much to Kate and anyone else.

But wait, hadn't she said she didn't think much of Prof. Chavez? Called her rude?

This was hopeless. All she had was a cloud of vague suspicion about all the students except Kareem and Phoebe.

She tried another angle. Who would have a motive to poison mice?

Maybe the midnight visitor didn't know the difference between white-footed and black-footed, and was trying to wipe out the endangered mice. The Reserve might be easier to sell if it weren't a haven for a species on the brink of extinction.

It sure would help to have somebody to talk things over with. Sean? She was still reluctant to call him. Besides, it would be useful to talk to someone right in Hunterville, someone who knew the Otterlin scene. She scrubbed her mind clean and tried to think of anyone she'd met in her brief time in Hunterville whom she trusted for sure. Besides Aunt Sarah. Kate would trust her with her life, but she didn't want to upset her. Uncle Pete? Too busy. And volatile. He was at his calmest in class.

Brew? Maybe Brew.

Ah, Myra. Head of the aviary, she couldn't be anything but a tree-hugger, bird-lover, mouse advocate. Kate had liked her. Pick Flowers not Fights, her T-shirt had read. It might be safer to hang out with her than with Rosa.

It was late, getting toward dusk. She didn't have time to do the loop around the pond. She stood above it for a couple of minutes, enjoying the cold, quiet place.

If Prof. Chavez had been murdered, of course, Kate couldn't trust anyone completely. But talking to sensible Myra would help balance Rosa's wild ideas.

On her way back to the house, a thought surfaced in her mind she didn't like one bit. Only three other people had known she was going to the HCDC meeting: Azul, Brenda, and Rosa. It didn't make sense for any of them to sabotage something they'd asked her to do in the first place. Unless it was a trap. If Azul had something to hide, could he have arranged for the attack?

Kate stopped. Could he have transported a live bee to the Reserve the night his fiancée died? Was that jewel-like insect an instrument of murder?

She started up, slowly. Focused on her glide, her breathing, the swish of the skis. Thank goodness her muscles were benefitting from this outing. She'd wanted to be outdoors and moving, believing it would help her think, but her brain was in a worse muddle of suspicions than when she'd started.

THIRTEEN

"Kate, how nice," Myra said on the phone that Monday. "I've been meaning to call you myself. Want to meet at the student union? I'm free between classes, from ten to eleven."

Kate had found her office phone number on the Otterlin website. She'd browsed around a bit, deciding Uncle Pete's picture was out of date—he'd had more hair when it was taken—and finding on Dave Simmons' site a fascinating article comparing human inner ears to lobster statocysts, the organs that give the animal a sense of balance. On the aviary site she'd been impressed at its international standing. Ornithologists, botanists and entomologists from Germany, England, Holland and Brazil were currently running experiments, which they paid the college to manage between their visits. Kate hoped none of the frozen birds was an experimental subject. Zoe was right: whoever had turned off the thermostat might be trying to hurt Otterlin's bottom line as well as its reputation.

The food court at the union was crowded with students who seemed to be both sleepy and in a hurry; at their age Kate had read into the wee hours and would have been in the same state. But that morning she'd awakened early and worked on some drawings before walking to campus. The coffee she'd just bought was recreational, not the required morning fix.

Tim had been ahead of her as she passed the library. He carried a toolbox in one hand and a cup of coffee in the other, despite the bright orange coil of extension cord slung over that shoulder. Kate wondered how much he liked being a college handyman. Enrolling in Uncle Pete's night class suggested Tim wanted to do something else for a living.

Cardboard cup warming her hand, she scanned the food court for Myra but was distracted by a familiar head of big red hair. Zoe stood next to a table where Justin and Tim were eating. Tim's face was turned up toward hers, and he pushed out a chair in invitation.

Way to go, Tim, Kate thought. Ironic that he was doing Zoe an unintentional favor, giving her an opportunity to sit with Justin. Did he know Zoe was wild about his friend? Kate guessed the answer was yes. Zoe wasn't subtle.

Justin ate a sandwich with military speed. Zoe was focused on him, but he didn't look up. Good luck, kiddo, Kate thought, resuming her search for Myra. Spotting her, she moved through the crowded space toward her table. Just before she got there, she took another look at the three students. Zoe must be thrilled to be having lunch with Justin.

But she wasn't there. Justin was still paying full attention to his lunch, and there were three trays on the table. But Tim had half-risen, looking toward the big exit doors. Doors Zoe was running toward, pushing through.

They closed behind her, and Tim fell back into his chair.

A vicious triangle, Kate thought. Nearly everyone had been involved in such a painful constellation when they were young. An unlucky few got lost there, in the emotional Bermuda Triangle of adolescence. Kate hoped

Zoe would recover her internal compass of wants and needs, and not spin out of control around Justin.

Myra was sitting alone. In jeans and a turtleneck, she blended in with the students. As Kate got closer she saw the tweedy jacket hanging on the chair and the half-moon glasses perched on the professor's nose: no, not an undergrad. She was reading the top term paper from a stack.

She looked up. "Hey," she said, a student-like greeting. During her own college years, Kate remembered, the greeting was "What's up," pronounced *Wassup?* and accompanied by a forward thrust of the chin.

"Myra," Kate said, slipping into the chair opposite her. "Thanks for coming to the house after the funeral. Aunt Sarah was really glad to see you."

"I'm embarrassed I didn't go to see her sooner. I'm glad you're here for her."

"She's getting stronger, but it's been a slow recovery. Losing Prof. Chavez was a blow."

"It was for all of us. I wasn't close to Camila, but I respected her a great deal and her death stunned me. All of us. So sudden, and way too soon. I keep half-expecting to see her march into the aviary, shouting about the latest environmental outrage."

"I hear she was a firecracker," Kate said. "A dragon."

"She would have been totally bat-shit about the sabotage at the college, some sadistic creep turning off the heat. I've never lost a bird except to natural causes before." Myra rubbed her face with her hands. "It's a crazy time."

"Were any of your experiments disrupted?" Kate asked. "I read about them on your website."

"Holland isn't going to be happy, but the biggest project, for a German botanist, is still on track, thank heaven." She'd pushed the term papers aside and put her elbow on them, as if to keep them from coming back.

High above Myra's head, a flutter caught Kate's eye. "There's a bird in the union?" she asked.

Myra sighed. "Yes. Not good for the sparrow, or for us. One flies in occasionally through the main doors. B and G—Buildings and Grounds—has to come at night and, ah, relocate it."

"A second aviary," Kate said. The brown-and-white creature fluttered against a window, confused by the patch of air that was mysteriously solid.

"An accidental aviary," Myra said.

The sparrow swooped at a farther window and bounced off. The sound was lost in the clamor of human voices and clatter of dishes, but the collision had looked substantial. A few window-strikes like that and B and G wouldn't have to hunt for a sleeping bird.

"So tell me, Kate. What's up?"

"I know you're busy, but you seem smart and sympatico, and you have your feet on the ground. I really need someone I trust to talk to."

Myra's eyebrows went up. "I'm glad I'm that person, Kate. I think." She smiled. "But this sounds serious. Let's hit my office." She put her glasses in her pocket, grabbed the stack of papers and stood, all in one motion. Kate scrambled after her, threading through tables and down the stairs. Outside, she almost bumped into Kareem, who flashed her a smile as he skidded past her on the snowy sidewalk. Myra nodded at several other students and a passing colleague as she led the way, waved at Brew through the bookstore window, and turned into the next building.

She breezed by the elevators and took the stairs fast enough that Kate couldn't say a word. She caught her breath as Myra unlocked the door to her office, gave her a conspiratorial smile and said, "I have to warn you, this office is bugged."

It was true. All manner of insects infested the small room: pinned and framed specimens, poster-sized illustrations, plastic models, and a glass box that held what looked like chrysalises.

Ordinarily, Kate would have explored the collection and asked questions, but her time with the busy professor was limited. She quickly described her visit with Rosa to the HCDC meeting, their narrow escape, and the intruder who'd poisoned mice at her uncle's house.

"So many strange things have been happening, there must be a pattern. I was hoping to bat some ideas around with you."

"Hmm." Myra leaned back in her chair and gazed at the ceiling, where a hairy tarantula clung. Kate hoped it wasn't a live one. "Maybe the first thing to consider is what the target is," the professor said. "Because of Bascomb and then the aviary, I'd assumed the college. But mice getting poisoned off-campus suggests otherwise. And so does violence toward you and Rosa, who aren't connected to the college." She frowned at the spider, then at Kate. "The greatest loss, of course, was Camila. Could some anti-environmentalist have wanted to shut her down?" She leaned forward. "Do you think Camila was murdered?"

Kate sighed. "The police seem pretty sure no foul play was involved, but Rosa is convinced they're wrong. And it does seem strange that someone who grew up in Alaska would be overcome by a Massachusetts snowstorm."

"I thought that, too. But the newspaper said she had an allergic reaction to something." Myra's gray eyes were trained on Kate, undistracted by the clutter on her desk. The woman knew how to focus.

"Mark, my Aunt Sarah's friend, do you know him? The detective? He said she hadn't eaten anything that night."

Myra nodded. "When I saw that in the newspaper I talked to an M.D. friend of mine, a researcher. There are non-food triggers for anaphylaxis. One of them is exercise. It's rare, but it happens. And some drugs, just over-the-counter medications, can trigger it in some people."

"Exercise?" Kate said slowly. "That's strange. But I suppose that could be it. It fits the circumstances."

Myra watched her take it in, then said, "I know. I don't quite believe it either. Camila was fit and tough. Yes, stranger things have happened. But it's not a very satisfying explanation, is it?"

"I'm sure Rosa isn't going to accept an exercise-induced allergic reaction as the cause of death," Kate said. "She's sure it was murder." She hesitated. "She says she has a psychic connection with her sister. Feels her presence."

"Oh, dear." Myra's kind face was sympathetic.

"She also thinks she can read people's minds. That's why we went to the meeting—she's on a crusade to find her sister's killer, using her, um, powers." Kate felt her face get hot. She was talking to a very successful scientist.

"A sister, any family member, would have the most trouble accepting the situation, naturally." Myra's voice was guarded. "But that sounds—well, frankly, delusional."

"I know. I don't believe in parapsychology—most of the time. But when I'm with Rosa she sometimes half-convinces me she can see things I can't." She was blushing as badly as Tim. "It started with me wanting to help Rosa process what's happened."

"And then, spending time with her, you got drawn in?"

"Exactly." Kate wiped her face with her sleeve. "It's great to talk to you, Myra."

"Anytime." The entomologist shrugged. "Who knows? Sometimes a new angle shakes ideas loose. I can't disprove mind-reading."

The two of them looked at each other for a moment. Kate's instincts said she could trust this woman. But there was a question she had to ask.

"The most common cause of anaphylaxis is bee stings," she said. "And there are thousands of bees in your hives. Could Camila have been stung at the aviary and had a delayed reaction because of the cold weather?"

"No, the reaction is immediate. Once the neurotoxin is in the blood, it doesn't matter how cold it is outside."

"And wild bees wouldn't be flying around Massachusetts in the winter?"

"That would be a safe assumption." Myra smiled.

She seemed relaxed, but Kate knew from Uncle Pete that academia was highly competitive. Had Prof. Chavez and the entomologist been rivals? Perhaps the world-wide attention the former had gained for the plight of the black-footed field mouse had left other Otterlin biologists feeling neglected.

"Sometimes talking things over with someone else uncovers connections and new ideas," Myra continued. "I can't see a pattern in all these events, Kate. Yet. But keep digging. And keep me posted on any thoughts you have— you or your psychic friend. If Camila was murdered, I want to see justice done."

"Okay." Kate's suspicions were ebbing. "The police haven't closed the investigation, and sometimes I pick things up from Mark when he visits Aunt Sarah."

"If you can untangle this mess, the whole college would thank you." She leaned forward. "Now I'd like to ask you something, Kate. I've seen your drawings at the bookstore, and I think they're excellent. I'd like you to do some more. Would you consider it? I'd pay you well."

"I've never worked to an assignment. What sort of subject did you have in mind?"

"Insects, duh," Myra laughed. "I'm putting together an entomology textbook and I need illustrations. Photos just don't cut it."

"That's right, you liked my bee," Kate said. "The one I was drawing in the aviary the first time I met you."

"I liked your bee so much I bought it from Brew at the bookstore. I'm going to have it framed. It'll join the menagerie." Myra waved a hand at the office and beamed. "So. What do you say to my proposal?"

"Do you have specimens of the insects you want me to draw? I could do a few, we could see how things went," Kate said. "Would the specimens be live?"

"Some live, some dead and mounted. A few rare ones from photos only."

"Yikes," Kate said. "How many drawings are you thinking of?"

"Dozens."

"Yikes," Kate said again.

"Why don't we meet at the aviary? I've got some live specimens there, and drawing from life might be the most fun for you." Myra tucked her glasses in a pocket. "I want you to like the work. Are you free this afternoon?"

* * *

Kate went home and chopped celery and onions to put in the tuna salad. The snarl of a circular saw meeting wood came from the back yard. Aunt Sarah was downstairs, watering plants. She'd gotten much better at using her left hand.

"I'll be ambidextrous by the time I get this wretched cast off," she said.

"That's not a bad outcome," Kate said.

"It wasn't worth it, believe me."

While they had sandwiches and tea, the carpenter knocked and put his head inside the door. He looked worried.

"What's the matter, Frankie?" Aunt Sarah said. "You want some water? Want to use the bathroom?"

"No, but thanks," he said. "Is Pete around? I'd like to show him something."

"He's in Boston today, but he'll be back tomorrow. Is it something you can tell me about?"

"I can have a look at it," Kate said.

"Would you?" her aunt said. "Thank you, dear."

The snow in the back yard was packed down to icy grayness. Frankie had set up a portable table for the saw, and sawdust from cutting two-by-fours made the footing secure instead of treacherous. He'd torn apart the old steps and piled the pieces at the edge of the yard, so the back door opened into space, a disconcerting sight. Kate decided to put a sign on the inside; her aunt and uncle had lived in this house for more than ten years, and one of them might forget, open the door, step out—

She turned away from the imaginary scene. The woods in the Reserve below were beautiful, the dark branches glistening with ice. A chickadee called.

Frankie went to the pile of old lumber. "So I was taking the old stairs apart with a crowbar, and first thing I notice was it was easier than it should have been. But I didn't look too close until after I was done."

He picked up a board that had been a step. A nail fell out, pinging onto the scrap pile. "Now don't you worry. I'm going to build it right, I'm going to use screws, and countersink 'em. But the guy before me, he used nails, and they didn't hold."

"Bad construction?" Kate asked.

"It's more than that," Frankie said. "See how the wood is dark around the nail hole? Dark and soft? It's rotten. That's why the stairs gave way."

"So they were old."

"But that's the thing. The wood's in great shape everywhere else. And look at these six nail holes. See the gouges right next to them? Like somebody dug a hole in the wood next to each nail."

Fear ran a cold hand along Kate's spine. "Are you saying somebody deliberately damaged the stairs?"

"I'm just saying there's no earthly reason for these dings to be here next to the nail holes. Oh, and I found this." He held out a scrap of paper. "It was caught under one of the boards on the ground."

Crumpled and torn. Kate flattened it against her thigh and read the untidy scribble. "'Know' and 'comment.' Do you know what this means?"

"No idea." Frankie looked at her, blue eyes narrowing. "But I know what these boards mean. If somebody wanted to make the stairs fail, wanted to rot out the wood around the fasteners, they might take a knife and make a kind of well like this, and then put something in there to chew up the wood."

"Do me a favor, Frankie, and don't dispose of this scrap pile. I want Uncle Pete to have a look at it. And the cops."

"Sure," he said, and shrugged. "People are crazy."

The woods Kate had admired a minute ago glittered with menace.

* * *

"So somebody booby-trapped the steps?" Marjorie asked. "You're turning me into a detective instead of a therapist. Who are your Aunt Sarah's enemies?"

"I can't imagine she has any," Kate said. "Everybody thinks she's an angel."

"Start with the spouse. Isn't that what a real detective would say?"

Kate laughed. "You don't know Uncle Pete. He'd be a total flop as a handyman. When he tries to fix things, Aunt Sarah says he makes them worse. This sabotage took some dexterity."

She'd decided not to talk about her foray to the HCDC meeting because she didn't want Marjorie to worry. But she thought her friend would be interested in a woman who claimed, essentially, to read minds. So she skipped the meeting and just described Rosa and her psychic abilities.

"She's a flake."

Kate was startled. She'd always taken Marjorie's nonjudgmental attitude as the bedrock of her personality. Openness and acceptance of other people's mental states, their ideas and their values—wasn't that the gold standard in the therapist's role that Marjorie aspired to?

Not that Kate didn't agree with her. Rosa had a persuasive effect in person, but on reflection Kate wasn't convinced of her powers.

"Do you have even a hint of evidence," Marjorie said, "that she can read men's minds or intentions the way she describes? All you have is her say-so, right?"

"Right." Kate thought back to the pizza evening. "Well, she knew which chair was her sister's, at Brenda's house. She'd never been there before."

"Look, Brenda and this professor lived together. Brenda sits in her usual place, and all Rosa has to do is look for the natural other place—the most comfortable chair left, or the most worn place on the sofa."

"I guess she could have done that," Kate said. "But Brenda thinks she's for real."

"Brenda has just lost a close friend, and according to your aunt she's insecure and depressed. So she's in a state to be easily taken in."

Marjorie was probably right, but Kate found herself resisting. "Rosa says this ability of hers has been around since childhood. Something she and her sister shared." Maybe she was being what Uncle Pete would call a devil's advocate.

"Did her sister ever mention it to her boyfriend or to Brenda? You might check that out."

"Why would Rosa make this up?"

"For all sorts of reasons. To impress you. To influence you. To give her power over a difficult situation."

"You think she's a fraud." Sometimes Kate accused herself of being too easily influenced, and now she felt herself swaying between Rosa's certainties and Marjorie's.

"I don't know that. She may sincerely believe she can feel her sister's spirit and evaluate the minds of strangers. But I suggest you take this power of hers with an entire shaker of salt."

"Or maybe with a silo instead of a shaker?"

Marjorie's tone lightened. "Ha! I've always thought silos looked like salt and pepper for giants. You too? "

* * *

The aviary was bright and steamy, leaves dazzling green where they were backlit by the sun. Amazing to be in this tropical bubble, knowing the building was surrounded by miles of ice and snow.

"Both Dave Simmons and I got inspired by Pete," Myra said, "when he started his textbook project. For a while Dave and I were going to be competitors." She laughed. "Then we saw how much work Pete had to do, so we joined forces."

"I've met Dave," Kate said. "Uncle Pete introduced us at the reception. He does arthropods, right?"

"Right." Myra had on the muddy boots she'd worn when Kate first met her. The brick and gravel paths they strolled together were dry enough, but the professor often had to bushwhack to monitor the insect populations throughout the aviary. "Lots of people think tropical soil is thin, but it's among the deepest in the world. Natch. It's been protected by trees for millions of years, with warm temperatures and tons of rain to foster rock breakdown." Despite the grungy boots, she sometimes sounded like she was in front of a classroom.

"Oh, so soil gets built from the bottom up as well as top down?"

"Exactly," Myra said. "Rainforest soil is only thin in the sense of nutrients. So many plants grabbing what they need, the life-cycles going so fast—" She stopped next to a bush and smiled at it. She touched one of the branches and cocked her head at Kate. "See it?"

An ordinary branch, its bark an anthology of shades of brown. Then Kate saw the twig that wasn't a twig. "Amazing camouflage," she said. "A stick insect, right? I've read about them, seen pictures, but I've never met one before. In person, so to speak."

"A lot of interesting creatures will come your way if you join the textbook project with Dave and me," Myra said. "See the imitation bud scars on this guy's side?"

"Realer than real," Kate said, which made her think of the HCDC guy who'd introduced McCoy as realer than real estate. "You know what we were talking about in your office? There's another item to add." She told the entomologist what Frankie had said about the stairs.

"That's disturbing," Myra said. "Have you told the police?"

"Uh, no." Damn. Why hadn't she thought of that? Was stress building up in her psyche, like rock turning into soil in a rainforest?

"I can't imagine anyone wanting to hurt Sarah, but your uncle has a few enemies. He can be kind of outspoken sometimes." She laughed at the look on Kate's face.

"Kind of? Sometimes?"

"All right, he can be a royal pain. Is that more accurate?"

"That's my Uncle Pete."

"And you haven't even seen him at faculty meetings."

The curve in the path looked familiar, and in a few more steps they were at the line of hives. A figure wearing gloves and a face net was lifting the top off one of the wooden boxes.

"Let's go a different way," Myra said. "Azul's checking on his AHB babies."

Kate took a second look. Yes, the thick beard was flattened under netting. "AHB?"

"Africanized honey bees. They're more aggressive than EHBs, the European bees, but a lot more productive. They're active earlier in the day and work later, and they'll even fly in light rain. Azul's trying to come up with a calmer hybrid. Calmer but just as hard-working as the AHBs."

"Africanized bees are called killer bees, aren't they? And they're more venomous?"

"Don't use 'killer bees' in front of Azul," Myra said, "or he'll kill you."

Her laugh went unanswered. In the last few months Kate had lost her sense of humor about murder.

Myra caught her expression and moved on. "Their venom's not any more potent, but they're more sensitive to threats and they chase their victims much farther, in larger numbers. They were developed in Brazil, and Azul's patriotic intent is to create a new Brazilianized bee that produces lots of honey but has a calmer temperament. He's making good progress, and it'll be a commercial blockbuster." Myra strode away from the hives. "But hey, let me find you another insect, someone more congenial."

Did she say *someone?* Apparently Myra was getting insects and people mixed up.

A huge blue butterfly landed on her sleeve. "Look, I've got a volunteer."

* * *

Kate hurried on the walk home. Pete was away, Aunt Sarah was alone. What if she was the intended victim? Anyone who knew the household routine knew she filled the bird feeder most mornings. Kate had a bad feeling. Kicking herself for not thinking faster after Frankie told her his suspicions, she tried to fling herself through the front door and instead bumped her nose hard. It was locked.

Good for Aunt Sarah. Kate pulled out her key, tears from the impact with the door still brightening her vision. The voice from behind her made her jump.

"Sarah left a message for me. Is she okay?" It was Mark.

Kate's hands were shaking, but she finally got the door open and they both piled in. Aunt Sarah was calmly doing a crossword puzzle in the dining room. "Hello, dears. What's a three-letter word for an alt-rock genre? I haven't got a clue." She looked from one to the other. "What's the matter?"

"Nothing," said Kate, who didn't like being worried about and therefore tried not to worry about others. Or at least not let them see that she did.

"We were worried about you," Mark said. "You called me?"

"Goodness, what could happen to me sitting in my little house?" Aunt Sarah said. She glanced at the cast. "I mean, that hasn't already happened? I called you because of what Frankie told me before he left."

Kate wanted to hug her aunt. Instead she said, "Why don't I take Mark out back and show him?"

The carpenter had sprinkled sawdust along the icy trail along the side of the house. Nice of him. Kate didn't know how he could get around in the winter wearing sneakers, unless he carried a pouch of sawdust in his pocket.

She gave Mark two of the damaged boards and poked through the scrap pile for another, then showed him the dings beside the nail holes, the rotted wood.

He looked grim. "This probably explains what your midnight sneak was doing. Let's have a look."

He led the way to the front steps. Two of the nails on the top one had crescents of wood carved away next to the heads.

"That was a sharp knife he had," Mark said. Then he snapped his fingers and patted his pockets. He flipped his notebook open and read aloud. "This is what the lab tech said potassium nitrate is used in: fertilizer, fireworks, food preservative, gunpowder. Rocket fuel, rodenticide, toothpaste. And tree stump remover. Our guy wasn't trying to poison mice—that was an accident. He was trying to rot wood."

"Not for the first time, either," Kate said. "Aunt Sarah didn't fall down the stairs out back. The stairs were made to fall out from under her."

"I'm going to talk to the lab and get an idea of the time frame. How long would it take this stuff to weaken the wood enough for the nails to loosen?" He turned to her. "I'll also put this house on a watch list for more frequent patrols."

"I guess that's a good thing," Kate said. "But the house is set back pretty far from the street. Can someone in a cruiser see much from out there? Especially with my camper parked in the driveway?"

Mark looked toward the street. "These steps have a line of sight to the end of the driveway, so if this perp tries the same thing again he could be spotted. But if he wants to cause harm, he might come up with something else next time." He tapped the notebook, looking up at the house. "Tell you what, I'll recommend the patrolman take a stroll up to the house, flash a light around, see if anything looks fishy."

"Great," Kate said. "I wonder if the stair saboteur is the same guy who turned off the heat at the college. That's happened twice now, and it caused a lot of damage both times."

He gave her an appreciative look. "Right, the damage here and on campus could be connected. Pete's a big wheel at the college, and his house is among the closest faculty-owned houses. If you want to hurt Otterlin, he could be seen as part of the target."

"I wonder if it's one of the students in the class that meets here?"

"What? A class meets here at the house?"

"Yes, because of the flood in Bascomb Hall," Kate said. "I don't know how long it's supposed to take to get the plumbing replaced and the walls repaired, but the last couple of weeks Uncle Pete's had eight students here, Tuesday and Thursday nights."

"That's good to know, Kate. If our guy's a student, he might be emboldened by familiarity with the house. I'll get a class list from Pete, and talk to him. I should coordinate with the college, too. But I'd rather talk to Pete first."

Kate followed him to his car. "Do you still think Prof. Chavez died accidentally?" she asked. "The property crimes here were dangerous. My aunt could have hit her head on the concrete at the bottom of the steps and died herself. Another carpenter might have assumed the boards had rotted by themselves, and it'd be called an accident."

Mark took a long look at the house, nodding. "Sarah's safety is at the top of my agenda. And don't worry, I haven't forgotten about Chavez." He met her eyes.

"The jury's still out?"

"Yes." He got into the car, put the window down. "The ME says she wasn't stung by a bee, but I'm not closing the file until I've gotten to the bottom of all the vandalism, just in case there's some connection." He started the engine. "I'll talk to Pete when he gets back, recommend some motion-detector lights, especially out back. Somebody's up to no good around here."

FOURTEEN

She was uneasy for the next few days. Uncle Pete got back, and they all were being careful about keeping the door locked. Kate met with Myra a couple of afternoons and filled her notebooks with butterflies, stick insects, a wide-winged creature that looked like a dragonfly but that Myra called a skimmer. "You don't have to know the names," she said.

Kate's favorite at first was a weevil, with big eyes and such a long nose that it made her think of an anteater—not that she'd ever seen one of those.

But then she found more favorites: the flag-footed bug, with a geometric pattern on its back and such big flags at the end of two of its legs that it looked like a boat with pontoons. The furry white plant-hopper, the tiger beetle, the glass-winged butterfly: she had plenty of invertebrate models. The glass-winged butterfly would be the greatest challenge to draw.

Myra was as busy as ever. Her stack of student papers didn't get smaller, but she enjoyed reading them in the aviary. She'd find Kate an insect and then sit on one of the benches, perusing the papers and writing vigorously in the margins until it was time to find the next subject.

She didn't mind waiting. "I get more work done out here," she said, turning off her cell phone. "I'm away from the phone and that blasted email."

The insects were magical. Kate took plenty of reference photos so she could refine her sketches into finished drawings. When she shut her sketchbook she felt as if she were closing the lid on a jewelry box.

Aunt Sarah was stronger, getting herself down the stairs some mornings before Kate was up and turning on the coffeemaker. She read the paper and did crosswords, awkwardly, and used her phone for email, typing on the tiny screen with her left index finger. Kate sometimes skied with Rosa after breakfast and worked on drawings at the aviary in the afternoon, the two activities giving a pleasant balance to her days. The Alaskan was perhaps uncharacteristically quiet, and Kate thought it had to be good for her to be outside and active.

It was certainly good for Kate.

She still felt disturbed about the damage to the college and Uncle Pete's house, but as the days went by she started to relax. Several nights when she worked late in her camper, she saw police cars pass slowly, and twice a uniform came up the driveway past the camper, his flashlight glancing across the porch. The new back stairs were finished: they looked overbuilt, and Frankie had used screws as promised. When Kate filled the bird feeder, she checked the stairs for holes near the heads of the screws.

Whatever had happened to Prof. Chavez, she was sure Mark would get to the bottom of it.

The morning after her uncle got back from his latest trip, Kate joined him for coffee and volunteered to get lights installed on the back porch as Mark had suggested. "Just give me your electrician's phone number," she said. "I'll make the appointment and plan to be here."

Her uncle looked up from *The Scientist*. "Thanks, Katie."

She had his attention. "Mark and I were talking about your students as suspects for damage to the back stairs."

"My students? Oh, you mean the ones who come here. Sarah calls them my home-schoolers."

"Feelings are running pretty high at the college. Prof. Chavez was popular, and rumor is that she was murdered. In your back yard. Could that make you a target?"

"Doesn't sound very rational." His hand was still on the journal. "Although nobody said nineteen-year-olds are always rational."

"Or people in general. At any age," Kate said, and gave him her best cynical smile.

"Yes. So who do you think is porch-surfing at midnight, sowing mayhem and murdering mice?"

"And breaking Aunt Sarah's arm, indirectly."

His face sobered. "Yes." He pushed the journal away.

"I think we can eliminate Kareem and Phoebe. They asked me for advice about ways to oppose the golf-condo development on the Reserve. Kareem is a mature, no-nonsense guy. Phoebe's more excitable, a lot younger emotionally than he is. But she's no sneak or vandal. So that's two down," she said. "If you agree."

He nodded. "I think we can also eliminate Grace and Maddie," he said. "Grace is afraid of the sound of her own voice, and while Maddie is gutsier she wouldn't do anything to endanger her scholarship."

Kate remembered Grace, surprised at street lights. Aside from her apparent timidity, she had such a slight build Kate didn't think she was the person who'd scrambled away in the night. "Maddie's the one who doesn't think she belongs at Otterlin. She might resent being the poorest student on campus."

Uncle Pete nodded. "You might be right. But when it comes to sneaking around at night, pardon my sexism, but I'd think first of the male students. If you're right about Kareem, that leaves only Justin and Tim." He gave her a thoughtful look. "Justin has military training."

"He does. And Tim is a klutz." She described his coming to ask her advice after class, ripping his course-pack and stumbling over his feet and his words.

"I'd suspect Justin, if I had to choose someone from that class," her uncle said.

"Just to touch all the bases, who else? Zoe, right? That's seven. Who am I forgetting?"

"Chaya," he said. "I can't see her taking divots out of boards with a knife. She might mess up her manicure."

"Zoe was the only one of them that first night who said she wasn't a fan of Dr. Chavez's. Everybody else thought she was great."

Uncle Pete frowned. "I don't see a motive there."

"I don't see a motive for any student," Kate said. "Why attack a school you're enrolled in? It's like hurting the horse you're riding out of town."

"Unless it's something personal." He stared at the table for a moment. "Someone who's angry about a grade, or who just doesn't like me. Not necessarily a current student."

"The damage to the college buildings? The dead birds? That's aimed at the whole department. The whole faculty, not just you."

"We can't assume it's the same person at the house and at Otterlin," he said. "I flunked a couple of dolts last spring. I'll talk to Arnie Thorne about those two, and Justin. I don't have a shred of proof about any of them, but the dean should know what's going on over here."

"It's worrisome, with Aunt Sarah half-incapacitated," Kate said.

"Yes." He looked down at his mug. "Maybe the back stairs were supposed to collapse under me instead of her."

Kate had thought of that. "In that case we'd know the vandal didn't do surveillance, right? How often did you go out the back and fill the bird feeder?"

"Nine times out of ten it was Sarah. Big fan of birds. And cats. Separately, of course." He looked out at the feeder, busy with chickadees and juncos. "I'm actually glad, now, that the class meets here. After all that's happened I don't like leaving her at night." His laugh was pained. "Or during the day, either."

"It's okay, Uncle Pete. I'm here a lot of the time, and I don't have a teaching schedule on the Otterlin website for anybody to look up," Kate said. "Plus we're locking the door now. Right?"

He smiled. "You've got me trained, Katie." He ran a palm across his comb-over and stood. "And you're doing the best you can with Sarah. I just wish she'd move back into our bedroom."

* * *

A Thursday, Kate's third week at her aunt's. Brenda phoned Aunt Sarah. She was on her way to Otterlin, and would it be all right for her to drop Rosa off so she and Kate could ski this side of the Reserve?

Rosa was restless. She zipped along the trail, now well established, down the first hill and up the second and past Azul's house to the pond. When Kate caught up to her, she was poking holes in the snow with a pole. "We aren't doing anything."

Kate had hoped Rosa had been slowly accepting the fact that her sister's death was an accident. An odd accident. Kate had never heard of exercise inducing an allergic reaction, but after Myra described it she got online and read about it. Rare, but it happens. The victim's level of fitness doesn't seem to be a factor.

The attacks aren't necessarily fatal, but in this case once Prof. Chavez was down, she would have succumbed to the cold and the lack of oxygen in the well around the tree trunk where she'd fallen. She'd have suffocated, like people swept away by avalanches.

Too many demands on her body, all at once.

"What is there to do?" Kate was reluctant to ask, because she figured Rosa had a plan. Considering how the last one had gone, she wasn't sure she wanted to hear the successor. But it was important to know what Rosa was thinking.

"I want to meet the developer guy who was speaking at the meeting we got chased away from."

"Don McCoy?"

"Yeah, Mr. Realer than Real Estate," Rosa said. "I got bad vibes at the meeting, but there was a crowd of people and I was nowhere near him. He's their leader. I want to know if he's behind what happened to my sister."

"It might not be so easy to get close to him at a public event. He'll be mobbed with fans."

"I have to get close. Eye contact's the best."

Oh, man, here we go again, Kate thought. "You know, I got a bad feeling from the meeting, too. Based entirely on the fact that a couple of guys tried to beat us up."

Rosa laughed. Apparently a couple of thugs didn't scare her.

"What about the two men who knew who I was? We still haven't figured out how they recognized me."

"You don't need to go," Rosa said. "I'll go alone to his next rally, early, and get close, trust me. I'll watch the newspaper for his schedule."

"Online would be—" The words were out of her mouth before she could catch herself. Reflexive helpfulness was not always an asset.

"Right. I never think of that. No WiFi on fishing boats."

"But what if the same thing happens to you? They somehow know who you are, that you're only pretending to be a supporter?"

"I can take care of myself."

"I know you can, but there are lots more of them than there are of you." Kate liked the tough woman and wanted to help her reconcile to what had happened to her sister, but she didn't want to put her in harm's way.

Rosa shrugged. "Something I have to do."

Kate sighed. There was no deflecting this woman. "I could give you a ride, and wait with the truck running."

"You'll be my getaway driver?" Rosa shook her head. "No, your truck with its camper on top is too easy to spot. Borrow your uncle's car?"

"No, he's too well known around here, and a sky-blue Volvo would stand out as much as my camper."

"I'll ask Brenda if she'll loan us her Jeep. It's got to be ten years old, black, totally boring. Just what we need, and she never goes out at night."

"It's a plan," Kate said. "But this is going to be the end of it, okay? McCoy is the leader of the pro-development movement. If he passes your test there's no where else to go."

* * *

Brenda didn't think it was such a great idea. "Oh no, Rosa, you don't want to get yourself into any more trouble."

191

"That wasn't trouble. That was a minor disagreement." She had the paper open, folded to the local section. Kate hadn't gotten around to checking out McCoy's website, but that hadn't slowed Rosa down. "He's giving a talk at the Clarion Hotel tomorrow night. Perfect."

"How long do you need to be close to him to get your, um, data?" Kate asked.

Rosa shrugged. "Not very long. Half a minute? It's like radar. I just need time for a ping. A scan. I don't know what to call it. Eye contact helps a lot."

"Maybe you could be by the door when he walks in," Kate said. "You ping, we get the hell out of there."

"Works for me," Rosa said. "So, Brenda, could I borrow your car tomorrow night?"

Kate wasn't convinced of the Alaskan's powers, but she couldn't let her go alone. Who knew? Maybe they'd find something out anyway.

* * *

Washing her face before bed, Kate reconsidered what she'd gotten herself into. She was going to help Rosa ping somebody? Marjorie would think she'd lost her marbles.

Kate didn't think Rosa's take on Don McCoy was worth much. She was humoring Rosa, trying to get her a little further down the road of grieving, a process that could take some time. Would Marjorie say she was encouraging a delusion?

As she slipped into bed, she wondered if Rosa's unusual psychological talents included hypnotizing friends to support her in her hare-brained schemes.

Eclipse was favoring Kate with his furry presence, laying claim to half her pillow. She stroked the purring cat and met his gold-foil eyes. They brought Sean to mind. She'd sent the FBI agent an email, keeping it short and breezy: where she was and why, since the last he knew she'd been heading for Arizona from Pennsylvania. How great the skiing was.

She hadn't heard back.

Yet, she told herself, yet.

She drifted to sleep with the inscrutable gold eyes shining on her, two moons in a dark sky.

* * *

Headlights out. The engine was running, partly to be ready for action and partly because it was so darn cold. A watch cap pulled low on her head, Kate surveyed the people going into the hotel. According to plan, she and Rosa had come early and gotten a great parking space right near the door. She'd parked nose in, so the Jeep wouldn't stand out from the cars around it. A slower getaway, but at least she'd see Rosa coming out.

This was a larger, more cosmopolitan venue than the Hunterville school. She didn't expect Rosa to be pursued by assailants.

It was mostly a middle-aged crowd, more couples and women than the last time. Rosa was wearing a decent-looking jacket, taken from her sister's closet of teaching clothes. Brenda had volunteered to give Rosa a make-up job on what was left of the black eye. Kate had laughed: this rowdy woman in make-up was a contradiction in terms. "Like a cat wearing jewelry."

Rosa had given her a look, and said, in a tone of weary patience, "Kate. It's a disguise." And she made an effort to stop laughing.

Some younger faces in the crowd. Was there some other event going on at the hotel tonight? Were any of the twenty-somethings Otterlin students? If so, maybe they were up to the same thing Rosa was, scoping out the enemy.

Fighting the human current, Rosa came out of the big glass doors. Nice coat or not, her walk was a swagger and her expression smug. She looked like a sailor.

"Success," she said as she got into the car. "He was coming out of the restaurant, got on the elevator. I got on with him, gave him a nod and a smile. He smiled back. Full-on eye contact for several seconds."

"Great," Kate said. "You pinged away?"

"I did," Rosa said. "I got nothing. He may be a jerk, but he didn't have anything to do with Camila going down."

"Oh," Kate said. "That's not much help. We didn't learn a thing?"

"I got a wicked ping from someone else. Two someones. They came in as I was going out, so I made a U-turn and got their pictures."

Kate had backed out of the parking space, and the car was sideways to the hotel. She looked at the front door to see if Rosa had been followed. "How'd you do that without giving yourself away? They didn't pose, I'm sure."

"I pretended to be taking a selfie, but I made sure they were in the background." She looked at the screen. "Not bad for my first selfy ever."

Kate stopped the car at the exit. Nobody was behind them, so she took the phone from Rosa.

Not bad at all. The two young men were standing together outside the elevator, as if in conversation, but they'd glanced Rosa's way just as she hit the button.

Justin and Tim.

"Holy cats," Kate said. "I know them. They're a couple of students in the class that meets at Uncle Pete's house."

"I got a bad ping off them."

"Both of them?"

"I wasn't close enough to tell if it was one or both. I'd already gone up in the elevator once, and I'd rubbed my eyes and was worried I'd screwed up the artwork Brenda did on my face. So I bailed. But if you know them, that's great. I can hang out at Pete's. I'll get his permission or else I'll hide in the bushes."

"I wish we had more to go on than your pings," Kate said. "They're hard to show to other people, like Uncle Pete or Mark, Aunt Sarah's policeman friend."

Rosa's personal radar. Impossible to convince skeptical Marjorie of it. As scientific as tarot cards or astrology. Only Rosa's unassailable belief in her own powers kept Kate from dismissing them outright. She'd always thought of herself as a scientist at heart, like her uncle. A psychic Alaskan fisherwoman? Come on, Kate.

Baffled by the events of the past month, she was willing to listen even to Rosa's oddball ideas.

FIFTEEN

Kate took the stairs in the Bio Building two at a time, her first set of finished drawings for Myra tucked in a cardboard portfolio. The entomologist's office was small, and crowded; good thing she had the aviary, which she affectionately called the bug-house, to escape to. Even though an aviary is for birds, people on campus not connected with the biology department called this one a greenhouse because that's what it looked like. A scaled-up greenhouse, a pet jungle.

Voices carried out the door of the entomologist's office, so Kate waited in the hall.

"I'm telling you, she said the computer was on the fritz. Said she'd send me the check in the mail as soon as it was back up. That was over three weeks ago and I haven't gotten it."

Myra's voice was a soothing murmur.

"Look, Myra," the man said, "we've been doing business together for a long time. I trust you. Wish you'd been here that day, that's all I can say. I can't afford to give away a three-pound box for nothing. Not to mention the cold-weather packaging."

A large man in a shearling coat and dirty jeans came out of the office, with Myra behind him. "Your word's good with me," she said. "Let's go get you paid right now. It'll wipe out petty cash, and the secretary will yell bad things at me, but she won't mean them." Seeing Kate, she winked. "Paperwork, ugh. Go on inside, I'll be right back."

The man's boots left wet tracks down the hall.

Kate made herself at home in Myra's office. She'd spent enough time here by this time to see through the clutter and appreciate how functional it was. Piles of notebooks tilted toward each other on the long credenza with a microscope at one end. The desk was clear, with only a few papers and a big computer screen. Pristine compared to Uncle Pete's academic midden pile on the coffee table. She hated to think what her desk might look like if she had a workload like these professors. When she was a reporter, most of her work was electronic; before that, as an ambulance tech, it was hands-on.

Myra swooped back in. "Never take a day off," she said. "It'll come back to bite you."

"Was he talking about a three-pound box of insects?" Kate asked. "I've never thought about bugs in terms of pounds. Not sure I want to."

"Not bugs, bees. Luke's our local beekeeper, and somebody ordered a flat of bees and didn't tell the office. Must have been Azul, though he's usually pretty good about paperwork."

"I hate to think how many bees you get in three pounds." She was fine with insects, but hordes of them gave her the creeps. Or gave them to some part of her brain, well hidden from the modern biologist part.

"Ten thousand or so," Myra said. But she was distracted, eager for the drawings. She opened the portfolio, missing the startled look on Kate's face at the number. The entomologist's lips compressed in concentration as she studied the work, turning pages slowly.

Kate waited, a little breathless with anticipation and with the vision of ten thousand stinger-bearers stuffed in a box. Ugh. Nobody actually had to count them, of course. Still, she liked the kind she drew better.

Nodding occasionally, Myra went through the whole set. She nodded again as she looked up. "These are excellent, Kate. Just what we need. I want Dave to have a look at them, but I'll bet he'll be delighted, too."

"I'm glad," Kate said. "It's fun to draw them, and I probably wouldn't get as much work done if I didn't have a nice warm bug-house to hang out in. Want to find me some more models?"

"You bet," Myra said. "And remind me to check that little desk out by the hives for the order for Luke. Sometimes people write up orders out there and forget to log them in."

Azul was in the aviary, writing at the wooden desk. His size made it look like something from a kindergarten classroom. Kate was glad to see him. The last time she'd spent time with him had been at Brenda's, when they'd had pizza and hatched the plan that had nearly gotten Rosa and Kate beaten up. He could have had tipped off the HCDC. But when he looked up, his friendly face made it hard to believe he'd had anything to do with that hostile encounter.

"Hi, Azul. How's bees-ness?" Myra asked. Kate hung back, not wanting to get too close to the hives.

"Buzzing," he said.

"Natch."

"Nuthatch." He winked at Kate. Must be their standard greeting. What a couple of wacky profs.

They were both at ease around the insects, neither of them wearing gloves or those hats with nets hanging down from the brim. Azul's thick beard protected half his face, at least. His big frame at the undersized desk make Kate think she'd fallen down a rabbit hole and was in a personal version of *Alice in Wonderland*. Next the bees would talk, telling her where to go to find flowers with the most nectar.

"Your queen's good?" Myra asked. "I saw in the log you took the frames out right down to the bottom."

"Yep, she's pumping out eggs like the royalty she is. I didn't harvest any honey, though. Thought I'd let them get over the open-window trauma."

"The cold air shouldn't have made it back as far as this corner," Myra said.

"I know, I know," Azul said. "But it was windy, And anything different, you know, upsets them."

Myra rolled her eyes at Kate. "I told you they're his babies."

"Baby bees?"

"They need their daddy," Azul said. He stood up, and the little desk fell over. "You know, Myra, one of these days this thing needs to be replaced."

"You're right," she said. "By the way, did you order a three-pound package from Luke a couple of weeks ago?"

"Nope," Azul said. "Why?"

"Just trying to chase down the darn paperwork. Anything like that in the log?"

"Don't think so. But have a look." He set the desk back on its legs, opened the lid and took out a ledger-style notebook. Myra looked over his shoulder as he paged backwards.

"Not much going on," she said. "Not since before Thanksgiving."

"Well, get Luke paid. He's the best," Azul said. "Not his fault if we can't figure out who put in the order."

"I already got him paid. Almost zeroed out petty cash, so my name is mud in the office," Myra said. "Especially after I reminded them it's their job, in the end, to deal with this kind of admin chore."

Azul shut the notebook. The hive nearest to him looked increasingly busy, with dozens of bees flying out of the slot at the top. A few landed on his shoulders and arms, and Kate edged back even farther. For some reason the insects crawling on the ledge under the slot made her more uneasy than the ones in the air. She wasn't afraid of spiders or snakes the way many people were, but the human genome must have passed this aversion to multiple crawling critters along to her. Ah, the evolution of everyday life.

One of Azul's shoulders had some yellow blobs on it. Bee keeper's epaulettes.

"Azul, what's that yellow goo on your shirt?" Where had she seen similar stuff?

"Probably frass," he said, putting the notebook back in the desk. Then he looked up and saw her puzzlement. "Oh, you don't know the word?"

"Bee poo," Myra said. "It's actually pretty clean."

"I'm always happy to see it," Azul said. "It means the bees are healthy—out foraging, coming back, feeding the larvae, packing honey away for the future. Investors in gold."

"Amber," Myra said.

"Literalist," Azul said. "Frass sticks like glue," he said to Kate. "Like plastic. Water doesn't touch it. If you find some on your clothes, scrape it off with a dull knife before you throw your shirt in the laundry. Otherwise it will be there after it's washed."

"Not likely I'll have the problem," Kate said. "No offense, but I won't be spending a lot of time back here with your babies."

"Oh, you can get frassed on anywhere," Myra said. "In fact, they usually do it away from the hive. Like a lot of animals, they'd rather not dump on their own homes."

Kate remembered where she'd seen the yellow stuff. "When the heat went off," she asked Azul, "and the windows were open, did any of the bees escape?"

"They would not be tempted. A cold draft would be something to avoid. If it got cool enough they'd go inside the hive. They keep warm with muscle-power, like people shivering. Not that they have to do much of that here in the aviary. Normally."

"Well, suppose a bee did get out. How far would it fly?"

"A block, maybe?" Azul looked at Myra, who shrugged. "Not even that far. The metabolism would start shutting down as soon as its body temperature dropped, and that would take just a minute or two. Those bodies are small."

"So an aviary bee couldn't fly as far as Topper Reserve," Kate said.

Azul looked startled. "Certainly not."

"Could someone *take* a bee that far? Keep it alive somehow?"

He shook his head. "My dear Houston, you hallucinate. Perhaps you could make a tiny snowsuit? No, of course—a space capsule!" A rumble of laughter. "For a bee to go out of here, that would be a trip to the moon."

His laugh went on, and Kate felt her face burning. Her question was easy to ridicule, but she'd asked it to see if Azul seemed uncomfortable at the idea of a live bee near where Prof. Chavez had died.

If he did, he was covering it well. But being charming and funny didn't mean he was above suspicion. There wasn't anyone in the country who knew more about bees and how to handle them.

"Well, let's go find you a nice bug," Myra said, a little too brightly. "See you, Azul."

"Later," he said, still chuckling.

After they were a couple of gravelled turns away from the hives, Kate said in a low voice, "A bee did make it to the Reserve. That's where I found the bee I drew, the one that first got you interested in my work."

"You told me you found it, but I thought you found it here," Myra said.

"Something strange is going on," Kate said. She looked around. Could they be overheard? Sight distance wasn't good in this jungle, shorter than hearing range.

Myra must have read her mind. "Let's go back to my office."

* * *

"I never thought about how far bees could fly in the cold until after Luke was here, and I heard him talking to you about the bees he delivered," Kate said. "He mentioned cold-weather packaging, and that made me have second thoughts about that bee I found." They'd settled in Myra's office, in the chairs in front of the desk; Kate had shut the door.

"It was in the Reserve, the first full day I was here. How could that have happened?"

"It had to have been transported," Myra said. "That's a mile, as the bee flies. Not a snowball's chance it got there on its own."

"Okay, listen, I'm getting worried about something." A familiar kind of excitement was stirring in Kate. It was such a relief to be able to talk to someone she trusted. "I found that bee when I was skiing the morning after I got here."

"You said that," Myra said. There was no impatience in her voice; she was used to dealing with students. But she didn't want to waste time, either.

"That was the morning after I'd found Dr. Chavez." Kate waited for understanding to show on Myra's face.

Something in her eyes shifted. "You found Camila, and the next day you found a bee. And Camila died of anaphylaxis," Myra said.

"Or was incapacitated by it," Kate said, "and froze."

"Same difference," Myra said. "The question is how the bee got there, and whether it stung her, and whether that caused or contributed to her death. If so, the question becomes whether somebody arranged for it to be there."

"I think the answer is yes," Kate said. "I saw some frass in her pack."

"When her body was removed from the scene?"

"No, I didn't stay around for that. I saw it when Rosa and I skied in the Reserve. She was treating her sister's things like the relics of a saint—wearing her clothes and pack, eating the stale sandwich."

"She's an odd one," Myra said. "Not that I'd expect Camila's sister to be ordinary. Was the frass on the outside of the pack? Camila could have worn it near the hives."

"There was some on the cap of an empty water bottle. But inside the bottle, too."

"You couldn't put a bee in a bottle in Camila's pack when she was going out for a few hours to check on her mice," Myra said. "The temperature would kill it in a few minutes, and it would be lethargic right away."

"Maybe I should have another look at that pack," Kate said. "But I don't want to tell Rosa I have any suspicions. She's sure her sister was killed, and I don't want to get her hopes up without some decent evidence."

"You might be on to something," Myra said. "Although to be honest I think it's a long shot. Keeping a bee alive in cold weather? Hard to do."

"Might have been a bunch of bees. Once they got out, they'd freeze and blow away, or get buried in the snow. Just a fluke I found the one."

Myra stared at the spider on the ceiling for a minute, thinking. "Camila was so goal-oriented, working every minute she was awake. She was so happy to have someone else do the cooking and housework. Brenda sometimes packed Camila's lunch on her teaching days, especially if she wasn't going in that day herself and wasn't in a rush."

"I wonder if Brenda made her a sandwich on the last night she spent checking on the mice. The one left in the pack."

Myra shook her head. "I can't wrap my head around her doing Camila in. But look, if there's frass inside the pack, then anyone who has access to the hives and the pack could have done it," Myra said. "That includes our student workers here." Her eyes widened. "We can't even dismiss Azul."

"Right," Kate said. "That's why I didn't mention where I'd found the bee while we were in the aviary. Did Dr. Chavez leave her pack around where other people could get at it? The students who work for you, for instance?"

"Sure. She might have left it around, here or at a table in the union while she went up for a refill. Anybody might. I've done that myself. It's not a purse, after all." Myra looked rattled. "That means we have hundreds of suspects. A meditation class meets in the aviary every week, and other classes take tours sometimes."

"Not hundreds. Only the ones closest to her. If this was murder, it took a lot of effort and care, and that means a significant motive. Nobody's going to knock off a prof after seeing them on a tour. Or even after getting a bad grade on a test."

"The way they complain sometimes, they sound like they would. Grades are like money to them," Myra said. "But you're probably right."

"Who are the students who work in the aviary?"

Myra told her the six names, only two of them familiar. "Chaya's trying to graduate in three years. She's totally responsible and mature. Maddie? She's work-study. Feels sorry for herself, but she does her work okay."

"Brenda's suggested dinner and a ski party tomorrow night," Kate said. "Why don't I ask her to invite you, too? You and me, Rosa, Azul. We can ski for a while, out under a full moon, and go to Brenda's afterwards for dinner. Then one of us can scope out the pack."

"Good plan," Myra said. "We can do a little snooping, nobody the wiser. Skiing, food, and snooping. What's not to like?"

* * *

Kate was in her camper when there was a volley of knocks on her door. Not Tim's uncertain knock or Kareem's polite one. She put her pencil down reluctantly.

"Aren't you coming to class?" Rosa was simmering with energy, convinced she was on the brink of discovery. "I'm ready to roll. Haven't taken notes since high school." She smiled and held up a brand-new notebook.

Who the heck are we all fooling? Kate wondered. A bunch of actors, all in different plays. "No, I decided not to go after the first week. Too much like being an undergrad again," Kate said. "I come out here—this is my art studio this winter—to get some work done while Uncle Pete probes the inner life of plants with the gang."

"Oh, that's too bad," Rosa said. "I was looking forward to passing notes and kicking you under the table." In her current mood Rosa reminded Kate of a blue jay, loud and brash, and she guessed that's what her personality was like under ordinary circumstances. "Okay if I come out to debrief after the class?"

"Or I'll come in. Depends on whether I'm in the middle of something or not."

"Okay."

Back at work, Kate looked at the butterfly. She'd taken the photo on her cell phone, and translating it to paper was proving difficult. Challenging. She remembered how much she'd hated that word when she was in college. A challenge was something the professors or administrators wanted her to do that she'd rather avoid. Now it was something that drew her to it, something she wanted to do and had to figure out how.

Like finding out what had happened to Prof. Chavez.

Life was coming at her in volleys, like Rosa's knocking. The fight to reclaim a life in art, encouragement from a mentor at the art colony in Maine, his murder, her travels in the Adirondacks and in southern Pennsylvania, the later murders there—too much to contemplate all together.

One day at a time. Her mother's mantra, at least in her better moments.

Kate felt a wave of sympathy for the students in Uncle Pete's class and for all the Otterlin students, in their dorm rooms or in the union, drinking coffee or beer or curled in those orb-like chairs Uncle Pete called "womb chairs" or spread-eagle on their beds, reading and reading and reading. They didn't know how much they would have to go through to live a life.

Or maybe they did. Maybe they were smarter than she was.

Kate forced her squirrelly mind back to the present. On her phone the butterfly's wing was transparent, but it didn't have the uniformity of glass so the leaf on the other side of it looked blurred. The body was a bundle of lines, distinct. She'd need her finest pens for this.

Rosa was convinced she'd found the bad guy, just had to narrow it down between Justin and Tim. Kate would bet on Justin. She'd volunteered to ask Uncle Pete if Rosa could attend his class, and they'd talked that afternoon when he came out of the living room for coffee.

"How's the bug artist doing?" he'd asked her.

"Fine," she said. "The aviary is a trip, like being on another planet. After I spend enough time working on one of Myra's critters, I feel like they're the same size as I am. "

"Sounds a little scary."

Kate laughed. "Are you open to a visitor to class tonight? Rosa's interested in dropping in."

He looked surprised. "Sure, that would be okay. I'll have to run it by the students, of course, the way I did with you. She's interested in botany?"

"I guess so," Kate said.

Rosa had argued hard against telling Uncle Pete her motive. "How do we know he won't defend his students, or even alert them by accident?" she'd asked.

Fine with Kate. She didn't want to tell Uncle Pete that Rosa believed she could feel other people's auras and know their intentions. He was a scientist through and through; he would scoff, and not gently. Aunt Sarah was more open, but even she would probably have trouble with Rosa's mental sonar being able to probe people's minds.

Kate didn't want to talk to Mark about it, either, until she and Myra came up with something more substantial.

If they could.

* * *

After class, Rosa was disappointed. "Tim was all shy and embarrassed and wouldn't look at me, and Justin didn't look at anybody," she said. "It's such a bummer. I'm going to have to come back on Tuesday and howl like a wolf or stomp on their toes to get decent eye contact. Tim's just shy. What's with Justin?"

"I don't know either of them very well," Kate said, "but Justin's out of sync with the rest. Flew choppers in the army, he told us at the first class, so he's a couple of years older. He's pretty quiet, doesn't join in."

"The other problem is they stick together," Rosa said. "They came together and left together. Are they gay?"

"I don't think so," Kate said, keeping Tim's crush on Zoe in confidence. She suspected Tim was sticking close to Justin because that's where Zoe's attention was. Or maybe he was trying to figure out what Justin did to attract women. Tim was definitely a puppy running beside the alpha dog. "Tim tags along. I think he wants to be like Justin, cool and remote. But it's just not him. And if you stomp on his toes I guarantee he'll hop around looking at his foot, not at you."

Rosa peered at the drawing on the table. "That's one cool butterfly. But its wings don't match."

If Kate had to explain, the drawing didn't work.

"I like the one of the birds at the feeder better."

Everybody's an art critic.

SIXTEEN

Kate swung down from her camper and unlocked the front door. It had been a good morning's work. She hated to stop, but she was out of water and that meant no coffee, the black fuel of her art.

In the kitchen, filling the plastic jug, she heard voices.

"It wasn't me. You're barking up the wrong tree."

She wasn't sure who the speaker was, but the voice came from Uncle Pete's improvised office in the living room.

"That doesn't mean anything." The voice was angry, and coming closer. Now she could see the speaker, who'd walked into the dining room. Justin.

Uncle Pete moved to the other side of the table, facing the kitchen, but he hadn't seen Kate yet. Focused on Justin, he was uncharacteristically still, his voice lower than usual. "It's in the same font you've used for everything you've turned in. I don't have another student in any of my classes who uses that font. And a number of words are underlined in green pen. I haven't seen a drop of green ink from anyone but you."

"Everybody with a computer has access to thousands of fonts these days, okay? And the bookstore probably sells six kinds of green pen. Anybody could have written that note."

"It even sounds like you. Do you know how often you use the word 'frankly'?"

Justin didn't answer right away, and a look of triumph spread across Uncle Pete's face.

"All right," Justin said. "Then it must be somebody who knows me. Must be somebody in one of my classes, because he knows what my papers look like. Knows how I talk, that I like green."

"Very clever. But I'm not falling for it."

"I'm telling you—"

"No, I'm telling *you.*" Uncle Pete leaned forward, palms on the table. His voice rose. "This note is going straight to the dean of students, young man. I'm sure he'll be in touch. You're going to be in a lot of trouble."

Justin stood for a moment, then moved out of Kate's sight, toward the door. His footsteps paused. "Frankly, you're a stupid old fool."

Kate waited for the door slam, but it closed quietly.

She stepped into the dining room just as Aunt Sarah reached the bottom of the stairs. "What's the matter? Who was that?"

"One of my students."

"What's he going to be in trouble for?"

"He wrote a note that said I'm an anachronism who's gumming up the wheels of progress. Wait, I'll get it." He went into the living room and came back with a sheet of paper. *"Professor,"* he read. *"Frankly, you're a joke. An old joke that isn't funny. You should retire before somebody does it for you."* He looked up at his wife, then Kate. "Doesn't that sound like a threat?"

"Yes." Aunt Sarah was holding onto the back of a chair hard with her good hand.

Kate moved beside her and put an arm around her waist. This was the last thing either one of them needed, but Uncle Pete had more energy to deal with it.

"Here's the rest of it," he said. *"Forget about BFF. Keep your head down and your mouth shut or you'll wish you had."*

"When did you get the note?" Kate asked.

"This morning, tucked into one of the books I use for the botany class," Pete said. "I don't know when it was left. I recognized the font and the pen as Justin's, and I emailed him right away, and then he was here."

Kate had been working so hard she hadn't noticed Justin walk past her camper on his way to the house.

"I think you should call Mark," Aunt Sarah said.

"And the campus police," Kate said. "Ask them to keep an eye on him. Although he's right, both the typeface and the pen color are easy for anyone to access."

Uncle Pete sat down. "Maybe I shouldn't have emailed so quickly. I was upset." He rubbed his face with both hands. "I shouldn't have yelled at him."

"What's Mark's number?" Kate asked her aunt. She put the numbers into her phone and handed it to Aunt Sarah. "Why don't you sit down?"

* * *

Mark was there in half an hour. He slipped the note into a plastic bag. "Did you handle this a lot? Sometimes we can pick up fingerprints from paper, or at least helpful partials."

Uncle Pete looked embarrassed. "I did. I waved it around in the boy's face."

Mark stood by Aunt Sarah's chair and rested a hand on her left shoulder. "It's a good thing I can get involved, since we're in the city and not on campus. If this had happened in your office you'd be talking to campus security."

"Wouldn't they be helpful?" Aunt Sarah asked.

"Yes, indeed. I'm going to bring them in. They'll have a file on Justin that might give me some insight." the detective said. "The kid's right: the font and the pen suggest, but they don't prove. Fingerprints, now they'd be conclusive."

* * *

Like the aviary, the camper was a bubble of warmth in a glittering landscape of snow. Instead of birds, it was full of insects. On paper. As real as Kate could make them.

This kind of pressure was new. Last summer she'd been searching for her identity as an artist, recovering the ability to work at all. It had been a wrenching battle, but an internal one. Now the pressure was external: Myra and Dave were in the final stages of revising their textbook manuscript and the faster Kate could produce drawings the better.

She'd lucked into the job, and she loved it. Myra kept introducing her to wonderful, exotic creatures to draw, sometimes asking for close-ups of the head, or thorax, or some special feature like the plumes on moth antennas or the spines on a mantis foreleg. Aunt Sarah was stronger every day; in a week or two her cast would come off, and she'd start a series of physical therapy appointments.

Excited and fulfilled, Kate had been spending hours in her camper-studio. With work stretching ahead of her, she realized how much she'd missed it. She loved exploring back country in her camper, but she loved working, too. Maybe this free-lance artist idea, only a month old, was something to develop. This job might lead her to others.

But she wasn't ready to give up her traveling lifestyle. How would that mesh with getting jobs?

Today she became so engrossed in the delicate face of an orchid mantis that she'd actually forgotten to drink her coffee. The cup was three-quarters full, and cold. She stood and put it in the microwave, pushing the two-minute button.

Her mind roamed. Whoever had damaged the back stairs and caused Aunt Sarah to fall hadn't been identified, and neither had the Otterlin campus vandal. Maybe it was the same person, or people. Kate stayed alert when she was outside after dark, and she was happy the motion-activated lights were installed on both the back and the front of the house.

Aunt Sarah still hadn't moved back into the master bedroom, and Kate was becoming concerned about that. Was her aunt putting a brave face on her condition, pretending to feel better than she did?

The microwave beeped, and she brushed the thoughts aside. She had work to do.

A hesitant knock on the door. Oh, for heaven's sake. It wasn't even class night.

"Tim," she said, at the door. "Is it about Zoe?" She was hardening her heart to turn him away. She really wanted to concentrate on that mantis. Disguising itself as a flower to attract prey, it looked as delicate as a classical ballerina.

"No, it's not that. I have something important to tell you." He looked around as if he were afraid he was being watched.

Rats. "C'mon in." Even as she said it, Kate scolded herself for being a pushover.

Across from her at the dinette, he looked older, somehow, than the last time he'd come on board. He didn't stutter as much and got right to the point.

"I've b-been hanging out a lot with Justin," he said. "We met up right after school started last fall, and I thought he was awesome. A copter pilot, you know? We're sort of friends, even though he doesn't talk much. But we study together, sometimes really late at night."

Kate nodded.

"Late one night I saw him out my window, and he had skis over his shoulder. I ran outside because I was hoping he'd let me go with him. He was walking really fast, though, and I c-couldn't catch up, so I kind of trailed him. I didn't mean to spy, but I was curious because it was so late and he was in such a hurry. And skiing at night? What the heck."

"He didn't see you, then?"

"No. Because, well, he left campus and went down that street that borders Topper. He took the easement between two of the houses and skied off. In this d-direction."

Kate blinked. "What night was this?"

He paused. "A week ago Thursday. I remember because it was botany class night, and I thought maybe he'd forgotten something and was going back for it. But it was way too late to knock on a professor's door. Anybody's door."

"What time was it?"

"Not sure. Around midnight?" He shrugged. "So I went back to my dorm."

"That's really helpful, Tim," Kate said. "Thank you for letting me know. But why didn't you tell me, or Prof. Stewart, sooner?"

"I didn't want to rat out a friend. But it kept nagging at me." He stood up. "I k-kept thinking about all the dead mice, and I thought maybe he was trying to scare the girls. A practical joke, you know? Although it didn't seem like him."

Kate stood, too. She felt a little sorry about how reluctant she'd been to talk to him. He was a decent guy, struggling with his loyalty to a friend. "Things going any better with Zoe?"

"Not really," he said, blushing. The old Tim was back. "She likes Justin, b-but he ignores her. I mean, he's really rude to her. When she sits at our t-table he just looks through her. The last time, she put her tray down on our table and said 'Mind if I join you?' in this cheery voice and he looked at me and said 'Frankly, I think some big dumb b-broad has a crush on you,' and she got so upset she ran off. Left her lunch and everything."

"Yikes, that's pretty rude, all right," Kate said. "I'm surprised. That sounds kind of juvenile for Justin. Didn't think he was like that."

Tim shrugged. "He can be mean." Now that the subject was Justin instead of Zoe, his stammer was gone. "So thanks for listening. You won't tell him I said anything, will you?"

"No, of course not."

"Good." Tim dropped his pack beside the step and climbed down after it. "Goodnight."

As the latch clicked into place, something clicked in Kate's mind as well. The two parts of Tim's conversation were connected. Attracted to Zoe, he was angry with Justin for treating her badly. So ratting out his friend wasn't as altruistic as it seemed. He wasn't only alerting Kate to Justin's sneaky post-midnight visit, he was also getting revenge. Justin's insulting Zoe so badly she ran out of the Union was the trigger.

She turned back to her splendid mantis. Bugs were a lot easier to deal with than people.

SEVENTEEN

The moon was almost full, rising above the trees. Topper Reserve was still and bright as Kate and Rosa skied away from Aunt Sarah's house.

"Maybe I've been trying to use it too much since I got here, this ping thing," Rosa said. "It fades in and out, you know? I think I've worn it out for now."

"You're still convinced your sister was murdered?" Kate asked. She and Myra hadn't told Rosa about their suspicions arising from the bee Kate found. She'd turned it over to Mark as possible evidence. He'd thanked her and said he'd factor her theory into his investigation, but she didn't think he gave it much credence.

"Absolutely." Rosa sighed. "I didn't get a thing from the second class and it was really too bad, because Tim and Justin got there separately. I just couldn't read anything."

"Bummer," Kate said. Suppose one of the students could have gotten access to Prof. Chavez's pack, how would they have acquired a bee, and have known how to handle it? Or suppose they were working together? Justin, as a full-time student, had access to the aviary. Maybe he'd taken an entomology course. She'd ask Uncle Pete to find out.

"They're guilty of something. I just don't know how bad it is, and whether it has to do with Camila."

"Everybody's done something," Kate said. "You must get pings all the time." She and Rosa were matching strides, which meant Kate wasn't working too hard because of her companion's shorter legs.

But Rosa wasn't about to be distracted. "It's okay, though. I have a feeling. I'm excited. Something's going to happen tonight." Her grin was bright in the moonlight. "That's another thing. My pings work better when I'm sad, and this feeling is getting in the way."

"Tonight? Really?" Half of Kate's mind was intrigued, the other half accused herself of being gullible.

"Yessirree." Rosa double-poled hard, twice, and glided ahead of Kate down to the lean-to. Two figures were already there, in the moonshadow: Azul and Myra. They'd come from his house, where Myra had left her car.

Rosa and Myra each said "hey" as a greeting. Azul said "Good evening, Houston."

"I'm about as Texan as a lady-slipper," Kate said. "Or a saguaro cactus."

"Ladies in Texas don't wear slippers?"

"It's a Massachusetts wildflower, Azul. Pink, mostly. Yellow ones are rare. It's an orchid."

"Ah, I know orchids. The rainforest in Brazil is full of them, big as saucers." He looked pleased at the reminder of home. "Symbiotic with fungi."

It was getting colder, the air stinging as Kate inhaled. The four of them looked like scuba divers in the darkness, putting out bubbles of white air that rose and dissipated.

"This has been great, but I'm freezing," Myra said. "I'm heading for Brenda's. If the dinner isn't ready, I'll have to eat dessert first."

She's impatient, Kate thought. She wants to get to the point of the evening, which was not dinner or dessert or skiing but having a look around Brenda's kitchen and Camila's former bedroom, now Rosa's.

"Freezing?" Rosa said. "It's only about zero. And no wind. This is a walk in the park."

"I'll go around the lake with you again," Azul said to her. "Just give me a minute to go behind a tree. Excuse me, ladies."

"I hope it doesn't freeze and fall off," Rosa said. Wow, she was wild tonight.

Myra pushed out toward the pond. Kate followed, the two of them swooping in s-curves toward the dark ice, Myra shouting "Woo-HOO" in a high voice.

Kate felt it too: the night was exhilarating. Do snow crystals sparkle more in moonlight than in sun? A research project for some aspiring Ph.D. in physics. Kate carved her turns sharply to shower the slope below her with blue sparks of snow.

Then the slope flattened out, and she and Myra moved side by side.

"We're telling the police if we see one single thing that doesn't look right," Myra said. "I know it's a little embarrassing to say we're going on the intuitions of a psychic, but I don't mind sounding a little nuts. We just need to explain the bee frass to ourselves, and then we're out of there."

"Fine by me," Kate said. "I have Mark's number in my phone, but we probably aren't going to find anything. The cops went over Brenda's house right after Prof. Chavez died."

They climbed the slope to the edge of Brenda's circular driveway, took off their skis and clumped onto the porch. The house was dark, the door ajar. Myra pushed it open and patted the wall for a switch. Light.

Brenda sat up on the couch, blinking.

"Oh, you're here," she said. "I'm sorry, I fell asleep." She threw off an afghan and yawned, then got up heavily and turned on the lamp by the couch. Shot her guests a smile. "Don't worry, the pizza's okay. I put it in the oven and set a timer. But I haven't even started the salad."

Pizza again? Aunt Sarah had called Brenda a good cook, but of course she wasn't at her best. "We'll help," Kate said. She and Myra followed their host to the galley kitchen, where she pulled a head of Romaine lettuce out of the fridge. "There's not a lot of room out here," Brenda said. "It's kind of a one-woman set-up." She glanced at them in the doorway. Blue eyes had turned from sleepy to alert. Friendly face, a look over her shoulder and she put the Romaine on the counter. "I've got this. Why don't you put on some music?"

Myra picked something classical and slipped the CD into the slot. Bright trumpets filled the room, strings behind them.

A few minutes later, thumps on the porch. Azul and Rosa. They tumbled through the door, talking like a flute and a bassoon. Azul got more conversation from Rosa than anyone else; he was good at putting people at ease. And Rosa was on some kind of a high.

"Can I see where you're staying?" Myra asked her.

Go, Myra.

"Sure. And hey, I found an article Camila was working on, with a note that says it needs editing. At least I think that's what it says. It's kind of technical. Could you figure out what it needs?"

"You should probably take all her papers to the Bio department. I bet she left more than one paper that's nearly finished," Myra said. "When you're ready, of course."

Azul stood in the kitchen door, talking to Brenda while she chopped a red onion. Kate saw her opportunity and sat down on the couch, unzipping the little fanny pack Rosa had taken off. The green bottle was clean and half full of water. Not a bit of frass, not even on the knurled sides of the cap. Damn. Rosa must have scrubbed it clean.

Underneath the bottle Kate found two hand-warmers, the small packets tucked in mittens or pockets and activated by snapping an interior vial to start a chemical reaction. Unused ones have a baggy feel, as if filled with loose sand, but after the reaction ends they go rigid. She pinched one. Hard as a marble. Trash, in anybody else's book, but Rosa must have left them in the pack in memory of her sister.

Things were falling into place. But two spent hand-warmers weren't strong evidence.

Kate went to the door of the kitchen, hoping the excitement buzzing through her brain wasn't showing on her face. She turned away from Rosa as she and Myra thumped back to the living room in their boots, not wanting to risk getting pinged even if Rosa was off her game.

"Anything I can do out there?" Myra called.

"No, I've got it." Brenda opened the oven door, and the aroma of hot bread and cheese made Kate's mouth water.

"What would everybody like to drink?" Azul asked. "Brenda's got Pepsi and orange juice, and I brought beer."

Kate usually avoided soda, but orange juice didn't go with pizza and she didn't feel like beer. "Pepsi," she said. "Thanks, Azul."

"Outta my way," Brenda said with a smile. Kate stepped back and the pizza went by, Brenda's hands in thick blue pot-holder mitts. She was humming, literally this time, but Kate didn't recognize the song.

According to Aunt Sarah, Brenda suffered from depression. She must know how to hide it well.

As they settled in the living room, the cell on the coffee table barked like a dog. Brenda poked it to silence. "Timer. Pizza's ready," she said, taking a bite. Beside her on the couch, Azul rumbled a laugh.

"Uncle Pete says Bascomb Hall will be finished before Christmas," Kate said, ending a few minutes of silence and disappearing pizza. "Replacing sections of pipe and sheetrock, and painting. He won't have to teach in his dining room anymore."

"Sarah will like that very much," Brenda said.

"She's a saint," Azul said. "A fountain of energy for the church and the community. And Pete is the same way for the college." He popped a beer open. "So he must be a saint, too." He didn't sound convinced.

"If saints wave their hands a lot," Kate said. And throw tantrums.

"How do you know they didn't?' He gave her a look of academic mischief. "Does scripture give us any clues about the body language of saints?"

"Who's your favorite saint?" Myra asked.

"Antonio de Sant'Anna Galvao," Azul said. "A mystic and a healer. An angel who could be in two places at once to minister to the dying."

"My kind of guy," Rosa said. "Who's yours, Kate?"

"St. Francis of Assisi."

"Ah, well chosen," Azul said. "Frei Galvao was also of the Franciscan order."

"My favorite saint is Camila," Rosa said.

A pause.

"Mine's Rachel Carson," Myra said.

"I can't think of a single saint," Brenda said. Then she put down her beer and sang. *The moment I wake up, before I put on my makeup, I say a little prayer for you—*

Kate recognized the old tune. Her mother had loved it. Was it Dionne Warwick or Aretha Franklin who'd made it a hit, way back?

Forever, forever, you'll stay in my heart— Brenda was throwing herself into the chorus. *Together, together, that's how it must be, to live without you would only be heartbreak for—* She stopped abruptly, put her face into Azul's shoulder and sobbed.

Okay, she wasn't as good at hiding her grief and depression as Kate had thought.

* * *

The conversation was subdued after that. Out the window, moonlight held the dark trees in a blue trance.

Kate looked at her watch and drained her Pepsi. "I should go. Thanks for having us over." She stood and piled the plates on the coffee table together, adding her Pepsi can on top. Myra looked up at her carefully.

"Thanks, but I can clean up," Brenda said. Her tears had subsided to hiccups and then to a dullness in her face and voice. "Not much to it with paper plates."

But Kate was already in the kitchen. She dropped the plates in the trash and tossed the can into the blue recycling bin, where an Otterlin logo caught her eye: a green water bottle like the one in Rosa's pack.

She picked it up. It was dirty, stuff clinging to it on the inside. She screwed off the lid and looked. Was that frass?

"What are you doing?" Brenda stood in the doorway.

Kate jumped. "It looked like a nice bottle. I wondered why you threw it out," she said, forcing a smile. "But it's full of gunk." She tossed it back into the bin.

"Yeah, that stuff wouldn't come off." Brenda moved past Kate and dropped the rest of the plates into the trash. "But you're right, it's a nice one. Maybe I'll try again." She snatched the bottle out of the bin and set it in the sink.

Kate turned. Myra was behind her. They gave each other quick looks of disappointment.

Goodnights all around, and the commotion of putting skis down and stepping into the bindings, the clacks resounding off the porch and out into the blue night. Then

Kate was skiing with Azul and Myra toward the pond, past it, their earlier tracks slick and fast.

"It doesn't seem so cold when you've just had pizza and beer," Myra said.

"Don't let that beer fool you," Azul said. "Beer lies."

"Vascular dilation lies big-time," Myra said.

"My stop," Azul said when they got to his house. "Good night, Houston. C'mon, Bug Hugger. Or have you forgotten your car's in my driveway?"

Kate put a hand on Myra's sleeve. "Wait, could I talk to you for a minute?"

The big man shrugged and skied through the gate to his back door.

As soon as he was out of earshot she said, "Hey. I know who took the picture of me that blew my cover with the HCDC when Rosa and I went to their meeting. Brenda. She tipped them off we were going."

"What? Why? I mean, why do you think that?"

"Because when Brenda's timer went off tonight it barked like a dog. That's the same sound it made when I was over at her house a couple of weeks ago. The night Azul asked me to go to that meeting."

Myra's frown was clear in the moonlight. "So?"

"That night she had the phone pointed right at me, and it clicked. I noticed the click at the time, but I didn't notice I noticed. Know what I mean?"

"Yeah," Myra laughed. "I do that a lot, especially when I'm thinking about too many things at once."

"It was a trick. That was her timer barking, not an incoming call. She needed an excuse to pick up the phone."

"But how do you know?"

"I heard her take an actual call once, when she came to visit Aunt Sarah at the house. The ringtone sounded like chirping birds, not a dog."

The frown didn't disappear completely. "Let's call that a hypothesis, since she could have changed her ringtone." Myra was poking holes in the snow with her ski pole. "What about that bottle you were looking at?"

"It had frass in it. She must have gotten a bee in there, and kept it from freezing with handwarmers."

The pole poked faster. Maybe it was helping Myra think. "She could have packed it with bees. The more bees, the more dangerous the outcome. They'd keep each other warm, and excite each other with attack pheromones."

Kate thought back. "There was crumpled newspaper in the bottle the first time Rosa and I skied together. What was that for?"

"Something for the bees to hold onto. So they wouldn't get thrown around as Camila moved. Still, they'd be pretty upset by the time she opened the bottle."

They gave each a long look.

"So we're thinking Brenda killed Camila?" Myra's eyes glistened.

"It'd be the perfect murder kit, that fanny pack, for someone allergic to bees. But she wasn't, was she? Surely Rosa would know that about her sister."

Back to poking holes. The tip of the ski pole looked like an enormous stinger, and Kate wished Myra would stop.

"She could have been allergic and not known it," the entomologist said. "But if there were enough pissed-off bees she'd be in trouble whether she was allergic before or not. She was a small person, without a lot of body mass to absorb the venom. So the dose would be effectively larger for her than for you or me or Azul." Now she seemed to be writing letters with her pole. Better. "The stuff causes vasodilation and a drop in blood pressure. She could have passed out from that."

"That's the same thing alcohol does—expands blood vessels. The way Azul was just warning us about."

"Right. But drinking is voluntary. If we're right about this, Camila didn't have a choice."

Kate imagined Prof. Chavez unscrewing the cap of the warm bottle, looking forward to some unusual treat Brenda had made. Dropping the bottle as bees boiled out to attack her, the only moving thing, the only target. She'd have died knowing her friend had betrayed her.

"I wish I could have kept that bottle I took out of the recycling bin. She's going to get rid of it. Throw it in the woods somewhere and we'll never find it."

"Not a problem," Myra said. "I stole it." She laughed wildly.

"Myra! you've been holding out on me." Kate laughed. "And you sound like a coyote."

"You thought fast. I came up behind Brenda when she caught you checking out the water bottle."

"I did my best, but she probably saw right through me." Kate thought a moment. "She'd want to take care of it as soon as we left, wash out the frass, to get rid of the evidence. And when it's not in the recycling bin, she'll figure out one of us took it."

"So what's she going to do about it? She's not much of a skier, so she won't be able to catch up to us. Let's take this evidence to your aunt's house and call the cops."

"Sounds like a plan." Kate smiled at Myra. "Fast thinking yourself, Myra. You saved the day."

"Oh, damn, it's gone!" Myra patted her coat frantically. "Fell out of my pocket. C'mon, we've got to go back and get it." She did a jump-turn and was speeding away before Kate could answer.

Kate did a somewhat rattled version of her own one-eighty and followed. Myra's tracks shone silver in the moonlight, swooping toward the pond, then straightening to whiz through the dog-hair section. Kate caught up at the bottom of the open rise toward Brenda's house.

"I don't see the bottle," Myra said. "It could have rolled somewhere out of sight. Damn, I wish I hadn't dropped it."

"Brenda's got it," Kate said. "She came out and picked it up. Or at least looked for it."

"What? She did?"

"Yes, see the tracks? She didn't ski, she walked. Really wrecked the snow, put holes all over the place." The ragged post-holes looked black, like a dotted line that came from Brenda's driveway and then doubled back a quarter of the way to the pond.

"Ouch," Myra said. "The snow's crusty, and she broke through. She was wearing a skirt. Her shins must be hurting."

"Maybe we're not too late to stop her from washing out the frass." Kate moved in front of Myra and started toward the rise. "C'mon, it's worth a shot."

"You bet. Two of us to one of her. And she's out of bees."

Kate slipped on the way up. It had gotten colder, icier, and it was hard to avoid the gouges in the snow left by Brenda's plunging footsteps.

Near the top Myra must have hit one of them, because she went down and couldn't stop herself from sliding almost to the bottom of the slope. "Don't stop!" she shouted, struggling to get back on her feet. "I'll catch up!"

Kate kept going, out onto the circular driveway. The moon lit it up like a skating rink and touched blue highlights into the old black Jeep.

In fact the driveway would have made a good rink. Her skis clattered on the ice and she slipped twice. The heck with this. She knelt to release the bindings.

An engine roared to life.

The old Jeep. Ice crackled under its tires.

Kate popped her boots free and ran for the island in the middle of the circle. She slipped, put her hands down and managed not to fall, slipped again, fell, got up, trailing her poles. Behind her the Jeep skidded, engine revving, then quieted as it got traction. She glanced over her shoulder and the headlights came on, blinding her.

She skittered toward the island. At the edge, the snow was softer. Bushes she didn't see grabbed at her legs and small branches zinged off her nylon pants. The ground was uneven and she staggered, something hit her hard behind her knees, shoving her forward—

Her head hit a tree and her field of vision filled with exploding stars.

Groggy. Snow in her mouth. Twigs in her hair. She was lying face-down with one of her poles caught underneath her, hard against her ribs.

The Jeep's engine roared as the driver tried to back up. Was it Brenda? The wheels must have dropped into the soft snow like Kate's boots had.

The vehicle wasn't going anywhere, because the driver was flooring it, didn't have the know-how or patience to go easy on the gas and let the tires bite. The rear wheels spun, making that whining sound that meant friction was melting a smooth, tire-shaped rut that would freeze into an icy trap when the tires stopped moving.

Silence.

The door unlatched. Kate rolled over, sat up. The vehicle was tilted steeply: one of its front wheels had dropped into a hole.

The driver's door swung open. A statuesque figure, made bulky by a down coat, half-fell out. Stood.

Kate sat in the snow, her head spinning. "Hey, Brenda, didn't you see me? You didn't have your lights on at first." She was sure Brenda meant to hit her with the Jeep, but having failed at that maybe she'd accept a fairy-tale version of what had just happened, an innocent excuse. Kate needed a minute or two to recover. Pretending to be unsuspecting might give her that.

It didn't.

Against Brenda's silhouette, moonlight glinted on the bright shape of a blade. A chef's knife Kate had last seen chopping red onions.

It wasn't icy under the trees; Kate got to her feet slowly, still dizzy. She wanted to lie down for a nice long nap. She wanted two Ibuprofen tablets and a warm blanket. She was going to have one heck of a headache.

But first she had to deal with a crazy person.

"Brenda," Kate said. "Don't make things worse." She was leaning on the two ski poles, but she couldn't use them for support and as weapons too. She put her weight on the left one, freeing the right. Brenda noticed and moved to Kate's left. She was coming closer, slowly, backlit by the moon. Her vision blurry, Kate couldn't read the other woman's expression.

Turning her head to the left hurt. More stars. Kate couldn't keep herself from swaying. Damn. She had to stop Brenda from getting close to her with that knife.

Putting her weight on the right pole, she changed her grip on the left one to point it forward instead of down. Jammed it toward the big black coat, felt it hit.

Was that a chuckle? Brenda grabbed the pole with her free hand and shoved it back against Kate.

With the wrist strap in place, Kate couldn't drop the pole. The handle hit her in the stomach and she folded over it, her breath gone. She fell backwards, blacking out.

She never hit the ground. She kept falling, and Brenda's form turned into a towering grizzly bear, its teeth shining ice-blue in the moonlight.

The night was peaceful. The bear was tall, and taller, and nothing mattered anymore.

Then she was awake and Brenda's form had jump-cut much too close. Kate wriggled her right hand out of the strap and then her left. Grabbed a pole and aimed the point at Brenda's face.

The grizzly bear smiled and knocked the pole away, stepping closer. Kate smashed her ski boot into the woman's shin and the smile changed into the rictus of a death-mask.

Brenda slashed at Kate's leg. The blade whispered through cloth. Kate kicked again, aiming for the hand with the knife, missed.

She didn't have much strength left. Got both hands on a pole, giving her more control, and struck it at Brenda's thigh. A hit. A yelp. Brenda fell to her knees.

The bear slashed, and Kate felt a sting in her arm. The knife came up, poised to strike. Kate grabbed the pole halfway down and put all she had into shoving it at her attacker's throat.

Had she made contact? She fell back into the blackness that said nothing mattered.

* * *

Kate found herself lying under a blanket with her feet up. She'd gotten most of what she'd wished for so fervently just before the bear-woman came at her with a knife: no Ibuprofen, but a warm blanket. And a nap. While it hadn't been the restful kind, it accounted for the fact that she had no idea how she'd gotten inside.

Her memory of the attack was confused and spotty. The Jeep engine starting, her scramble for the island, headlights blinding her, the soft snow—that much was clear. Then a series of disconnected images, a knife blade flashing white, the ski pole in her hand—

A voice came out of the dark. "Kate. How are you doing?"

Slowly the details of the room revealed themselves: Myra's face, Brenda on the couch with Rosa standing over her.

"I'm here. Not with the bear." A perfectly logical thing to say, but she got an odd look. Talking wasn't as easy as it used to be. "Hair feels tight. You pulling it?"

"Matted blood." Ah, trust Myra to be straightforward. She finished tending to the cut on Kate's arm, wrapping gauze firmly over the slashed anorak. "Here's a glass of water and the Ibuprofen you've been moaning about. Open up."

Kate opened her mouth and happily swallowed the pills and the water chaser. "You find the bottle?"

"No. Not in the sink. Or the recycling bin."

Kate had to concentrate to follow her friend's words.

"Major bulletins: the coffeemaker's doing its thing. We haven't called the police yet."

Coffee. Bless Myra. An everyday saint. "Police. Good idea. Soon."

"Some of us don't want to." Kate followed Myra's nod: Rosa, pacing in circles in front of the exhausted-looking woman slumped on the couch. Brenda held a dish towel against the wound just above her collarbone. A bad place for a puncture.

"Rosa?" A series of thoughts faltered on their way from Kate's brain to her tongue.

"Kate! Good, you're back."

Feeling oddly understood, she managed a single word. "Jail."

"Yeah, yeah, I know," Rosa said. "Procedures and rights and all that. We'll get there."

Camila's sister was running this show: the stakes were highest for her. And she apparently wanted some time with Brenda, on her own terms, before the authorities got involved.

Myra came out of the kitchen with two cups of coffee, one of which she set on the table beside the lounge chair.

Kate looked up. "I'm—not all here. I didn't see you go to get this." The cup shook in her hands as she took a grateful sip.

"You wouldn't be here at all if it weren't for that short woman obstructing justice over there," Myra said.

"I heard the Jeep's tire spinning and I went out to help." Speaking to Kate, Rosa kept her eyes on Brenda.

Yes, someone from the Last Frontier would know what a stuck vehicle sounded like.

"Otherwise you'd be toast like my sister," Rosa said. "But the killer wouldn't have gotten far." The next word, wrenched out of her, was hurled at Brenda. *"Why?"*

"I don't know what you're talking about." Brenda sounded unperturbed, but when she took the blood-soaked towel away from her throat and looked at it her eyes widened. "I need medical help here."

"Yeah, right. You'll get it when you've answered my question," Rosa said. "C'mon. You owe me."

No answer. The towel went back to the throat, but the cloth was saturated: blood dripped down Brenda's arm.

"Press harder," Kate said.

Rosa reached to her ankle and came up holding a knife. Not a chef's knife, only about five inches long. But it would do.

Kate felt completely herself again. She looked at Myra, sitting beside her on the arm of the lounge chair, who was staring at Rosa in alarm. Myra grabbed Kate's hand.

"I'm waiting," Rosa said. "You owe me a sister." She tilted the knife, but it didn't catch the light. Matte black finish, curved blade. She held it up. "Sharpened it yesterday."

No answer. Brenda had tensed, her shoulders back hard in the chair, her focus of fear no longer her wound.

When the knife touched Brenda's wrist she jerked and whimpered. The edge of the blade ran sideways up her arm to the elbow, leaving a strip of skin that the lamplight showed to be smooth. Shaved.

"There's more where that came from," Rosa said. "I've got all night, and you most certainly don't." She wiped the blade on her pants. "And just so you know? Life in prison is a price I would pay to find out the truth about my sister."

Kate's ears filled with a rushing noise. She could barely hear Rosa.

"Believe this: I will kill you if you don't tell me what happened."

Brenda swallowed. "It was personal," she said. "You wouldn't get it."

"Try me," Rosa said.

Kate hadn't noticed earlier, but the Alaskan's jeans were slit above her knee, the denim dark with blood. The patch wasn't spreading, but Brenda must not have gone down easily despite her ski-pole wound. Rosa had saved Kate's life.

Brenda was hunched, her hair in her face. "When Camila first moved in she told me she wasn't a person who made friends," Brenda said. "'I'm all about work,' she said. 'So don't get attached to me. You are warned.'" Brenda's face exploded into tears, and she put her head down on her knees and howled. Blood ran from her neck wound.

Kate had never seen anyone cry so hard. Myra's face was drawn in sympathetic pain, as Kate was sure her own was.

Rosa stood stone-faced.

Brenda's sobs lessened, then stopped, but she didn't look up. She stared at her lap.

"More," Rosa said. "Hurry up. You're bleeding harder."

Kate and Myra looked at each other again. If she hadn't hit a tree trunk and been stabbed in the arm, Kate wondered if she would be trying to restrain Rosa. Her interrogation was putting Brenda's life in danger.

Restrain Rosa? A dangerous task. Like trying to tie up lightning. This was the sister of a dragon, after all, and a person in great emotional pain.

Myra must be having the same thoughts. She shook her head at Kate. Even unhurt, she wasn't going up against Rosa's knife.

"Camila was so smart, and so dedicated. At first I just admired her, and then?" Brenda rocked back and forth. "We got to have these little jokes together, and she was fun, really she was. Nobody knew that, she was so serious with her work, with everyone at the college. But we had something special. I know we did." She looked up at Rosa and took a shuddering breath, her face pleading. "She was my friend. She *was.*"

"More." Rosa flipped the knife in the air. Caught it. "Everything."

Brenda coughed, and wiped her nose with her arm. A smear of blood. She grabbed a small pillow and put it to her throat. Her voice was weaker. "She didn't have friends from anyplace she'd been before. She never got personal letters, or phone calls. She'd told me the truth: she wasn't interested in friends. But okay, that didn't mean *we* weren't friends, whether she liked it or not." She twisted in her seat, as if she could get away from the memory. "Then *he* came along."

"Azul," Rosa said.

"She started spending time with him, more time than she'd spent with anyone. He stole her. Two years we had together. We had such a good time. And then she threw me away."

Kate got it. What she was looking at was fury, not sadness. Kate remembered a phrase Marjorie had used once: grievance collector. Behind her grief for Camila was Brenda's grief for herself. The rejection from Otterlin College, the family rejections Aunt Sarah had hinted at. Other failed relationships, probably. Camila's rejection had been the last straw.

"She warned me, she did. But I didn't think it would hurt like that." Brenda's voice was harder. "She warned me too early, before I cared about her. Before we built what I thought was a friendship. But I was wrong. She didn't do friendship." Brenda slumped against the arm of the chair. "You are warned. *Warned*? I—I loved her. She dumped me like trash."

"You killed her because you *loved* her?"

"Of course. I had to. See? I knew you wouldn't get it."

She looked spent, but Kate didn't trust her. She was hurt for sure, but she was also a pretty good actor. She'd done a great job of enlisting Aunt Sarah's sympathy. Was she playing possum, soon to explode again? Tears or violence could be coming. And Rosa wouldn't turn down an opportunity to have a full measure of revenge for her sister's murder.

Kate fished her cell out of her anorak pocket. "I'm calling Mark," she said in a low voice to Myra.

Brenda's head snapped up. "I'll deny everything I just said. You don't have a shred of proof."

"There were three witnesses to that confession," Myra said.

"You don't have a thing." Brenda was gathering herself. "You three witches are out to get me, and you cooked up this crazy story."

Rosa's body tensed, too. She'd put her knife back in the ankle sheath, but her hands curled into fists.

In Brenda's position, Kate wouldn't move an inch. Rosa would welcome a struggle that gave her an excuse to beat the daylights out of her sister's killer. But the mention of police had energized Brenda. She looked like a rattlesnake positioning itself for a strike. Still calculating. Kate could see it in her eyes.

"I've got the whole thing. Recorded it on my phone." Kate held the cell up. "Ever hear of an app called Audio Track? Your voice, your words. Every one of them."

She touched the screen to talk to Mark, or at least to his voicemail.

Brenda sat back, angry but contained. For the moment.

Kate lucked out and got the detective. "Hey, Mark. Could you come over to Brenda's house? We have a development."

"Ten minutes," Mark said, and her phone went dead.

"That was brilliant, Kate," Myra said. "To record everything Brenda said."

"You're a smart cookie," Rosa said. "Can you print it out for the cops?"

"Sure," Kate said. "Why not?"

* * *

Two cars came, a dark sedan and a cruiser. They zipped into the circle and the drivers got out, Mark and a uniformed officer, both of them studying the marooned Jeep for a moment before coming inside.

Now it was Myra's turn to be master of ceremonies. She explained everything to the patrolman. She described the bottle with the frass and what it meant, then showed him the small pack, using Kate's phrase "death kit." She described the attack on Kate, or as much of it as she'd seen after struggling up the icy hill: the Jeep going at Kate and then stalling, Brenda and Kate fighting, Kate falling, Rosa running out of the house and throwing herself on top of Brenda.

Throughout the summary, Rosa sat on the arm of the couch next to Brenda as if she were still capable of running away. After Myra was finished, Rosa said, "I wish I'd figured out sooner what was going on tonight. I didn't hear Brenda leave the house."

Mark listened to it all. Then, while the uniform read Brenda her Miranda rights, the detective squatted next to Kate. "You three have been having too much fun tonight," he said. "Especially you. Next time you're fixing for a fight, pick something smaller than a Jeep, okay?"

Kate managed a smile. "It was the knife that scared me silly," she said. "Fortunately for me, Rosa pounced on Brenda before she got too far with her chef skills. Rosa has a bad cut on her leg, by the way—she probably should have it cleaned up at an urgent care place."

"You could use a head X-ray yourself."

"I guess so." Kate wasn't excited about another X-ray, having had one a month earlier after being knocked out by a dropped rock.

"You're going to press charges against Brenda, I assume."

"You bet," Kate said. "She's dangerous. So quiet nobody noticed her. Like a snake under a log."

The uniformed cop helped Brenda out of her chair and took her to the door. "Time for a ride downtown," he said. She leaned heavily on him and stumbled a little, either from her injuries or as an appeal for sympathy. Kate didn't care which. The woman looked strong enough to survive. That was the important thing, that she survive and stand trial.

When the door closed behind them, the dynamics in the room changed. The tension drained out of Rosa and she collapsed on the couch. Myra spun in a circle and said, "That woman is a nut case. Seriously, I am so glad she's going to get herself locked up for a good long time."

"Innocent until proven guilty, of course," Mark said.

"Oh, she'll be proven guilty, all right," Myra said, beaming. "Kate taped her whole confession."

"Good work, Kate," Mark laughed. "You trying to steal my job?"

She looked away from his pleased expression. "I made that up."

Myra and Mark stared at her; even Rosa lifted her head.

"I said it to keep her from thinking about ways to get around what she'd told us," Kate said. "And I was afraid she'd get violent. She could have done some damage. She's physically a lot stronger than I expected." She turned back to Mark. "The three of us heard her confess. Won't our testimony be enough to convict her?"

"It should do the job."

"Wait a sec," Myra said. "Brenda was in the Jeep when you got here, right, Kate?" She shot out the door and came back grinning, holding the water bottle by its strap. "Here's the evidence to back us up."

Mark stood and pulled a plastic bag from his pocket. "Good work, Myra. Drop that right in here, thanks. Now would you like to go with your friends to the hospital?"

* * *

"Oh, honey, you fell into a real hornet's nest this time."

"You're confused, Marjorie. Hornets don't make honey."

"All right, killer bees," her friend laughed. "So Brenda knew Camila was allergic to stings?"

"Mark told me that's what she said, under intense questioning. Even Rosa didn't know. That allergy gets worse with each exposure, and Brenda must have seen enough to know even a few more stings might prove fatal."

"Might? A smart lawyer would say she couldn't be sure, that she was trying to punish, not kill. Intent matters."

"Three women are available to testify that she said she had to kill. Had to. I think that settles the intent question."

The momentary silence was dark.

"Bottled bees," Marjorie said, finally. "That sounds horrible. Are you having nightmares?"

"I had a bad dream about being chased by a bear, but that particular bear's locked up now. And the judge denied bail."

"Good. She does sound dangerous."

"So much pain in her. I keep hearing her cry. And repeating what Prof. Chavez said: 'You are warned.'"

"It might have been better," Marjorie said slowly, "if Camila hadn't told her that. You can't warn people away from their natural, human feelings."

"She wasn't warning Brenda about her feelings—"

"But she was able to look ahead, and knew the relationship was temporary, however important it was to Brenda. Lots of friendships get made and then peter out when people move on with their lives. You don't have to make a production out of it. You don't have to announce it."

"You mean Camila made it sound sort of deliberate, the pain she knew was inevitable?"

"Yes, that's right. As if she was planning it, which of course she wasn't. She was just being who she was."

"I wonder if Brenda would agree," Kate said, "that a turn of phrase, a well-intentioned comment, could turn her toward murder?"

"Words are powerful things," Marjorie said. "For better and for worse."

* * *

In her camper the next day, Kate figured something out. She wasn't calling Sean because it had been close to a year since the collapse of her longest relationship. She still didn't know why Mike had ended it. After spending five years with him, she would have expected him to talk to her, to tell her what was wrong and give her a chance to work things out. But he'd taken the coward's route and left her a note.

It asked her to move out. It didn't explain anything.

She was working on a portrait of Uncle Pete when the thought popped into her mind that she was afraid of another serious relationship. Her fingers, powdered with black dust from the charcoal stick, stalled over her uncle's chin.

She'd been thinking the chin looked a bit stubborn, which made her think of Mike. The anniversary of reading that awful note had been on her mind without her being aware of it.

She didn't like being afraid of things. And not realizing she was afraid of something was emotionally crippling— she'd had enough conversations about psychological issues with Marjorie to know that.

Kate put down the charcoal stick and sprayed the portrait with workable fixative. Wiped her hands on a rag and logged into email on her tablet.

Sean had come to Pennsylvania in an RV, hoping to spend some time with her. He didn't think she was boring. He didn't think she was weird for traveling the country in her truck camper.

He likes me, she muttered to herself as she worked on the message.

He liked her. And she liked him. She didn't know a lot about his life, but he was smart and careful and kind. He'd given her mixed signals because he was a complicated person. The break-up with Mike didn't mean she was unfit to be in a relationship.

Hey, Sean. Wondering if you got my last— No. Whiny.

*Hey, Sean. Had a murder here in—*No. Worrisome.

Hey, Sean. Otterlin College has been wild this past month. Her last email hadn't mentioned the college by name. If he looked it up he'd get the whole story. *Vandalism, arson, even murder. Your kind of place? JJ.* Would he understand? She spelled it out. *Just joking. All the crimes are already solved, the major perp in jail. Thinking of you and hoping all your cases are going as well as this one.*

She hit SEND. If he answered, great. If he didn't, at least she hadn't let fear be in the driver's seat.

EIGHTEEN

Warblers flickered through the trees, which had just leafed out. The lime-green canopy turned neon in the late-morning sun.

"Those little birds are so good at hiding themselves that it seems like the leaves are twittering," Aunt Sarah said.

"They sure make a racket first thing in the morning." Uncle Pete scowled over his coffee. "Now that the days are getting longer, that means earlier and earlier."

"A nice racket," Kate said.

The three sat on folding chairs set out on the concrete apron at the bottom of the new stairs. Kate had been surprised, as the snow melted, to see how large the backyard was. Yellow and purple crocuses salted the lawn, and finches mobbed the feeder. Then the land sloped down to the Reserve.

"It's pleasant to sit here now that we don't have to worry about seeing bulldozers," Aunt Sarah said, massaging her forearm. The cast had come off weeks ago, but the skin was still dry and flaky, the muscle thin. "My bone has knit itself back together, and so has the community."

Kate had been shocked when she'd seen the newspaper headline, RESERVE SOLD! But it turned out the city of

Hunterville had bought it, and deeded it to be forever undeveloped. With help from Otterlin College, which retained the right to conduct research on the grounds.

"I'm sorry you're leaving, Kate," Aunt Sarah said. "You know you're welcome back any time."

"Thank you. It does feel like home here. Maybe I'll come back at the end of my trip, whenever that turns out to be."

"You sure are welcome," Uncle Pete said. "I guarantee you one thing—your next visit will be less exciting."

"It has been an unusual few months," Aunt Sarah said. "I wake up at night sometimes and find myself listening for Camila, hoping she'll stop by for her midnight lunch and tell me about her wonderful mice. I'll miss her forever."

"Yes," Kate said. They sat quietly for a few moments.

"Her murder was the biggest event at Otterlin since it was founded," Uncle Pete said. "But the outbreak of campus vandalism just before Christmas was memorable, too. If only Brenda had stopped there."

"She couldn't, according to Rosa," Kate said. "She said the astrological equivalent of an earthquake pushed Brenda over the edge. Rosa tried to explain it with star maps, but it didn't make sense to me."

"I'll go for the rational explanation every time," Uncle Pete said. "And sometimes that gets me in trouble. I was convinced Justin was up to no good—too quiet in class, aloof from the other students, leaving a threatening note in my book, acting belligerent when confronted. I was pretty sure he was the one who used potassium nitrate to make the back stairs fail."

"That was the beginning," Kate said. "The first move in what turned out to be a long campaign against the college by Brenda, her accomplice Tim, and the HCDC."

"But it was my arm that got broken," Aunt Sarah said. "Not Pete's. It was a lousy campaign."

"It stunk. Pure vindictiveness." Kate sighed. "I wish I'd recognized KNO3 as the chemical formula for potassium nitrate. Remember that scrap of paper I found when Frankie was replacing the steps? I thought it said 'know.' And 'Commando' was written next to it. That's the name of a popular brand of the stuff. I thought it said 'comment.' It sounded like a student's shorthand for studying harder and speaking up in class."

"Criminals should write more clearly." A sly smile from Aunt Sarah.

"Fortunately for us, Justin figured out he was being set up," Uncle Pete said. "And he didn't have to look very far to find the culprit."

"Mark was pretty impressed with Justin's file from the college," Aunt Sarah said. "His military service was in his favor, and Mark said he was quite calm when questioned. He did better with the cops than with you, Pete. Something to do with how excited you got."

"Hogwash. I just asked him a few simple questions. He was the one who got all exercised."

That wasn't how Kate remembered it. "Tim might have gotten away with a lot more if he hadn't tried to frame Justin with that note," she said. "That tipped Justin off. Which tipped Mark off. "

"Tim confessed in minutes," Aunt Sarah said. "Mark said he put him in a bright room at the station, started a video camera and he sang like a canary."

"It helped that Brenda had already ratted him out," Kate said. "She did it in hopes of more lenient treatment by the prosecutor."

"I still have a hard time seeing her as the source of all those horrible events," Aunt Sarah said. "She had such a sweet singing voice."

Uncle Pete snorted.

"Brenda's distress fooled me, too." Kate considered the woman's situation. "I took it for grief, and it was that, but mixed with guilt. And anxiety about whether she'd be discovered. She took a big risk inciting Tim to vandalize the college. She must have known he was a weak link in her scheme to make the police think Prof. Chavez was killed by someone in the HCDC. If they figured out it was murder at all."

"Mark says he's still looking into the HCDC. Brenda recruited Tim, but somebody paid him to disrupt the campus." Aunt Sarah turned the mug in her hands. CATS ARE BETTER, it said. She patted Kate's knee. "I'm so sorry I told Brenda you'd solved a couple of murders. I think that's why she took that sneaky picture of you and alerted the HCDC folks you were going to their meeting."

"They gave me fright," Kate said. "It might have turned out differently if Rosa hadn't been with me."

"She was the reason you were there in the first place," Aunt Sarah said.

The sun had shifted, shining into Kate's eyes. She scooted her chair back, the scrape of aluminum on concrete falling into the comfortable silence. The three of them had discussed the ins and outs of the case over many weeks as the facts became known, of course, but Kate's departure prompted them to talk it through again.

Mark had provided behind-the-scenes updates that mixed the results of police work with plain old gossip. He'd stopped by for a cup of cider on Christmas Eve and told them that Shannon Quigley was Arnold Thorne's "woman friend," and was fervently anti-HCDC.

So Kate had been right—she'd attended that meeting to scope out the opposition.

Eventually Uncle Pete spoke. "Good old Tim had me fooled with the blush-and-stammer routine," he said. "I was stunned when Mark said the kid confessed to all the vandalism. The restitution the court ordered will keep him in the poorhouse for years."

"A frightening few months," Aunt Sarah said. "I don't feel sorry for that boy. I feel sorry for Brenda, but she deserved the sentence she got. And I don't plan to visit her."

Uncle Pete grunted. "I'm going to mail her a bomb."

"Pete! That's nothing to joke about."

"She really hated the college," Kate said. "Years of frustration because she couldn't get a permanent job there. What she saw as rejection by a professor friend was the last straw. So she killed that friend in a way that had a good chance of looking accidental, getting her revenge and hurting the college at the same time."

"And if the police decided it was murder, Azul would be their top suspect," Uncle Pete said. "The bee guy."

"The whole situation would have been cleared up sooner if the medical examiner had noticed Camila had been stung by bees," Aunt Sarah said.

"You should have heard him over at Bascomb Hall, making all kinds of excuses," Uncle Pete said. "The main one was that the cold shut Camila down so fast that there was virtually no swelling at the sting sites." He shook his head. "He thinks he missed the barbed stinger bees leave behind. If he'd paid any attention to Azul's research, he'd know he wasn't dealing with an ordinary bee, European or Africanized."

"Azul told me the smooth stinger wasn't something he was breeding for, but it came along with the docility that was his goal," Kate said.

"Happens." Uncle Pete smiled. "Genes are tangled-up bits of biology with hidden connections. You never know what you're going to get. One researcher did an experiment breeding for the least aggressive wild foxes. Five or ten generations down the road, he got tame foxes all right. But they had spotted coats. Like beagles. And their ears went floppy."

Kate laughed. "Yes, co-determined. Azul says it's ironic that his bees' smooth stingers mean they can sting multiple times and not leave much of a mark. Like hornets. They had to be pretty angry when they got out of that bottle, because they're generally more docile than Africanized bees."

"Like that children's book," Aunt Sarah said. "The one about Ferdinand, the bull that would rather meditate under a tree than swipe his horns at matadors. My kind of bull." She turned to Kate. "I'm glad something good came out of the winter. You finished your project with Myra and Dave."

"That was an education. I met a lot of amazing creatures." The glow of accomplishment added to the sun's warmth, and Kate unzipped her fleece. "Stick insects and hummingbird moths were my favorites."

"You like things that look like something else?" Uncle Pete asked. "You must be into camouflage. Who are you, really? Fess up."

Kate didn't know what to say.

"She's a cat," her aunt said. "Obviously. A cat who talks and wears clothes."

"Okay, Katie-cat," Uncle Pete said. "If I ever do another textbook on plants I'm going to hire you."

"That could be arranged. I love drawing plants."

* * *

In the truck cab, Kate got out her atlas. The previous night she'd taken an orange marker and highlighted her route from the beginning, last August: from Marjorie's house near Boston to the artists' colony way down east in

Maine, then to upstate New York's Adirondacks, then south to the Laurel Highlands of western Pennsylvania. She wouldn't be on the road forever, and wherever she settled in the future she wanted a visual record of her wanderings.

What other roads would she color orange during her year of adventure?

Her eventual destination was Tucson, where her mother lived, but the next stop was a lot closer: Marjorie's place again. Kate stayed in touch with other friends, but none as closely as this smart, calm woman who'd talked her through the shocks and troubles that had come her way after she'd taken to the road.

She tried not to think too much about it, but she'd see Sean. He'd answered her second email the day after she'd sent it, apologizing for the silence after her first email and saying he'd been on a case in Colorado but would be in the Boston office next. These FBI guys moved all over the country, apparently. Or some of them did.

Thinking of seeing him again was a little scary. But at least she was aware of that now. There was something compelling about him, as if she'd entered the gravitational field of a newly discovered planet.

She found herself staring absently out the windshield. Turned her attention back to the map.

Up over the top of the Quabbin Reservoir, then, and an hour along scenic Route Two. Kate had driven it often enough to various hiking trailheads in the Berkshires back when she'd lived in Danvers. Somewhere fairly close to the city—near Concord, or Acton?—the trees in a swampy area visible from the road were crowned with the huge messy nests of herons. No place to pull over, but she'd steal some looks. Or maybe take an exit and find a place to pull over and put her binoculars on the heronry, something she'd never taken the time to do when she'd been working.

After a week or so visiting Marjorie she'd decide her next move. She might even drive north through Vermont, into Canada, and west from there. Across the whole continent, then south to Tucson. It was wilder north of the border: only the southern rim of the country had major cities, and the population dropped off dramatically above them.

Fewer people meant more wildlife, and more wild land. That sounded good.

First a renewal of her friendship with Marjorie. And maybe some time with Sean. Then she'd decide.

She would find her way.

Thank you for joining Kate and me!

If you enjoyed this book, please leave a review on Amazon, Goodreads, or wherever you spend time online. Even a few words can make a major different to an author.

Look for other novels in the Art of Murder series: *Drawing Fire*, *Boat Camp Killer*, and *Double Magpie Murders,* all available now on Amazon as e-books and paperbacks.

See www.PamFoxAuthor.com for news about Kate's adventures.

Comments? Email the author at PamFoxAuthor@gmail.com. I'd love to hear from you.